AUSTIN

LEARNING TO LOVE #4

CON RILEY

Austin: Learning to Love #4

Cover artist: Natasha Snow

Editor: Posy Roberts, Boho Edits

Production team: Annabelle, Garrett, Louise, Mel, Valerie, and Victoria

C/W: Non-explicit mention of bereavement.

For lovely Lily Morton who was the best company while writing.

And for everyone who helped me find my way when I was lost in Holland.

1

Austin Russell's last day as a school bursar could have started better. Almost falling into a seaside rock pool hadn't been on his agenda, and neither had swearing so loudly that a student overheard him.

It's summer break, for God's sake.

How was I to know little Tor Trelawney would pop up miles from Glynn Harber?

Yet here Tor was, six years old and startled, eyes wide and mouth hanging open as if he'd never seen a grown man slip on seaweed while yelping, "Fuck, shit, bollocks."

Tor yelped too. "Charles Heppel!" He waved until his teacher, Austin's housemate, picked his way across rocks towards them. "Your brother said three bad words!"

Austin brushed down a suit he'd worn for a business meeting, not for this soggy detour. "How many times do I have to tell you, Tor? I'm not his brother. And if you think those were bad words, here's a worse one for you. Snitch."

Tor didn't listen, too busy bouncing with excitement that,

snitch or not, Austin helped to steady, holding his hand until Charles reached them with Glynn Harber's padre, Hugo.

Tor whispered Austin's bad words into their ears in turn, both men stifling laughter. "Well," Hugo said, wrestling his tone to pious. "We can only pray that the poor crabs didn't hear that."

"Let's hope so." Charles reached into the water, lifting a strand of seaweed, tiny creatures scuttling for cover. "And let's hope the bravest of all rock-pool dwellers didn't either."

"Bravest?" Tor lifted some seaweed, copying the man Austin had watched him hero-worship during his time at Glynn Harber.

Best months of my life.

Can't believe it's almost over.

Austin checked his jacket pocket, his resignation letter still safe despite his stumble.

Tor checked as well, only by lifting more seaweed, searching for something fiercer. "You mean brave like a shark?"

Charles shook his head, put a finger to his lips, and spoke quietly, drawing Tor closer to him. Austin too, who also listened to his lesson. "No," Charles whispered. "I mean brave like a sea anemone." He moved one more emerald strand, uncovering what looked like a blob of jelly.

"That titchy thing can't be brave, can it?" Tor's nose scrunched. "It's all squishy."

"That's what makes it brave, Tor." Charles found another anemone, this time underwater, its tiny tentacles swaying. "See those wiggly feelers?" He nodded as Tor waggled his fingers. "Yes. Imagine being brave enough to open up like it has. The anemone doesn't know if its feelers will find something tasty for its breakfast or if they'll get munched on by something hungry." He met Austin's eyes. "Opening up must feel scary, but all anemones do it. Brave, see? Taking a risk instead of staying closed up."

Nearby, a whistle blew three shrill blasts.

Tor's head shot up. "That's Sealife Simon." He got to his feet, pointing to an older man a few rock pools over surrounded by small children. Tor mimed blowing an invisible whistle of his own. "Three peeps means that sealife school is starting." He frowned, aiming sudden worry at Charles. "You could come too if you're sad that Glynn Harber's closed for the summer." He held a hand out to him, surprising Austin by offering him his other. "Want to come with me?"

"That's very kind." Charles pointed to the sea wall where Porthperrin's harbour started. "But we're waiting for the pub to open so we can have a breakfast meeting."

"Why?"

"So that Austin not-my-brother Russell here can magic up some money for a big rebuilding project."

My last one here.

I've got to make it happen.

Tor wasn't done with his questions. "What for?"

"For the old art building," Charles told him, standing. He offered Hugo a hand, who rose more stiffly. "It's falling down, but Austin is the absolute best at finding money to save things."

Tor held up all his fingers, wiggling again. "This many hundreds?"

Austin shook his head. "Nope. Ten hundreds is only a thousand. I need to find a lot more thousands than that, Tor." Many more than he'd originally calculated, all the bids

submitted so far stratospheric, hence this meeting to pitch for
more cash from the school's new backers.

He watched Hugo take up Tor's offer, but not before Tor
offered a glimpse of the man he might grow into when Austin
was long gone from Cornwall. Concern creased his little forehead. "I usually go to sealife school with Maisie. But when
Mummy knocked on her door today, no one answered."

Hugo did what he did best, offering the quiet comfort
Austin knew he'd miss soon. "She's probably on a summer
holiday with her family, Tor. No need to worry." He turned to
lead Tor away.

Austin turned too, finding Charles watching him, his eyes
narrowed.

"What?"

Charles studied him for a moment before crouching
again, lifting more seaweed, revealing another jelly-like blob.
"This reminds me of you."

"Me? Why?"

"Because what I forgot to mention to Tor is that each
tentacle comes with a sting. That's what you were like when
you first rolled up to shut down the school in your swish
company car, wearing your flash designer watch while you
snipped all our budgets to nothing." He plucked a whelk
shell from the water, showed Austin the hermit crab inside it,
then put it back and made pincers with his fingers. "Snip,
snip, snip. Like that." He found a sea urchin next, holding it
with the tips of his fingers. "You were twice as prickly as this
beauty."

"Yes, yes, I was a cut-throat bastard, I remember." Austin
pressed his lips together before blurting, "You do know that's
what it takes to climb the corporate ladder, don't you?" A
ladder Austin would have to get back to sooner rather than

later. He touched that resignation letter in his pocket again, and Charles noticed, his eyebrows rising.

"I'm just saying that all of that stinging and snipping and being prickly was an act, wasn't it? You're actually quite squishy."

"I am fucking not." Austin drew a finger across his neck as a cut-throat reminder.

Charles ignored it.

"I'm just saying that someone cut-throat wouldn't have a fan club of five- and six-year-olds headed by Maisie Dymond, would they?"

"I don't have a fan club." Austin told his real truth. "I'm awful with kids." He stalked away, or did his best to, Charles catching his arm when he skidded on more seaweed.

Now real concern rose instead of teasing. "Austin, you're so wrong about that, but whatever's in your pocket *is* making you look all prickly again."

"I don't look prickly." Austin climbed up the few steps leading to the end of Porthperrin's harbour, waiting for Charles to catch up, which was a mistake—he'd pulled out his phone, taking a photo before Austin could dodge him.

"Look," Charles ordered, thrusting his phone at him. His voice lowered, gentling, but he didn't name the pinched look he'd captured. He didn't need to when it was right there in perfect focus. "That's how you looked when you moved into the stables with me and Hugo before you learned to love us. It's how you look whenever you dodge your mother's phone calls as well." He squinted. "As if you'd rather be anywhere else on the planet. That's how you look right now too, so what could be in your pocket to make you feel so awful?"

"Nothing."

Charles could move fast when he wanted. He swiped the

envelope before Austin could stop him. "This is addressed to Luke." He peered around Austin at where Glynn Harber's headmaster sat outside the Anchor, showing the new backers' legal counsel something on Austin's tablet. "He's right there with Keir. Why would you write him a lett—"

Austin saw the penny drop.

Wished he hadn't.

Charles crumpled. "You're *not* leaving us."

"This was always temporary. You knew that."

"But you're still needed."

Austin was, only not here.

Charles tried another angle. "Is it because I made you watch *Love Island*?"

"No."

"Then it must be because of that wretched spreadsheet you keep opening."

"Wretched?"

"It must be. I can tell each time you open it. You go pale. I saw the chart as well." Charles sketched a plummeting line in the air, his turn to look worried. "The school is going to be okay, isn't it?"

"Yes. Of course it is. That wasn't anything to do with the school's finances."

Charles brightened, smiling, which prompted the first real one Austin had managed that morning.

Once again, Charles noticed. "Oh, that's so much better."

"What is?"

"That grin right there. It's a traffic stopper." He sobered. "I bet you never smiled like that at your old job."

No.

Austin hadn't.

"You're gorgeous when you lighten up. Could actually

pull someone if you wanted to instead of staying single. Do you really want to work again someplace pressured where you'd stay lonely?"

No, again.

Austin didn't.

He answered a previous question rather than tell an outright lie. "It's nothing to do with the school. That spreadsheet is . . ."

Personal.

A target I promised to hit but will miss if I don't work somewhere paying a whole lot more soon.

Charles saved his best shot for last. "But if you go back to the city, you won't get to ogle Maisie's dad anymore, will you? He's a looker when he smiles too. That's why you're always in the outdoor classroom at home time, helping her on the balance beam, right? So you can catch a glimpse of his lovely bottom?"

"No, I don't ogle his arse. I just keep her company because her dad's late so often."

Hugo had caught up with them. Had also heard that Austin planned on leaving. He did his best to inject some humour. "Is that what you miss now we're engaged, Charles? Getting to appreciate other men's bottoms?"

"Why would I miss that when I've got you?" Charles said simply. "Your body is a temple I'll worship forever, but look." He pointed along the quayside. "Even you've got to admit your boss excelled himself by giving Dominic Dymond that arse and those shoulders. That face too," he said as Maisie's dad hefted a set of ladders, muscles flexing, a deep frown describing concentration.

"See?" Charles elbowed Austin. "He's tall, dark, and

protective. That's your type, right? Must be if you and Sol used to be serious about each other."

"No, that isn't my type," Austin said, although Charles had described his ex, Glynn Harber's art master, to a tee. "Why'd you think that?"

"Because that's how Sol looks whenever he's around his nephew."

Another kid I was no good with.

Charles pointed at how Maisie's dad also took care not to knock the ladder into a crowd of passing tourists before propping it against a cottage. "He's careful too like Sol is with Cameron. Protective. Wants to see him happy." Charles tilted his head. "You too. Sol wants that so much he's even painted what it used to look like when you were together. I saw it the last time I went up to the old art building."

"Saw what?"

"A painting of you and Cameron smiling at each other."

That seemed unlikely to Austin after the way his and Sol's relationship had ended. "Smiling at me? Pretty sure Cameron's more likely to want to stab me."

"But—"

"No buts." Austin asked them both a favour. "I'd appreciate it if you could hold off saying anything to Luke until I get a chance to."

"Of course." Hugo clasped his shoulder. "Are you sure though, Austin? You'll be missed."

"I need . . ." What he needed was a way to hit his personal target. One he wished to God he'd never promised his mother to meet. "What I really need is to get back to networking. Make some new contacts." Leaving his last role in a hurry hadn't done him any favours, and the few offers he'd had weren't too inspiring.

"I could . . ." Charles looked torn as Hugo left them, heading for Luke at the Anchor, where Austin hoped he'd keep his secret. "I could always contact Heligan if you wanted?"

"Heligan?"

"An old school friend," Charles said. "He's something big in banking." For a scant second, his eyes twinkled. "Something big elsewhere too. Mostly in his trousers. Left quite a long-lasting impression." He waggled his eyebrows, his smile falling away as he scrolled through his phone contacts. He stopped, finger hovering over one named *Mr Fucking Fabulous*. "Want me to text him for you?"

Austin's heart must have been exactly as squishy as Charles had suggested, casting out feelers that would cling if he let them.

He made himself retract them, telling his head to take over.

The sun blazed over Porthperrin, seagulls crying, and Austin slowly nodded.

THE MEETING GOT off to a good start, the harbour-side location scenic, Porthperrin at its best in late summer sunshine, even if Austin couldn't make himself eat much once seated.

He passed his tablet to one of the school's new backers over a plate still holding most of his full English breakfast. "This is a similar project I found online. See how accessible they made the building?"

"And this is why you want more money?"

"Yes. Keep scrolling to see the whole galler—"

Something across the harbour flashed bright enough to distract him.

Is that...?

He shielded his eyes. Almost rose to his feet, mouth starting to shape a name. Sat again just as quickly. That wasn't a child he hadn't seen for years now. It was some other kid near a group of tourists, wearing something sparkly. Something bright, contrasting with the granite of the sea wall.

"These photos are amazing," Nick said, shoving back loose strands of hair the wind whipped. He handed the tablet to his partner. "Tom, look at these adaptations."

"Nice," Tom said, sun catching the silver at his temples like whatever that kid wore across the harbour. "But accessibility has always been a big part of the brief. The most important factor to us. Why wait until now to ask for enough cash to make it happen?"

"You're right. I knew what you wanted." Austin took back the tablet, scrolling to another renovation that had caught his eye. "But now bids have started to come in, I found a problem. Contractors are saying they can only keep to the original budget by cutting out what you told us was most important."

"What about this outfit?" Tom scrolled to the top of the page, reading the logo. "Balfour. Have they put in a bid?"

"No. Wouldn't expect them to, to be honest. They're not local. Not in our price range either, even with a higher budget, but their projects show what could be done if we didn't have to choose between accessibility or aesthetics. Currently, we can't have both because the building is grade two listed."

"Listed?"

Austin met Nick's quizzical look and translated. "The

building has historic value. All that old Victorian glass and ironwork might as well be held together with red tape. Legally, we have to prioritise its preservation, on the outside of the building, at least. Retain its character ahead of anything else. Look. Here's another example of what more money might buy us." He stopped short, rephrasing because he wouldn't be around to see the project through to completion once he'd secured this funding. "I mean, here's what it could buy for you and the school."

He watched both men study a similar building he'd found on the same website. "See how accessibility is integrated here? It's seamless. Doesn't detract from the character of the building at all. I'm . . ."

He wasn't sure whether to share this, deciding to go for it after seeing Tom's gaze shift to his yacht bobbing in the harbour. "You know I used to work for a company called Supernus, right?"

Tom nodded.

"They made me cut school budgets, not increase them, even if that meant schools were less inclusive." He tipped his head towards the water. "You renovated your yacht for disabled sailors?"

"The *Aphrodite*? Yes."

"Which adaptation would you cut first to save money?"

"None of them."

"Because each one matters?"

Tom and Nick both nodded.

"I know that's what Sol wants for his art building too. Wants to make art possible for more people. For the whole local community, not only—"

Another bright glint made him stop.

Squint.

Stay silent.

That kid across the harbour was alone, no adults in sight to stop her from clambering onto the sea wall where she balanced like a tightrope walker. The breeze caught something on her back that didn't only glint, it tugged, hauling a memory to the surface.

Fairy wings.

She's wearing a set of fairy wings like—

The child in the distance windmilled her arms to balance, reminding him for a fleeting moment of Maisie Dymond left waiting in the playground so often for her father, but the child across the harbour had to be older than six, out on her own like that, unsupervised. She steadied, and Austin breathed again, getting back to business. He pulled out his phone, opening the calculator app. "This is how much extra I think—"

"Think what?" Nick asked, but Austin didn't answer.

He'd already shot to his feet, aware of what no one else had noticed.

That steadiness had only lasted for a second.

Now the child windmilled her arms faster.

She stumbled.

Tumbled.

Fell near the mouth of the harbour into the open water.

Where it's deeper.

Austin's chair fell too, his phone dropped and forgotten, calculation on its screen unfinished.

The table rocked, tea spilling, Austin not looking back, already skidding on slippery cobbles as he took off running.

The harbour stretched in two directions, granite arms sheltering boats from waters that frothed where the child had fallen. Austin took the shortest arm and sprinted, shout of alarm frozen somewhere between his lungs and voice box, his eyes fixed on where the sea wall ended, no sign a child had ever been there.

He dodged lobster pots and hurdled a stack of fish crates, hearing thumping but only realising it wasn't his heart pounding when he rounded the curve. That sound came from someone sprinting from the opposite direction, his work boots heavy against the cobbles.

Austin caught a blurred impression of blue eyes wild with terror, there and gone, a man hurling himself headfirst into foaming water seconds before Austin followed. He lost sight of him right away, vision blurred by water and swirling sand before the current caught him.

Dragged him.

Tore Austin away from the harbour's calmer waters to smash him against rocks.

His head rang.

The sun darkened.

Austin sank, pulled one way, then another before the current shoved him back to the surface.

He gasped.

Choked.

Found a rock to cling to.

Gasped again before duck-diving, looking this way and that, still no sign of the child.

He surfaced again, this time having to fight hard to break the surface where he caught another glimpse of terror.

A wave crashed between him and the man who'd also jumped in, gone when it subsided. The next wave lifted Austin high enough to see something that sparkled as brightly as the edges of his vision.

His ears didn't ring now, they clamoured, his sight blurring, but not enough to miss the little face that emerged, spluttering, followed by arms that still windmilled, only not to stop a fall this time.

For survival.

Fuck.

Fuck.

It is Maisie.

She went under again, her mouth still open.

A wave crashed over the spot where he'd seen her, followed by another.

Maisie didn't resurface.

Austin threw himself in her direction, battling the clash of currents, this time grasping something—one of her arms, he hoped, slippery like a fish and struggling.

He held fast.

Kicked hard.

Aimed for the wavering disc of the sun rippling above him, then kicked harder still, his lungs burning, getting nowhere fast and tiring.

Austin fought the water over and over, but the current wrapped an arm around him, dragging them out where the sea was deeper—*darker*—the sun above receding.

A stronger arm caught hold of them both, yanking Austin close with Maisie clutched tight to him. When he kicked as well as Austin, the sun got bigger.

Brighter.

Austin broke the surface, choking again and gasping, hoisting her face above the water.

He heard her cough and splutter.

Heard a harsh sob of relief from behind him, that arm around his chest tightening.

More sound filtered through the roar of the waves—

shouting from the sea wall above; panted words in his ear, *thank God* repeating; a lifebelt splashing ahead of where they'd surfaced, Austin propelled towards it by more powerful kicks.

The rest was a blur until he lay flat on his back on the quayside, sun no longer rippling above him, and if the sky had ever been bluer, he'd never noticed. Only shaky hands trying to pry loose his hold on Maisie registered.

Austin grasped her, not letting go, both of them still coughing.

A broad set of shoulders eclipsed the sun then and a voice rasped, gritty like the sand Austin had swallowed.

"Give her to me."

Austin's ears still rang and salt water still blurred his vision, but he recognised who tried to take her from him.

Dominic always-too-late-fucking Dymond.

"No way." Austin levered himself up, wrapping both arms around her like a strand of seaweed did his forearm, clinging like she clung to him, small and shaking. "No bloody way."

Anger rose like the waves that had almost stolen this man's daughter, washing in so fast he couldn't stop it—didn't want to—but was surprised his yell came out as a hoarse croak. "She could have drowned. Why the hell was she on her own? When the fu—" Only Maisie's chokes turning to sobs stopped him from cursing again. "When will you start being there for her when she needs you?"

Maisie's father didn't answer. He coughed too, and maybe that helped him sound more like himself. "Daddy's here, sweetheart."

Maisie's death grip on Austin let up and she turned like a flower would to the sun, her eyes scrunched closed, but her arms raised, blindly searching.

Her father reached for her and Austin let go.

Dominic Dymond took his daughter and held her. Sheltered her, his head bent, those massive shoulders shaking. But that wasn't what caught Austin's attention.

Maisie's fairy wings were gone, like one of Austin's shoes was, ripped away by water so powerful it could have torn her away too.

Forever.

More water ran into Austin's eyes, stinging. He brushed it away, barely noticing while molten fury turned to ice inside him. "Because that's what you need to do," he continued between coughs that kept on coming. "Learn to be there for her and pay much more attention."

He said that to Dominic Dymond's back because he'd got to his feet, towering above him, Maisie's arms gripping his neck the same way she'd clasped Austin's.

He could still feel her tiny fingers digging in, desperate. It prompted a truth that hurt to let out. "You have to start. You *have* to. Because I won't be at Glynn Harber to watch her for you in September."

Maisie's father stilled.

Austin did too as a voice said, "You won't?" from behind him.

Luke was there with towels that he dropped along with the subject as soon as he saw what Austin had mistaken for water running into his eyes. "Ouch, that looks nasty." He grabbed one of the towels, touching it to Austin's forehead, blood vivid when he removed it, scarlet against white cotton.

No wonder his ears still rang, the chimes as hollow as what he thought next.

Christ, if it had been her head that hit the rocks instead of mine, it really could have killed her.

The world took on a green cast then, his stomach rolling. It took everything he had not to lose its contents onto stone that seemed to lurch beneath him.

He swallowed hard.

Swallowed again and shuddered.

Maybe Luke saw that as well. "Hospital for you," he said. "For all of you," the last Austin heard as the chiming in his head switched to thunder, the sun gone for the last time that morning.

2
——————

Hours later, a doctor checked an image on a tablet and gave a flippant verdict.

"Yup. Your brain's still in your noggin. You'll probably survive the night."

"Thanks." Austin sat on the edge of a cubicle bed and touched the dressing on his forehead. "Very reassuring." He winced against a penlight's brightness that moved from left to right. Austin followed the movement for what felt like the hundredth time since arriving.

The doctor seemed satisfied. "Come back if your brain leaks out of your ears."

"I can go?"

"Yes, if someone drives you." He held out a leaflet. "Concussion protocol. Read it. Follow it. Take it easy for a few days. Avoid screens too."

Avoid screens? He couldn't, not with the renovation bid deadline looming. "Why?"

"Because they'll set you back. And while you're listening to instructions, avoid braining yourself on rocks again in future." He tapped on the screen, an image showing the inside of a skull that made Austin queasy to see. "Because this isn't your first bump to the head, is it?"

"That was ages ago." Austin stood, but the doctor wasn't done yet. He pressed the leaflet into his hand. "Seriously," he said, actually sounding that way for the first time. "Don't put your head in the way of anything as hard as granite again. Looks like you've been lucky twice. *Very* lucky this time. The odds of long-term damage go up for repeat heroics."

Austin tested the margins of the dressing, its adhesive tugging at his hairline. "I wasn't being heroic. Either time. I saw her fall, that's all."

"Lucky for her that you did," The doctor said, cool gaze meeting with Austin's and holding, warming for a brief moment. "Brave of you to go in after her."

Austin shook his head and soon wished he hadn't. His headache rang louder for a moment, somehow connecting to his stomach, which rolled. "Is . . . is she okay?" he asked once the queasiness subsided. "I keep asking, but no one will tell me."

"I think someone's outside waiting to tell you."

The doctor pulled open the cubicle curtain.

Dominic Dymond leaned against the wall opposite. He straightened as the doctor swept off, leaving them facing each other.

Austin had witnessed him roll up late wearing a similar expression plenty of times, one he hadn't known how to label, too cross on Maisie's behalf to focus. Now he saw a raw version of it, worry chiselled right where he could see it.

Austin touched his forehead again, unthinking, that sick sensation crashing like the waves had, but he forced himself to say what he should have back on Porthperrin's harbour.

"Thank you." Then he gritted his teeth against nausea that, like all high tides, eventually receded.

"Me?" Maisie's father took the few steps to the opening in the curtain. "You're thanking *me*?"

Austin nodded. Yet again, he wished he hadn't, having to grasp the edge of the thin mattress before he puked right in front of this man who, regardless of being too late to stop his daughter from falling, had saved Austin from . . .

He bowed his head, which throbbed at the memory of being helpless—*hopeless*—reaching the water's surface impossible until this man had caught hold of them both and hadn't let go.

Austin took a couple of long, slow breaths. Finally managed to say, "I couldn't . . . I couldn't get her to the surface on my own. Didn't matter how hard I kicked, it was getting further away, not closer. I . . ."

Would have drowned if you hadn't grabbed me.

Wouldn't have lived long enough to yell at you for being too late for her ever again.

"Thank you," Austin repeated, suddenly aware he must look as wrecked as the man who watched him. He shoved a hand through hair that snagged his fingers, a tangled mess instead of his usual glossy.

Dominic Dymond still watched, haggard in a way that should make him less attractive, not more, hospital lighting harsh enough to show his red-rimmed gaze as he took the last few steps between the curtains and the bed. He towered there like he had at the harbour with his daughter safe in his arms, a big man who suddenly crumpled, kneeling.

"Don't thank me."

He lifted his gaze slowly as if the sea hadn't only snatched away a set of sparkling fairy wings but had also sapped strength built through manual labour. Even his words came out sounding heavy. Weary. Way past exhausted.

"You're the one who saved her. *You.* Not me."

He met Austin's eyes then, those red rims highlighting something else Austin hadn't noticed each time this man had rocked up to school late. Bloodshot yet full of care and worry, they were the same shade as his daughter's, soft blue like faded denim. His voice softened too. "Don't you dare thank me," he almost whispered. "Don't, because I . . . I don't know what I would have done if you hadn't found her. Grabbed her." He took a turn at scrubbing a hand through his own hair, a few silvering glints flashing before he rubbed the square of his jaw. Stubble rasped like his voice. "Don't know what I'd have done if she'd—"

Austin couldn't let him end that sentence. "Stop."

He couldn't let loose the hundred different versions of *take better care of her* that had crowded inside his throat either because, like those competing currents, another urge tugged at him to also pay more attention.

"You're . . ." Austin cleared his throat, still seawater-husky. "You're wearing work boots."

"Me?" Maisie's dad got up from kneeling, glancing at his own feet before meeting Austin's eyes again, this time a hint of humour gleaming. "Can't say I recommend swimming with steel toecaps." His humour seemed aimed at himself, gentle compared to Austin's experience in other cubicles, like at his old Supernus office where kindness equalled weakness.

Hearing it from this man encouraged another question. "Dymond and Son." Austin read faded lettering on the front of a paint-spattered and torn T-shirt. "You're a builder, right?"

"Something like that." He chuffed a soft snort as if the thought was funny. "Trained as a carpenter first, like Dad, but yeah, I can turn my hand to most trades. Brickwork. Plaster-ing. Plumbing, if I have to. A bit of painting," he said, touching a dried-on splatter. "Don't touch electrics though. Haven't actually got a death wish."

He blinked at that last phrase, casting a quick glance over his shoulder at the opening in the curtain. "I left Maisie with my ex." His face twisted with something Austin didn't have a word for. "She needed her mum, but Gemma's not handling what happened too well. I should get back—"

Austin fired another question, already guessing the answer. "You weren't looking after Maisie."

Any humour on Dominic Dymond's face faded. Folded, like he did his hands into fists, their knuckles scuffed as if he'd grazed them on the same rocks that had scraped Austin's forehead.

All of the softness he'd glimpsed vanished as well, leaving only bleakness.

"You're right, I wasn't looking after her. You already said that. A lot."

Austin had. Several times on Porthperrin's quayside, loud and clear while sitting in a puddle of seawater and clutching this man's daughter. He'd also thought and said as much at school. Now Austin added a correction. "No, I mean, someone else should have been looking after her for you? You thought she was in safe hands?"

Maisie's father nodded, a short, sharp movement, his gaze anywhere but on Austin.

"But they didn't," Austin said, understanding dawning. "Look after her while you were working, I mean, and that's why she ..."

Austin watched him nod again, slower this time, another

twist to his expression he might have guessed meant either sadness or anger if he'd known him better—and if he hadn't been so quick to judge, Austin had to admit, now that he'd glimpsed not only terror back at Porthperrin but something else that resonated, a core of caring under that rugged surface.

It led to a final question, Austin guessing he already knew the answer.

"And all of those times you were late for her at school, someone else should have collected her for you? You didn't know she'd been left waiting?"

Maisie's father nodded one last time, glancing over his shoulder again before turning back and squaring his shoulders. "It won't happen again. I won't let it, so thanks again, um . . . is it Russell?"

"Austin. Austin Russell."

"Dominic Dymond," Maisie's father offered. "Dom," he added. "Maisie's mentioned you. You're her favourite teacher."

"Teacher? Christ no, I don't teach. Kids are . . ." Austin faked a shudder and couldn't regret it despite his brain rattling, not when it prompted a smile marking another revelation.

Charles was right.

He really is a looker when he smiles.

Austin made himself stop staring. "I'm the school bursar. Or, I am for now, anyway. I balance the books. Send the bills. And—"

"Give parents a piece of your mind when they turn up late?" Dom asked dryly. "Like you did on the last day of term? Can't remember the last time anyone gave me a public spanking."

Austin winced for a whole new reason. "I was hoping you'd forgotten."

Dom didn't seem to bear a grudge. He extended a hand and they shook, Austin's hand enveloped by a work-hardened hold that lingered after he'd let go.

"Forget?" Dom's voice lowered. "Trust me, I didn't. I thought about what you said on the last day of term a lot. I'm thinking about it even harder now. This . . . Today . . . It was a shove I needed. That we all needed." He let go and took a step back, glancing over his shoulder again.

Austin took that as a signal to make a move as well. He looked around for his suit jacket, not sure if he'd worn it when he jumped in or had left it outside the pub, resignation letter still in one of its pockets. He stopped searching when Dom asked, "So you're really not staying at Glynn Harber?"

"Can't." That was easier than explaining. "I've already stayed longer than I meant to."

Dom backed towards the curtain opening. "Then I'll have to think of how to repay you before you move on."

"Repay me? You don't owe me anything."

"Oh, I think I do." Dom crossed thick arms over his chest, work boots squarely planted, still-damp jeans clinging to legs that looked equally as solid. "After what you did for Maisie . . . For my family . . ." He shook his head. "I thought she was gone. That I'd lost her . . ." His eyes closed for a long moment, anguish there when they opened. "The relief when I saw you had her . . . I swear that if we hadn't both been fighting that current, I could have kissed you."

Austin saw him blink as if that had slipped out without permission.

Blink again at Austin's reply popping out as quickly.

"I wouldn't have stopped you."

Before he could haul the words back or blame them on a bump to his head, Dom surged like the waves that had caused it, only he didn't shove Austin as hard as that water had, knocking the sense out of him.

No.

He took the few steps between them and followed through on what he'd promised.

His touch came first, lighter on Austin's jaw than he could have imagined if he'd ever pictured this moment, the size of Dom's hands also processing on some kind of delay because, by the time he'd parsed surprise or logged that they were gentle, they'd slid to the nape of his neck to hold him.

Austin sucked in a breath, ribs aching with pain he'd have to catalogue sometime later, too busy feeling stubble rasp the edge of his mouth, nerves firing off a tingling message only to short-circuit because Dom's lips were a shocking contrast.

Soft.

Giving.

And for a fleeting moment, Austin felt them open, Dom's breath warm compared to where he'd been cold to the core, that soft touch receding so fast Austin leaned in to chase it.

Dom pulled back further. "Yeah?" he murmured, and if a single word had ever had the power to stop time and reverse it, this was its moment, Austin needing this surprise kiss to continue, not end. To keep going for as long as it took for everything else to stop hurting. His head, his heart—even the ache of inhaling and exhaling—all eased while somewhere close by an alarm sounded.

People ran past the gap in the curtains, doctors and nurses rushing to save some other soul in crisis, but Austin barely noticed, his lips parting for a new tide to wash in, this time not trying to fight it.

Dom stood in the lea of Austin's legs, his arms a brand-new harbour, kissing him like this ebb and flow was more than the repayment of a debt, kiss deepening like the water that had tried to part him from his daughter.

That had also brought them together.

His arms enveloped Austin, and at any other time, he would have loved it. Would have encouraged Dom's strong hold to tighten. Because Charles hadn't been wrong: Dom *was* his type. And because, dammit, he must have hit his head harder than that scan had indicated.

He *must* have.

He broke off as abruptly as they'd come together, ache in his chest rushing back as soon as Dom also retreated, his steps slow, his lips reddened, which he wiped with the back of a hand that had held Austin twice now, both times close to drowning.

The first was explicable—a man reaching out for his child and doing whatever it took to save her. The second was less so, Austin having no idea what the hell he'd been thinking, his body saying yes to a kiss his head should have thought more than twice at.

This was a student's parent who was married to a woman. Or he had once been.

Now Dom stood framed by the cubicle curtains. "I don't . . . ," he started to say, fingers rising to his lips again, a flush climbing as fast. "I don't go about kissing—" He gestured in Austin's direction, then searched his face before making a promise, voice full of what Austin had judged him so often for lacking. Now his commitment couldn't be any clearer.

"I'll find a better way to thank you. You want something? I'll get it for you," he said as if he wasn't a jobbing builder in a torn and paint-stained T-shirt. "For Maisie." He touched his lips one last time, blinking. "I promise."

Dom tugged the curtain closed behind him, heavy footsteps receding, leaving Austin alone, wondering.

What else had he got wrong about him?

3

A ustin turned that thought over all the way back to Glynn Harber, his head still throbbing even though Luke must have heeded his earlier plea to slow down, taking each corner slow and steady.

He barely noticed, too busy rewinding and replaying what just happened. The fact that Luke was silent didn't register either, until they got back to the school, pulling up beside the old stable block Austin shared with Charles and Hugo. Luke broke that silence when Austin twisted to scan the empty seats behind them.

"Looking for something?"

"My jacket. It's bad enough that I lost a shoe." He touched the edge of the dressing on his forehead. "Can't remember if I still had it on before I . . ." He clenched his jaw, reliving almost drowning.

Perhaps Luke saw that. "Nauseous?" He turned off the engine and grabbed a leaflet from the dashboard. "This says it might last for a while. Especially if you don't take it easy. Need some help getting out?"

"No." Austin took a couple of the slow breaths that worked best to settle his stomach. "I'm fine." Even he knew that was a stupid answer. "It could have been much worse."

Luke took the keys from the ignition and focused on them instead of meeting his eye.

"It could have been," he finally agreed. Austin watched him draw in a long, slow breath of his own. "But no, you didn't have your jacket on when Nick pulled you out of the water."

"He pulled me out?" Austin must have blanked that. "I don't remember him being there."

A memory surfaced, rising as suddenly as that nausea, vivid enough he felt the cold splash of water in his face and Maisie clinging, coughing, choking, both of them sinking before Dom must have kicked even harder.

A hand *had* reached out for them.

He saw it again now and felt the same swell of a wave lifting him before suddenly dropping, that hand further away, not closer, Nick's desperation stark until he'd managed to haul Maisie to safety.

Dom hadn't let up once she was safe, he remembered.

He shoved me against the sea wall.

Held me there until Nick grabbed me too.

That's why my ribs ache.

Another thought swiftly followed.

Fuck me, he's strong. No way I could have done that. Neither of us would have made it.

He clenched his fist, the sting of abrasions a good distraction from an action replay that only made him feel sicker. "I'll . . . I'll call Nick later and thank him. Oh shit. My phone."

Luke nipped that worry in the bud. "Nick brought it and your tablet to the hospital. You dropped it on the table outside the Anchor. Found your jacket too." He glanced over his shoulder. "It's in the back of the bus. But yes, do call him. I know he wants to speak to you. He was . . ." Luke frowned. "What you did . . . diving in like that? It got to him. *Really* got to him. He said to tell you yes."

"Yes . . . You mean to upping the renovation budget?"

That should have been good news, but Luke's next glance was wary. "Yes, he asked his legal counsel to call an emergency meeting. Asked his board of directors to agree to another twenty percent." That was good news, no reason for Luke to sober. "Then he handed over your jacket. A letter fell out of one of its pockets. Addressed to me."

He made sure to meet Austin's eye, wariness shifting to worry. "I haven't opened it yet." He unfastened his seatbelt, reaching inside his own jacket to retrieve it, laying it over the bus keys on his lap. "Up until I saw this, I thought I'd misheard what you said back at the harbour. About leaving us." He clarified. "About leaving Glynn Harber, I mean."

Austin wondered how he'd ever seen Luke as icy—as a cold fish who couldn't show emotion. The man beside him showed plenty.

"Don't leave us."

"Luke—"

"No. Fuck it, Austin. Don't leave. Not when we're just getting started." And there was the fighting spirit that had been so easy to rally behind when the school had been at risk of sinking.

Like I was earlier.

Luke asked a simple question. "Why would you leave now?"

"Because you don't need me."

Luke denied that, shaking his head in a way that would

have made Austin's head pound if he'd tried it. "Of course I need you. We all do. Don't you believe me?" He continued before Austin could answer. "Tell me, who put together the refinancing proposal? The one that meant I could buy the school without selling off its biggest asset?"

Austin's gaze caught on the woods that made Glynn Harber feel sheltered. A sanctuary for so many children who'd been through tough times.

And for me.

"I put the proposal together, but—"

"And who sourced all of those grants so we get to offer twice as many free school places for children who need them?"

"I did, only—"

"Austin, you're the only reason we're getting a second chance to make the school a success."

"I'm really not. That's down to you, and you *don't* need me," Austin repeated. "Not now I've set everything up for you. Once the art building renovation is squared away, all you'll need is a bookkeeper."

"That isn't what you're qualified for?"

Austin shrugged. He was and Luke knew it.

"Or is it working in a small school that's not enough for you?" Luke asked quietly.

That came closer so Austin nodded. He shook his head just as quickly, wincing. "No, it's not the school. It's . . ." He made the mistake of looking into eyes he used to see as rock-hard. Now they were beseeching, begging him to share, but Austin averting his gaze only brought the stables into focus.

Luke must have seen the flinch Austin couldn't hold in at the sight of accommodation he'd shared for months now. He sounded surprised. "You don't like sharing with Charles and Hugo? That's why you want to leave?"

"No, I love sharing with them. Loved it, I mean. It's . . ."

Luke gave him a moment before filling Austin's silence. "You know, I've had moments here where it seemed like I was the odd one out. Everyone else was coupled up, you know? Complete. It's easy to feel on the outside around that kind of happiness." He turned in his seat, Austin not needing to turn as well to know he looked uphill where Sol lived with his new partner. "You and Sol seem to have put the past behind you. I've seen you chatting with his new partner. And Cameron—" It was Luke's turn to wince, no way to sugarcoat that Sol's nephew still blanked Austin more often than he managed to act civil.

"It's nothing to do with Sol being with Jace. And I've given up on Cameron."

"Given up on him? In what way?"

"On him ever forgetting what happened." The reason for that came out as rough as those rocks outside the harbour. "My boyfriend lost a parent and gained a child to raise out of the blue. Cameron didn't ask for that. None of us did. Everything changed overnight with no warning." He swallowed, still tasting sea salt. "I left right when they . . ."

"Needed your help?"

"No." Austin shook his head. "Cameron didn't need me. He couldn't have made it any clearer that he wanted me out of the picture. Didn't want *anyone*, full stop. Not even Sol."

Lately, he'd had to confront that self-sufficient first impression. He did so again now, sitting in the shadow of a school where he'd seen Cameron warm to plenty of people. To flourish as a gifted artist, like his uncle. To laugh and smile with anyone not called Austin Russell.

"Cameron needed someone to depend on. That wasn't ever going to be me." Austin rushed to finish when it looked as if Luke disagreed. "Sol used to be able to work anywhere. Came with me with each promotion. But Cameron needed to be in one place to feel steady. I could see it even if Sol couldn't. I couldn't stay put, not if I wanted to reach my targets."

If Luke had ever spoken more quietly, Austin didn't know when. "Targets? Whose?"

"Mine." He listed several, aware they sounded hollow. "For more challenge. For more control of multiple projects. The job I took when I split with Sol was a huge jump up the pay scale. The one after it was even better, plus it gave me access to extras."

"Extras? Like?"

"Bonuses. Matched giving. The chance of corporate sponsorship." At least, that's what he'd been promised.

"And that matters to you because?"

"My mother runs a charity."

"Ah," Luke said. "Well, she has my sympathy there. Fundraising never stops, does it?" He changed tack. "You've had challenge here though, yes?" Luke scanned his face. Must have seen his small nod because he continued. "And had control of multiple projects? You know they're only the start, don't you?"

Austin nodded again, not only his head aching now. His hand rose to his chest, rubbing. Of course he knew. He'd helped Luke plan to make this school rise from Supernus' ashes.

Luke shifted in his seat, angled to face him. "I'd mentally factored you into all of it. Got years of expansion projects that seemed doable with both of us driving them forward.

Sharing the management load together. Building something not only bigger but better." He paused. Pressed his lips together. Seemed to think twice before adding, "You leaving for a big jump up a pay scale doesn't . . ."

"What?"

"Ring true," Luke admitted. "Not now. Not compared to when I first met you. Back then I wouldn't have had a problem believing money was your motivation."

Austin's hand still rubbed his chest, stopping when Luke leaned over to tap the exposed face of his wristwatch.

"That's a Breitling, right?" He watched Austin nod. "Thought so. It was one of the bonuses you mentioned?" They both looked at the face of a watch worth thousands. Now its band sported a scuff those rocks must have gifted. "You turned up here from Supernus wearing that and driving a fifty-grand company car, but you haven't once moaned about doing without since you jumped ship to be my right-hand man."

"To be your temporary bursar," Austin reminded him bluntly. "*Temporary.* You knew I wasn't staying. I . . . I can't afford to. Not long-term."

"Because you're all about the money?" Luke sat back, his gaze still quizzical. Still warm as well. Austin avoided his eye as Luke asked, "If that's really the case, tell me when you last drew all of your wages?"

"My wages? I . . ."

"Haven't drawn them all since you got here?" Luke made a confession of his own. "You're not the only one who can read a balance sheet, you know. We're more alike than we're different, you and I. That's why I wonder if whatever it is you're looking for could be right here already. Like it was for me." He surveyed Austin for another long, quiet moment. "So, if we're really cut from the same cloth and wages aren't your driver—"

Austin was tired, so tired he couldn't be polite much longer. Couldn't keep his eyes open either. He closed them as he snapped, "I'm not the same as you. For a start, I'm no good with kids."

"I'm going to have to beg to differ. And I know plenty of children who'd line up to tell you the same when the summer break is over." Luke's voice lowered. "Especially the one you risked your life for this morning, but of course you need to do whatever makes you happy."

Austin rubbed his brow, shielding eyes he kept closed while Luke continued speaking, sure they must look as sore and red-rimmed as Dom's had under that stark hospital lighting.

"Think about that, will you?" Luke asked. "Your happiness, Austin. *Yours*. Not some definition of success you've used as a benchmark up until you came here." His voice softened. Thickened. Came out raw and honest. "I couldn't have found my own happiness without you. Any of it. I'll never forget that, and you shouldn't either."

Something landed on Austin's lap, his resignation letter there when he opened his eyes.

Luke spoke again. "I didn't open it. And I won't. Not yet, because I know that if I haven't had time to breathe these last few months, you can't have had time either. It hasn't been a usual summer break. We've been so busy." He placed the concussion protocol leaflet on top of Austin's resignation. "This says to take it easy, so that's what I want you to do now. At least until the kids get back at the start of September. Everyone else is taking some time off until then. You should too. Where's home for you?"

"Home? Exeter. Why?"

"Go there, maybe? Not thinking about targets for a while might make all the difference."

Targets were all he'd face if he went home to his mother.

Austin shook his head, instantly regretful. "I don't need any time off," he said through another rolling wave of nausea. "And I am going home soon, only not yet. Not until the renovation bids come in and the right firm gets chosen. For Sol." And for Cameron, he could admit to himself. Another mistake he could put right before leaving.

"Shadow me instead then," Luke countered. "The sixth-form boarding students come back early. They'll be here next Friday, half of them brand new to the school—don't know each other at all. That's why I take them up on the moor to start the bonding process. And they'll need to bond to get through the next few years of exam stress. You . . ."

He paused, searching Austin's face.

"You mentioned matched giving? I wouldn't have guessed that was important to you. You know we don't have the cash for anything like that, don't you?" He continued without waiting for an answer, aware like Austin that Glynn Harber was years away from profit. "But maybe seeing how we do our own version of matched giving each year might tick another happiness box for you?"

Austin didn't have the energy to explain the world of difference between the type of corporate sponsorship he'd been promised, which had made him stick out work he'd hated, and whatever version of it Luke did with his students.

He meant to say no.

Needed to.

Instead, he made the mistake of meeting Luke's eyes and nodding.

LATER THAT NIGHT, something dragged Austin from sleep, his mattress shifting, lurching like the waves had.

He rolled away, fighting his bedsheets, empty arms feeling all wrong. He flailed to find what was missing, shout cutting off when a familiar voice yelped, "Hey, mind my nuts, will you?"

"What the fuck?" he croaked, groggy. "Charles?"

"Of course it's me," Charles hissed. "Who else would risk getting kicked in the crown jewels at dark o'clock to check you're still alive and kicking?"

Austin sat up. "Your balls would be safe if you hadn't snuggled up to me with no warning."

"I did warn you, remember?" Charles said before blinding him with a beam of light so bright, Austin had to yank the sheets up.

"What the hell?" He fumbled for his bedside light before lowering the sheet again.

The lamp's glow gave Charles a halo. "Hi," he said as if sliding into Austin's bed after midnight was normal. "How are you feeling?"

"Feeling?" Austin took stock. "I'm . . ."

Disoriented fit best.

Aching came a close second.

Bone-tired washed in third.

"I feel like it's the middle of the bloody night." He squinted at the phone Charles brandished. "What are you doing with that?"

"What do you think I'm doing? Snapping nudes for your dating profile? Although, it's not the worst idea in the world." He lifted the sheets, peering before Austin wrestled them from him, pulling them down.

Charles continued undaunted. "You know what they say . . . There's someone out there for everybody, even a ghost-white body like yours. You really should consider ditching your suit and tie if you're taking some time off. How about you borrow a pair of my shorts to sunbathe with me tomorrow? Got a pair that would suit you, covered in crabs." He made a pincer with his free hand. "Snippy, just like you. I'll be in the garden all afternoon, going through the learning journeys for my new class of kids. Make sure I know all about them so I can plan the classroom for them."

"No. I'll need to . . ." Austin almost said *tie up loose ends before leaving.* He stopped himself, nowhere near ready to have that *don't leave* conversation with Charles again. "I'll need to get back to work tomorrow."

"That sounds a chore." Charles tugged at the sheet, drawing it a fraction lower. "Would you at least consider getting a spray tan? Might help you look a bit less consumptive."

He teased but he peered closely. At least he dropped his phone. He also finally dropped his teasing.

"Hugo and I said we'd take it in turns to check on your noggin, remember? Make sure your brains didn't actually leak out of your ears after that nasty bump to your head. Although, I could take a few headless torso shots while I'm here for anyone looking for a small yet perfectly formed power bottom with a ferocious temper."

"How about no?"

"How about I also add a voice note with some of your zingers I've recorded? There's bound to be some random who'd get off on your brand of fierce and brittle."

"Brittle? You woke me from a dead sleep, Charles. What

did you expect? I was right in the middle of a dream." One that now he was awake, he was glad to have escaped, his arms still weirdly empty.

Christ, I dreamed I let her go.

She sank, and I didn't even try to save her.

He wrapped both arms around his middle, then let himself go just as quickly, rubbing his eyes rather than see worry crease the brow of the closest he'd come to a best friend since . . .

Sol.

Maybe that knock on the head made him honest.

Since before I became responsible for a kid I didn't hang around for.

Now he looked into eyes that were usually full of laughter. That had brimmed with it every day since his and Charles' first meeting. Now he couldn't ignore that they were also full of caring.

For me.

Fuck, I'll miss him.

Austin pulled himself together. "No nudes." He grabbed his watch from the bedside table. "For fuck sake, it's barely two in the morning."

"Shame," Charles said, yawning. He lay down, looking comfy. "I'm good at taking nudes. Tasteful ones. Ask Hugo."

The bedroom door pushed open, Hugo there with a first-aid kit, sleep rumpled but smiling. "Or maybe we should ask the lucky recipient of your last naked selfies."

"That was an honest mistake." Charles sat up, the picture of innocence, blinking and still haloed. "Besides, the bishop never mentioned getting them, so maybe they didn't send properly."

"We can but pray," Hugo said, swinging his calm gaze to Austin. "How are you?"

"I'm fine. You don't need to look after me," he said, no idea why that came out exactly as brittle as Charles had stated.

Hugo must have heard it. He came around the bed to sit beside him, Austin now sandwiched between him and his partner. "Because you don't need caring for?" His voice dropped. "Or do you think you don't deserve it?" He continued before Austin could answer. "You know it isn't every day that we almost lose a housemate, so maybe you could humour us both and let yourself be coddled?"

"I only mean that I'm pretty self-sufficient."

"I can believe that too," Hugo said while rummaging in the first-aid kit and fishing out a penlight. "You're a very competent person, but even you might struggle to check if your own pupils are dilating correctly."

"That's what I tried to do," Charles protested. "With my phone."

"Yes," Hugo said, his smile as soft as his tousled bed head. "I heard how well that went. At least we all know there's nothing wrong with Austin's lungs." He raised the penlight, watching closely. "Nothing wrong here either." He clicked it off, compassion the first thing to come back into Austin's focus. "Now really, how are you feeling?" he asked again, kindness tugging the real truth from him.

"Tired." His eyelids were so heavy that keeping them open was hard work. "Achy," he added as Hugo nodded, every bone in his body begging him to lie down instead of sitting. "Worried."

"About little Maisie?" Hugo nodded again. "It's a miracle you noticed her." He plumped a pillow, his hand on Austin's shoulder gentle but firm until he sank, sighing, into the pillow's softness. "I know her parents must think so. I'm sure grateful doesn't come close to describing how her father must have felt that you were there for her when he wasn't."

That surprise kiss in a hospital cubicle flashed back, full of raw emotion.

Austin swallowed, glad that was the moment Hugo encouraged Charles to go back to their bedroom.

Hugo stayed a few minutes longer, repacking his first-aid kit, pausing before turning out the bedside light. "How did you?"

Austin rolled to face him. "How did I what?"

"Notice her. One little girl all the way across a bustling harbour." Hugo peered again as if searching for something. "The quayside was busy. Full of tourists. And you were busy too. Fully engaged, talking and tapping away on your phone one minute. Then the next, you'd gone, running hell for leather. None of us noticed why. Not even people who were much closer, but you homed in on her like a guided missile. Her father did too, but that's not uncommon with parents." He touched a scar slicing his cheek. "Seen it first-hand in Syria. People running towards danger to protect their children."

He searched Austin's face some more, and maybe if he hadn't been so wiped out, he would have rolled away from his next question.

"What did you see?"

The truth bobbed to the surface.

"Her wings."

"Wings?" Hugo asked with gentle amusement. "Like an angel?" Maybe he didn't expect an answer or had put Austin's silence down to the remnants of concussion. He clicked off the bedside light murmuring, "You were certainly Maisie's guardian angel today. A miracle for both her and her father. Her whole family will sleep better tonight because, wings or not, you didn't only watch over her, did you? You took action." In the dark, a ghost of a kiss touched his forehead. "Bless you for acting, Austin."

Austin tucked that blessing away like he had the resignation Luke had refused to accept. He added Charles waking to check up on him to it, sliding it next to a similarly affecting moment of Maisie's dad on his knees. Then he drifted, but what Hugo had asked still hovered before sleep took him.

Wings like an angel?

No.

They were like my little sister's.

4

The next week brought end-of-summer blue skies and Austin getting cockblocked. Or study-blocked, at least, Luke somehow knowing each time he tried to slip into their shared office, catching him yet again late on Friday morning.

Luke pushed down Austin's laptop lid, which closed with a click as firm as his tone. "No. No more of that."

"I wanted to—"

"Set yourself back? Spark another headache? Charles says you've been doing better for a bit of lazing in the garden with him."

"Yes." Austin touched where the dressing on his forehead had been. "But to be honest, there's only so many times I can listen to him rehash how last season's *Love Island* ended now I'm back to normal."

"Arguably, anyone normal would be making the most of some time off." He rounded the desk. "The deadline for bids will come no matter how many times you check the inbox, so leave it alone, yes? Maybe think about what you could bring to the moor walk later instead, if you're really feeling better?"

"Bring?"

"Yes." Luke sat at his side of their shared desk. "For our version of matched giving?" He focused on Austin's brow as if the scrape was still there. "You do remember me telling you, don't you?"

"Yes. I didn't lose my memory. I just thought it was for the sixth-form students, that's all."

"It usually is." Luke opened a desk drawer, digging through it. "I ask the upper-sixth students to give something they learned here to the new students joining the lower sixth. Something they want to pass on that helped them, and get them to explain why. It provokes conversation. Helps the friendship formation process."

"You said it's an exchange though?"

Luke rummaged in the next drawer down. "Yes."

"So, what do the new kids give in return?"

"Oh. That's always interesting. And often a mystery." He bent, digging in the furthest drawer down. "Some people arrive at Glynn Harber weighed down. Carrying something they'd much rather put down but feel that they can't. Only carrying it means they can't take on anything new while their hands are too full. Their heads and hearts too," he said simply, straightening to meeting Austin's eyes across their desk. "All I ask is that they let someone who's been here for years carry part of their load for them. To believe that we'd want to."

"Then what?"

"Then the new kids seal up something that symbolises whatever it is that's holding them back. Everyone knowing what's inside their envelope isn't the point. Trusting someone else to carry it for them so they don't have to manage it on their own is the real aim. That's what this moor walk is all about. Matching an old hand at trusting and sharing with someone newer to it. They can swap their envelopes back later in the year or let them go forever if they want to."

"Later in the year?" He wouldn't be here. Should be gone by the start of September if he was going to stand a chance of making up the deficit in his target. "What if . . . what if someone's partner doesn't stay here long enough to swap back?"

"I find these partnerships tend to last, whatever happens, but believe me, when you're ready to let go of whatever's held you back for good, you'll recognise the perfect moment. Ah!"

Luke found what he'd looked for, a couple of padded envelopes landing on the desk along with a Kit Kat that he unwrapped. Snapped in half. Passed two fingers to Austin.

"So, like I said, if you're determined to sit up here and watch the school's email inbox like a pot that won't boil, go ahead and have a think about what might fit in one of these." He slid one of the envelopes Austin's way. "Pretend you're brand new at Glynn Harber. What do you want to let go?" He held up a finger. "Don't tell me. Pop it in the envelope. Seal it and bring it with you later."

"How about you? What's going in yours?"

"Mine?" Luke scanned the study. "Hmm. Something to symbolise what I hope Glynn Harber gives back in return." Luke touched their empty chocolate-bar wrapper. "I've given a Kit Kat before because I can still remember the first time someone split one with me right here in this room. That was a turning point for me. A positive one. A difficult time made easier by sharing."

He got up, still searching for something that he finally located, returning with a framed photo of a knight in tarnished armour. "This is what I'll exchange this year. It marks another of my lowest moments."

"Who will you swap it with?"

"Not sure yet." Luke slid it into his envelope. "I've got an idea though." He flicked a glance Austin's way. "I think it'll be a positive message for them that bad times can end."

Austin pulled the spare envelope towards him. "So, you want me to do the opposite? Put something negative in here?"

"Exactly." Luke headed for the door, pausing at the threshold. "Don't think about it too hard. You could seal up a Kit Kat. Or seal up something more personal that you wished didn't rule you." He studied Austin as he had so often in this room that used to be a battleground between them. "Go with your gut. It hasn't let you down yet, has it?"

He left, a final order ringing out as he took the stairs, echoing through the empty hallway.

"And don't open that bloody laptop."

Austin waited until his footsteps faded, then went ahead and disobeyed him.

MAYBE THAT KNOCK to his head had more lasting impact than Austin had realised.

A headache thumped, no closer to deciding what to stuff in the envelope Luke had left him to fill. He raided the drawer for a couple of painkillers instead, then rested his head on folded arms, waiting for the ache to fade while watching a lone cloud scud across a soft blue sky framed by the window.

Its passage was easier on the eye than what he'd found in his email inbox.

The increased budget was still nowhere close to what the

latest contractors estimated, no way to avoid cutting corners on Sol's renovation.

He kept his head lowered as footsteps approached, slowing at the open doorway.

"Aus? You okay?"

Sol.

Austin still didn't lift his head, eyes fixed on that cloud. Or rather on the patch of blue sky it crossed, as pale as faded denim. "I'm fine."

Sol must have crossed the threshold. His voice next came from much closer, light like the hand he laid on Austin's shoulder. "You gonna be okay going up on the tors with Luke if your head's still bothering you?" Sol's other hand landed on the lid of the open laptop, pushing it closed. "Pretty sure Luke said he banned this."

"He banned *work*. I wasn't working." That summed up the last week. "I was only checking my email." And wishing he hadn't.

Sol crouched by the desk beside him. "You know it's a blast from the past finding you like this, don't you?"

"Like what?" Austin considered sitting up. Decided against it, still wary even though his queasiness had long passed, and because Sol *had* seen him during similar head-on-desk moments. Lots of them. "On second thoughts, don't remind me."

Sol ignored that instruction, his gaze so much warmer now than when Austin had first arrived at Glynn Harber—almost unbelievably so considering their break-up. Maybe time really was the healer Luke had promised. Sol certainly didn't seem to bear any lasting grudges.

"There only used to be two reasons for finding you like this, Aus. Back when we were together, you'd rest your head on the kitchen table when you had accounting exams or needed to go and see your mother." That twinkle faded. "Which is it this time?"

Austin pulled himself together, bracing himself for his head to pound before he sat upright. Thankfully, it didn't. "Neither this time." He glanced at his laptop. "It's the deadline for bids on Monday. Made the mistake of taking a quick look."

Sol's face fell. "And there weren't any?"

"No, there are bids." Only not for the project Sol wanted. Austin glanced at the designs pinned to the wall by his and Luke's desk, wondering which corner would hurt least to cut. He didn't get a chance to ask. Sol had shot to his feet, chuckling on his way to the open window where he leaned out.

"Hey! You sure you still want to bet that tenner?"

"Who are you shouting at?"

"Cameron."

He bet against me getting this done for Sol?

That shouldn't be surprising, no love lost between them. His heart still sank at the confirmation.

At least someone here will be pleased to see me go.

Sol looked over his shoulder. "He just got back from surf club. Ed gave him a lift. I was telling him about the project. Still can't believe I'm finally going to have somewhere flooded with light to work instead of my old dingy classroom."

"You deserve it," Austin said gruffly.

"The kids do. Anyway, that's what I was telling Ed when Cameron bet me a tenner."

"That I wouldn't find a contractor?" Austin sniffed to cover disappointment he told himself to let go—Cameron didn't like him, and he'd live with it. He aimed for the tone that used to be his armour. "His confidence in me is touching."

Sol glanced back. "Hey. Don't go getting all prickly. Cameron didn't bet that you *couldn't* organise the project. The opposite, actually. I'm just trying to wriggle out of paying. He was singing your praises to Ed."

"Really?" That seemed unlikely.

"Well, *singing* is probably a stretch," Sol allowed, his tone softening. "Did you know he's got his own group at Ed's surf club now? He teaches the little ones. Calls it Tiddlers. Maisie Dymond went for a taster session. He said she wasn't ready. Didn't have the arm and leg coordination yet for swimming. Hearing that you fished her out of the water . . ."

And if he'd thought Sol's tone had softened before, now it turned liquid.

"You saved her life, Aus."

Why did that leave him flustered? "Stop calling me Aus. It's not professional."

"And you stop changing the subject. You saved her life and Cameron's got a soft spot for her. Made her his special helper at the last art contest because she couldn't draw as well as the others. She still waves each time she sees him." He crossed his arms, gaze steady. "He also says there's no way she could have lasted longer than a minute or two in open water. Really fucking proud of you for getting to her so quickly."

"I . . ." He didn't know what to say. "Anyone would have done it."

"But *you* did. You're a good person. Deep down, Cameron knows that. That's why he bet there would be some bids." Sol turned back to the window at the sound of an engine. "Jesus, someone's in a hurry."

Gravel skittered, whoever drove fast enough to make it fly

gone by the time Austin got to the window. His gaze fixed on Cameron instead. Or on Sol's new partner Jace, rather, who stood with an arm slung around Cameron's shoulder, listening to his surf-club leader.

Austin backed away from a display of easy affection he'd never be granted.

"Don't go," Sol said, catching his arm, and for one, long difficult moment, Austin wondered if Luke or Charles or Hugo had told him about his resignation, the letter now buried in his desk drawer. Sol's stifled laughter suggested they hadn't. He tugged on Austin's arm and promised, "You really don't want to miss this. You know Ed, right?"

"I've met him."

"Watch him now."

Drawn back to the window, Austin watched Cameron's surf-club leader ease away, still talking, but also checking his appearance in his truck's wing mirror.

"What am I looking at?"

"Ed reliving his first crush. Keep watching."

Austin did, seeing Ed slide a hand through his hair, then mess up what he'd neatened, casting a nervous glance towards the car park.

"But why—"

"Shh. Keep watching," Sol murmured, laughter barely hidden.

Ed brushed down the front of his shirt next, straightening it before deciding to tuck it in. He changed his mind just as quickly, pulling it free.

Sol whispered as if Ed might hear him. "Cracks me up that Ed worships the ground his husband walks on, but the minute he sees Dom, he reverts to a teenager with a raging boner."

"Dom? You mean Dominic Dymond?"

The man himself rounded the corner from the car park, pocketing his keys, paying more attention to an envelope he held than to Ed, who'd raised his hand in greeting, his voice surely pitched lower than Austin had previously heard it.

"Hi, Dom."

In contrast, Sol pitched his voice higher. It came out quiet but breathy, edged with laughter Austin had almost forgotten. "Hi, Dom." Sol fluttered his eyelashes before explaining. "It's like he can't help reliving his first big gay awakening whenever he sees Dom. Happens every single time. Cracks me up."

"Big gay . . ." Austin watched Dom stop by Ed's truck. Saw him nod at something Cameron asked him. "Ed was *with* Maisie's dad?"

So that kiss hadn't only been high emotion or gratitude that had got out of hand, a once-in-a-lifetime stress-valve releasing.

Sol confirmed it. "Mate, he was Ed's first. Years before Dom met his ex-missus, obviously. He's bi, not a player."

Below them, Ed ran a hand through his hair again, still flustered.

Austin caught himself doing the same, his hand rising before he could stop himself from neatening what resting his head on the desk had flattened.

Sol caught that movement, his smile slipping before slowly returning. "You like him too?"

"Like him?" Austin lowered his hand, reliving the moment Dom had got to his knees to thank him. Had told him he owed him. Had also promised to repay him. "I don't know anything about him apart from that he's a student's parent." He recalled the Dymond and Son T-shirt. "And that he's a local chippie. Or builder. Something like that."

"And him being blue collar would be a problem? Not high flying enough for you, Mr. Rat Race? I'm pretty sure Dom's got more strings to his bow than his dad's old—"

Below them, Cameron turned, pointing up at the study window.

Austin jerked away. "Remind me. Why are we having this conversation?"

"Snippy, snippy, snippy," Sol said, craning his neck in a way that lured Austin to come back and copy, craning his own to see Dom take the path to the school's front door. "Save your brittle act for someone who doesn't know you. All I'm saying is that maybe Ed isn't the only one trying to make a good impression. Look."

Austin leaned further. Saw Dom repeat Ed's earlier actions, only using the glass pane in the door instead of a wing mirror. He watched Dom brush sawdust from his shirt before taking a deep breath.

Sol murmured, "I wonder what he's smartening himself up for?"

He backed away, leaving Austin alone in the study with a final question.

"Or who?"

5

Austin took his seat at his desk again as Sol's footsteps faded. Opened his laptop despite Luke's order. Better to appear busy if Dom came looking for him, he decided, than succumbing to the urge to shut the door and pretend the room was empty.

If?

Almost everyone else is on leave. There's no one but me in the building.

Besides, Cameron pointed right at me.

He pulled himself together because, yes, what had happened between them in the hospital might be awkward, but he could be professional.

I'll pretend it didn't happen.

Then another set of footsteps sounded, heavier than Sol's, climbing the stairs and coming closer.

Steel toecaps, he remembered.

He resisted the urge to straighten his hair again, making himself stop by opening his email. The latest renovation bid filled the screen as those footsteps drew closer. They stopped at the threshold, Austin turning before Dom could knock on the study's doorframe.

He meant to say, "*Hello*," but blurted something very different.

"If that was you who drove into the car park going hell for leather, make sure it's the last time."

"I—"

"Do you know how easy it is to kill a kid going that fast?"

Dom blinked. "Kill?" And just like that, Austin heard himself.

He closed his eyes. "Sorry. Let me try that again." He drew in a deep breath. Opened his eyes and said, "Hi. You look better than the last time I saw you."

Dom grinned, relieved, and what a difference that made to a man he'd only ever seen here looking harried. It prompted what he should have asked first.

"How's Maisie?"

"She's great, thanks to you. I mean, I've aged about a hundred years, but apart from her suddenly hating bath time and having bad dreams, you wouldn't know anything had happened to her. And sorry about driving too fast. I didn't think I was, but I'll watch it."

"Thanks."

"And so do you," Dom added. "Look better, I mean. Although you always look good to me." He took a turn at closing his eyes. Muttered a rueful, "For fuck sake," and rubbed the back of his neck. "Sorry, it's just that Maisie's been pointing you out to me for months, that's all. If you weren't around at home time, she'd make me stop under your window so she could wave goodbye and blow you kisses."

"She did?" Austin hadn't known that.

"Yes. Every single day it was my turn to collect her." There was that ruefulness again along with a small smile. "And a lot of the days that weren't mine, so I'd end up getting here late." His gaze met with Austin's, holding steady. "I got into the habit of looking out for you. *For Maisie.* Didn't need to be a genius to realise that her best days were the ones where you were anywhere near the classroom at home time."

"Like the last day of term?"

"When you gave me the mother of all bollockings?" Dom nodded. "Especially that day," he agreed, leaning against the doorframe, no blame in his tone that Austin noticed. If anything, it warmed. "She re-enacted it almost word for word for my dad when we got home, complete with you wagging your finger."

"I didn't—" Austin stopped. Thought. Took a turn at rubbing the back of his neck before he realised who he mirrored. "Ah."

"Yeah, ah. You wagged your finger, told me to try harder, then said, "You massive wanker," under your breath. Got to see and hear it all over again when she acted it out for her mum later at bath time too."

"That's nothing. I recently taught Tor Trelawney how to say shit, fuck, bollocks." Dom's laughter made every word of the apology he'd written to Tor and his parents worth it.

"Maisie added you to her prayer list at bedtime after you swore at me down on the harbour too." Dom steepled fingers Austin remembered could be both firm and gentle, pitching his voice higher, like Sol had only minutes earlier, this prayer one unbroken sentence that was pure Maisie Dymond.

"God bless Grampy and Mummy and Daddy and Tor and"—he aimed for girlish in a way that meant Austin couldn't hold a smile in—"help Austin Russell stop swearing at my daddy."

A laugh burst out before Austin could stop it. He bit his lip to stop a grin matching Dom's, which widened. "Did I apologise for that yet?" He thought he had but wasn't certain, not when their conversation at the hospital had competed with his ears still ringing.

"Doesn't matter," Dom said, plain and simple. "What does matter is that you do look better. Less in pain than when I last saw you." That smile faltered. "Are you? I . . . I've been worried." He took a step across the threshold before stopping. "Is it . . . Is it okay to come in?"

He hovered, neither in nor outside the study, hesitating with what Austin might have labelled as shyness if not for what still hung unspoken between them. There hadn't been *anything* shy about the way Dom had gathered him up and kissed him. No hesitation in how he'd prolonged it.

Austin could almost still feel it.

He swallowed, his mouth too dry to answer.

Dom came closer to the desk, frown a sudden reminder of how Austin had so often perceived him, but it was concern that threaded his words together, not brusqueness. "Are you sure you're recovered enough to be working?" He glanced at the window Austin and Sol had stood at. "Sol's son said you were up here with his dad, but you'd been banned from working. Said your headmaster would have your guts for garters if he found out."

"Sol's nephew."

"Sorry?"

"Cameron is Sol's nephew, not his son." Although that difference was marginal, Sol more of a father figure to Cameron than Austin could have ever mastered. He rushed on before getting mired in something that had crossed his mind increasingly often since diving head first after this man's daughter.

I would have done the same for Cameron in a heartbeat back then. But I'm pretty sure he wouldn't believe it.

And why would he after Austin had left with no explanation?

Maybe Dom noticed that thought scud like that cloud had, framed by the window. More frown lines appeared, which shouldn't be attractive, but Austin found himself looking first at lips he'd kissed the last time they'd been this close, then into eyes narrowed by worry.

They fixed on what was left of the abrasion at Austin's hairline. "That still bothering you?"

"This?" Austin touched the margin of a bruise the bathroom mirror had reflected as yellow that morning. A dressing had covered it the last time he and Dom had been this close. Now he felt strangely naked as Dom searched it. "N-no, it's not bothering me now. I'm fine. My boss is overcautious, that's all. And I'm not working. Not really. I was only ..." He gestured at his laptop.

Dom searched his face one more time before glancing at the laptop screen. "What's that?" He leaned closer. "A quote for some building work?"

He must have seen what had made Austin rest his head on the desk—an estimate far higher than he'd expected from a firm with none of the expertise they needed. The total quoted was eye-watering, higher than even the extended budget, blowing it out of the water.

"What exactly are you planning on building for that much?" Dom asked. "A whole new school?"

Austin snapped the laptop lid shut. "It's nothing." And there was that brittleness Sol had mentioned. And Charles.

Now Austin heard what they must have, no way to pretend that Dom's smile didn't freeze before fading. No way to ignore that he pulled back either, careful, as if on ice too thin to hold him.

Austin rushed to fill the silence. "Sorry. I didn't mean to sound . . ." He touched his brow without thinking, aware that Dom's gaze followed. Also aware that blaming snapping on an injury that had healed would be a cop out. He touched the laptop instead. "Of course that was something." He guessed that came out sounding warmer, Dom's arms uncrossing, thawing. "Only it's not an estimate for a whole new school. It's a bid to rebuild part of it."

Dom came closer. "Part? Which part?"

"An art building." He remembered that Dom had mentioned Sol by name. "You know Sol?"

"Vaguely." Dom's gaze skittered away, and he straightened, rubbing the back of his neck again. "I know one of his friends a bit better."

Ed.

Austin remembered what Ed had done while he'd watched from the window, checking his appearance in a wing mirror. Saw him run a hand through his hair all over again, wanting to look his best. Then he revisited Dom doing the exact same thing, using the glass in the school's front door as a mirror.

A new brittleness threaded through him then, but not one that would show in his voice if he spoke up. This version wasn't sharp-edged. It tingled instead of slicing, somehow both light and fragile.

For me.

He wanted to look his best for me.

Austin stood to escape a jittery feeling, gesturing at some

designs on the study wall as a diversion. "Sol's had to manage without a decent studio for years now. This is what he wants. Not only for himself, though, or for the kids who come here."

Dom followed. "What is it?"

"A community art centre. Something really special set in the school's original art building, but melding old with new bumps up the renovation costs."

Dom studied the drawings the same way he'd studied Austin's face, intent. *Intense.* Maybe making links between what he saw now and what he'd seen on the laptop screen before Austin had closed it. "That's a lot of ironwork and glass. What kind of condition is the original ironwork in? And how much of the glass is intact? Because that quote had to be for all new. How old is the original building?"

"Well over a hundred years. It's Victorian."

"Can't see the planners giving a green light to scrapping all the original glass if it's a listed building. Be cheaper too, if most of it can be salvaged."

"Salvaged?" Austin glanced back at his laptop. "I'm not sure that was mentioned. I didn't read the fine detail yet." Just the bottom line, which was as steep as the hill the art building stood on. "To be honest, I wasn't even meant to see that. Not until the deadline."

"Because you need to be impartial? It's you who'll decide which bid to accept?"

"God, no. I'll only make a recommendation. The final decision will be down to the backers. It's their money the school will spend, but they're busy people, so I'll need to rank the bids for them." If any of them fell within the budget, that was. A frisson of nerves about that made him honest. "Not sure how many I'll have to present to them."

"They're coming in higher than your budget?"

"Just a bit, and that's after it's been bumped up once." He ran a hand through his hair, Dom tracking the movement, a frown hovering as though he'd noticed a slight tremor Austin went ahead and gave a voice to. "I dealt with much bigger numbers in my last job. Multimillions. This project isn't anywhere in the same league, but..."

"But?" Dom asked while moving away to study the last drawing, the woody scent that hung around him combining with something sharper.

Paint and sawdust. He smells like his work.

Dom looked his way, his eyebrows lifting to ask, *"But?"* again.

"But it feels more important than anything else I've worked on."

"Because?" Dom wandered back, revisiting drawings he'd already looked at, tilting his head to read an annotation.

"Because I never needed to care before."

That caught Dom's attention. "About?" he asked, gaze the same shade as that patch of blue outside his window drawing far more from him. Or maybe that was down to Dom leaning a shoulder against the wall like it needed propping, posture relaxed and easy as if he had all the time in the world to listen.

"Because almost all of my old projects were on paper. I found budgets to trim. Made cuts. Pressed save. Moved on. Working here is nothing like that. *Nothing.* I never expected spending money instead of saving it to be harder." He hadn't verbalised this before. Hadn't needed to until Dom had asked and then waited for an answer, which finally emerged with a questioning edge. "Maybe because this project is for people I can picture?" He touched the edge of a drawing, as amazed now as when he'd first met Sol at what he could capture with ink on paper. "Getting this right matters so much to my ex—"

"Sol," Dom said quietly, nodding as if that answered an unasked question. He levered himself away from the wall, tilting his head to read another annotation Sol had left. "'Disability provision. Child and adult'." His gaze flashed Austin's way. "That matters to him?"

"To all of us." Austin blinked at how easily that *us* had rolled off his tongue. "The backers own the brain injury care home next door. And a sailing business for people with all kinds of disabilities. All their clients would get to use the art building once it's renovated. All of them were involved in the planning stages, consulted about what would make it work for them, so . . ." He shrugged. "Sol's prioritised making it inclusive, but that's brought its own problems."

"Why? Because it's listed?"

"Partly." He studied Sol's drawings of the finished building, glass seeming to shimmer on the paper before meeting eyes that asked for more detail. "It's hard to explain the scale of the work. How it needs so many different specialists." His gaze flicked to the lettering on Dom's T-shirt. "Not only carpenters or general builders." He tagged on a quick, "No offence."

"None taken. This is my dad's business, not mine." He touched the same Dymond & Son wording stretched across his chest. "What's the current state of the building?" He held a hand up, stopping Austin before he could answer.

Instead, he made an offer.

"Or maybe it would be easier to show me?"

6

Austin led the way out, pausing once at the foot of the stairs, the school's front door to his left, sunlight streaming through it.

He turned away from that exit, his footsteps echoing along the empty hallway.

Behind him, Dom faltered, Austin glancing over his shoulder to see him looking back at the door. "Isn't it that way?"

"The art building?" Austin hedged, still walking. "That's one way to get to it."

Leaving through the front door would be the quickest route, but it would also take them straight past an audience he wasn't ready to face. He continued in the opposite direction, trying to sound cool, calm, and collected instead of anxious. "This way's bet—"

"Hey."

Dom didn't only fill out that T-shirt Austin had watched him brush off outside the front door. He also didn't leave any room for Austin to avoid giving his real reason. Dom stood, unmoving despite the increasing distance between them, waiting for Austin to stop before asking him another, quieter question. "Or is it that you don't want your ex to see you with me?"

Austin did stop then, turning to see Dom with the sun behind him, his face in shadow, expression hidden.

He wanted to see it.

Needed to know what crossed it.

Austin walked back slowly, stopping a few paces away, no reason to feel out of his depth while on dry land, and yet . . .

I do.

I have no fucking idea why.

No clue why them seeing us together matters either.

It didn't, he realised as Dom watched him.

But I still want him to myself.

Dom asked another question, his voice quieter, even though there was no one to overhear them. "You and him are still a thing then?"

"Me and Sol? No. It's been years."

Dom shrugged. Glanced upstairs. Met his eye again and held it. "Seems like you're putting in a lot of effort for him, and time passing doesn't have to mean you're not still attracted."

That certainly seemed true for Ed. Austin couldn't help snorting. "I'm really not hung up on him. Sol's with someone else now."

Dom only raised his eyebrows, so Austin kept going.

"Someone who suits him better. Another artist. I'm happy for him. For both of them. We—" He stopped before saying, *wanted different things from life.* That was an old lie that would slither out all too easily if he let it. The truth sounded so much harsher. "I couldn't make myself be what he needed.

Part of a kid's life for the long haul." *A parent.* "I'm no good at it so I left."

"His nephew, Cameron?"

Austin nodded, not sure how Dom could listen to what he'd just said and still look at him like . . .

Like he's interested.

Because he was, no way to mistake it when he took the last few steps closer, his hand landing on Austin's shoulder and squeezing. "Kids are tough even when they're yours. He came to live with you both because . . . ?"

"No other option," Austin said baldly.

"And he was how old?"

"Thirteen."

Dom squeezed his shoulder again. "Teenagers. Already dreading it and I had months to get used to the idea of a baby." Something scudded across his face faster than that cloud had across the window upstairs, there and gone in a moment. "At least that's what I thought." His pat on Austin's shoulder felt strangely like consolation. "Nine months should have been long enough to wrap my head around her coming, right? Still learning every day that I don't have the first clue what I'm doing."

"She's yours though. I know it's different when you hold your own kids for the first—"

"The first time I held her was worse than jumping in the harbour. Never felt terror like it. Didn't trust my judgement back then. Still don't now, to be honest."

Austin opened his mouth, then closed it as Dom continued.

"Gemma and I had already split before we knew she was pregnant."

"Then you got back together?"

"We tried. Soon figured out that making it work for Maisie meant not using her as a sticking plaster. That we were better apart but friendly. Hasn't all been plain sailing. Lots of adjustment, like moving back here when—"

He looked away abruptly, gaze returning only slowly, something different in it.

Something familiar.

Talking about Cameron must have disturbed long-still waters, Austin decided. Silt stirred now and a memory surfaced.

Dom looked down at him but Austin saw himself reflected, only not in this school hallway. Instead he saw his and Sol's old London bathroom. Saw himself too, clutching the sink the night Cameron had moved in with them for good, the mirror reflecting something close to Dom's expression.

Is that fear?

Maybe not, because Dom picked up where he'd left off.

"Moving closer to family seemed best for Maisie. We did it for her, like we learned to compromise about work, covering for each other if that took us away for a while. It was a lot to start with. Still is in ways neither of us could have predicted, so having something like that dumped in your lap instead of building up to it gradually? Getting a surprise teen instead of a baby? Don't blame you for hesitating."

"Hesitating?" Austin blinked away that bathroom-mirror vision. "I did a lot more than that."

Dom tilted his head the same way he had upstairs, paying close attention. Then he asked, "If it had been Cameron in the water, would you have turned your back? Or jumped in like you did for my daughter?"

Funny how Austin had already asked and answered that question.

Maybe Dom saw that too, answering before Austin got to.

"You'd have done the right thing. Not sure why you thought leaving was the best thing for Cameron back then, but here you are trying to build something for his uncle. That feels like doing the right thing now to you?"

Austin nodded.

Dom did too, slow but steady. "Because sometimes going with our gut is all we can do, right? For ourselves. For our kids, like me and Gemma moving back here for Maisie. It's also why I didn't come to see you sooner. I felt like she needed all of our attention this week."

"You don't have to explain. Or need to come here to tell me."

"I wanted to," Dom said quietly. "A lot."

"You . . ." Austin stopped. Swallowed. Managed to ask, "Maisie's really okay?"

"She's Maisie." And there was another reminder, this time of Sol—love mixed with exasperation. "She bounces back after every stumble, and fuck knows she's had enough of them. She had a rough start. Already faced hurdles other kids won't. Hard not to feel guilt for that."

Splitting up while she'd been so young couldn't have been easy.

"But guilt's pointless. Can't do a thing with it apart from learn and move on. Make the most of the moment, you know, instead of looking back? Enjoy what we've got, not think about a future without her if you hadn't been there for her. That's what I've been telling Gemma all week, but almost losing Maisie like that was . . ."

Austin expected him to say it had been a shock. Dom chose a different way to describe it.

"It was a wake-up call for us both." He straightened. Crossed thick arms across his chest that Austin could almost still feel heaving for breath against his back like it had in the water. "It made us face the future. We'll pull together harder when she gets back."

"Who?"

"Gemma. She's away now, so me staying close to home is even more important. Reassures her that Maisie's safe and well while she's not with her. I want that peace of mind for Gemma these days. Took a few years, but yeah, I can see why you might want good things for Sol. Or maybe . . ." He glanced over his shoulder. "Do you think Cameron's more settled now?"

Austin nodded.

"Okay." He pressed full lips together. "Or maybe you two have unfinished business you can get back to now his nephew's not so needy?"

Austin shook his head, the movement slight to start. Then he shook it harder, clearing this up more important that staving off a headache. "I meant what I said. There's nothing between us, and even if there was . . . Parenting? Being responsible for someone?" He rubbed his arms. Mirrored Dom and crossed them. Said, "It's not for me," and heard more of that stupid fucking sharp edge he'd never noticed until just about everyone here pointed it out. "Besides, Cameron needed an anchor and I'm not done with moving on yet."

Dom's murmur carried in the quiet hallway. "Okay, so you're not seeing anyone or still holding a torch for your ex. I'm not either. Not for Gemma." He mentioned the other reason why not leaving through the front door had seemed a good plan. "And not for Ed Britten either, in case you wondered. Pretty sure he's married, and Maisie keeps me too busy."

He pulled an envelope from his back pocket.

"And yet here I am, bringing this as an excuse to see you again." He passed it over. "Don't ask me why, and don't open it here," he warned before Austin did. "Maisie made it for you. Almost a hundred percent glitter. You'll be sweeping for days."

Austin didn't know what to say. He settled for, "Thanks," but Dom wasn't finished.

"It's just that after I saw you at the hospital, and we . . ." He advanced, arms unfolding, Austin ending his sentence for him.

"Kissed?"

Dom nodded. Nodded again, harder. "Yeah. I couldn't stop thinking about it. Couldn't stop wondering what the fuck I was thinking." He drew in a slow breath as if steeling himself for rejection. "Most of all, I wondered if you'd—"

"Yes."

And there was another repeat, only of a relieved smile he'd last seen upstairs. "You don't know what I was going to ask you."

If there had been any space left between them, it vanished, Dom moving to cup Austin's elbows, drawing him close. They connected, chests meeting, and Austin's nerves somehow both settled and lit, senses heightened, woody scent stronger, the envelope he held creasing.

He also saw that Dom's eyes didn't darken. They warmed like a thick spill of something liquid. Honey maybe, sweet enough Austin could almost taste it. Wanted to. Was an inch away from leaning in and up for a re-do of what they'd last done after being in deep water.

Austin stood poised on the edge of what felt like another long drop while every cell in his body spiralled. Dust motes did too in the air around them, the edges of this moment gilded, just enough sunlight filtering past Dom to show his gaze dropping from Austin's eyes to his lips as though he wanted to replay the same moment, before rising again to the last remains of bruising on Austin's forehead.

He also saw worry flicker.

"I'm fine," Austin said before Dom's gaze dropped an inch or so more, followed by the pad of a thumb, which he brushed under one eye as if to sweep away a shadow.

"Fine, but not sleeping? You still dreaming about what happened as well? Losing sleep like I have?" He made to pull back.

"I am fine." Austin grasped Dom's T-shirt with his free hand, handful of well-worn cotton all that divided him from the warmth of his torso. "You can—"

This time, Dom's kiss was different.

Slow instead of desperate.

Soft, rather than harsh with relief.

At least, that's how it started, shifting gears the moment Austin let go of that twist of T-shirt, fingertips finding bare skin and splaying, hair on Dom's belly tickling until he gripped his hip and pulled him even closer.

Dom's mouth opened, tongue finding his, and it didn't matter that Austin had insisted he'd recovered—dizziness rushed back, surging, so he gripped even harder, fingers digging into firm flesh, holding on as if he'd sink without Dom to hold him. Drown without his mouth breathing for him.

They kissed where students so often crowded.

Austin didn't think about them. Didn't think of bids or targets either, not after Dom's mouth moved on, exploring. His lips slid to the hinge of Austin's jaw, lowered to skim down his throat, ribs expanding again under his palms as though he'd breathe Austin in too, if that was an option. As if he'd do more than inhale him, his mouth opening again to suck, his teeth grazing.

Austin stood where being professional had always mattered. Now he let out a sound that echoed, tipping his head back so Dom could keep going, clinging to him tightly.

Dom's arms came all the way around Austin then too, gathering him so close they cast one shadow. Neither of them noticed, Dom's eyes fixed on his after he raised his head, pupils huge and lips parting again for another kiss that the blast of a horn outside the building interrupted.

He jerked back, his hold loosening, but didn't let Austin go as he turned to the doorway, where more noise erupted, this time shouts and chatter from students, here for the moor walk Austin had agreed to.

The moment shifted, a tide that couldn't rise any higher receding.

Or couldn't rise yet, at least.

Austin pulled back. Wiped his mouth with the back of a hand, straightening his hair with the other. "I . . . I need to go and get changed."

"Changed?"

"For a hike on the moors soon." He gestured at the door the sunlight streamed through. "It's a school tradition. Sixth-form students only. A bonding thing before the school year starts for the younger students. Starts in an hour."

Dom checked his watch again. "I should get back too.

Maisie will be running rings around Dad." He fished out his phone, looking at it for a long moment, his voice still low as if someone listened. "But if you've got time, you could quickly show me the rebuilding project, if you wanted. I . . . I could text Dad? Ask if he's okay to watch her for a bit longer if you—"

"Yes."

It was only one word, but it echoed, worth blurting for a second time because Dom sent his message, smiling.

7

They only made it halfway up the hill before Dom's phone rang. He stopped to answer, Austin trying not to listen in by walking ahead.

"Hi, Dad. You got my message? Is Maisie—?"

His silence drew Austin back.

He drifted closer as Dom got out half a sentence.

"Yes, I know I said—"

He met Austin's eyes then, his own rolling. "Dad, I said I'd be back by lunchtime and I will. I won't let her down. It wasn't me who did last time, was it?" He flinched. Closed his eyes. Something like regret pooled when they opened. "Listen, is she there? Can you give her the phone?" He flinched again, this time holding the phone away, and Austin heard someone bellow.

"He's a bit deaf. Thinks everyone else is," Dom murmured. His focus switched back to his phone. "Okay, she's coming? Great. Now accept my video call, will you." He touched his phone before lifting it to his ear again. "The button should be on the screen now, Dad. Press it." He met

Austin's eye again, amusement so much better than that moment of flinching.

"Yeah. Accept the call. No. No! You don't have to hang up first. Listen. Give Maisie the phone, will you? She knows what to do." He mouthed, *sorry*. A beat later he held out a hand. "Come here," he rumbled, that low pitch as good as a rope tugging. As strong as one too, but Austin hesitated.

"I . . . I can always show you the art building another time."

Dom closed the distance, holding up his phone and sliding that outstretched arm around Austin's shoulder. He bent a little to bring their heads close together and said, "Hi, baby girl. Look who I found."

Maisie's face filled the screen. Or at least one eye and her nose did. "I'm not a baby. I'm a big girl," she said, giving them a great view up a nostril. The screen blurred and Austin pictured her jumping like he'd seen her do so often in the playground, bouncing.

"Stand still then, big girl, and hold the phone a bit further away from your face, will you?" Dom did the same, arm around Austin's shoulder pulling him into shot.

Maisie's sharp inhale was clearer. The rest of her face too, split by a smile that was another family likeness. "You found Austin Russell!"

"I did. I promised, didn't I?"

"That you'd try," Maisie said, switching to solemn and sounding more grown up than he'd ever heard her. "That was what you said. That you'd try your best . . ."

"Because that's all anyone can ever promise," Dom finished, just as serious for a moment that Austin broke with a question.

"How are you feeling, Maisie?"

Maybe that was the wrong question to ask. The phone wobbled like her voice did, and the screen froze for a second, or maybe she had, locked in the same fear Austin still had to shake off each time he woke gasping.

She said, "I . . . I fell in the water."

"Yes. You were so brave, Maisie."

"No, I wasn't." She cut to the chase, putting a different spin on what he'd replayed often at night, wishing he'd got to her sooner. "You were brave. You came to save me."

He tried to say, "*No, that was your daddy*," but couldn't, his throat thick, saved from answering right away by a low prompt in the background, her grandfather issuing a reminder.

"Thank you," she said primly, and there she was, screen unfreezing, curls wild instead of sodden like he'd last seen them, and Dom's arm settled more heavily across his shoulder as if he knew seeing that difference did something to him.

It also sent Austin straight back to both of them sinking, the sun above them shrinking. Rippling. Losing its brightness.

Fuck.

She was drowning. We both were.

"Good girl," Dom rumbled, echoing words that also came from his father in the background. He added a quiet, "She's doing so great."

Austin nodded. Couldn't speak. Nodded again.

Maisie broke the moment. "Did you like my picture?" She must have bounced from foot to foot again, her hair a tangled veil masking her eyes once she settled.

Dom spoke before he could answer. "Where's your head-band, sweetheart?"

"I'll find it!" The phone screen went dark, placed face down, maybe, and Dom snorted, taking the call off speaker.

"Christ. Nothing's ever quick with kids, is it?"

Austin pulled the envelope from his back pocket. "I better open this before she picks up again."

Dom hadn't exaggerated. Glitter exploded, scattering as he unfolded a picture. What remained caught the light, glinting, and the words *Thank you, Austin Russell* sparkled, a picture beneath them.

Dom said, "I did the writing. She did the drawing. That's you and her."

Austin touched stick figures surrounded by swirls of sea-green and gold, seeing right away what Maisie had tried to capture—sand stirred by fighting currents. Ones that had dragged them down to where pale green water had turned darker. Deeper. Obscuring his vision.

She saw all that too.

Still sees it well enough to recreate it.

"Is she having nightmares?"

Dom nodded. "Wakes up thinking she's choking. Calls out," he admitted. "For you."

Breathing around that was hard.

He couldn't.

Couldn't answer either when Dom pointed out a glitter free patch of paper. "You can tell this is meant to be you. Yellow crayon for your hair, and let me tell you, there were tears when she realised she'd used up all the gold glitter before she could copy this." He lifted a finger, his touch light, pushing back strands from Austin's brow that would have been stiff with product in his old life. Touched him again where a scrape was virtually healed now, fingers gentle.

Austin breathed again.

Blinked, although it wasn't seawater that blurred his vision.

The sting of it somehow lingered as he turned the picture over, an invitation to tea written there in a neat hand that she'd traced over with shaky crayon.

"She wrote her name almost all by herself. See?" Dom asked, pride not even close to hidden. "Her teachers this year have been fucking marvels. Helped her finally get to grips with the alphabet, and I don't mean parroting the letters. The sounds. She's starting to blend them. You know? Run them together. And unpick them. Never thought she'd . . ."

Austin blinked again, caught in a different flashback, this time of Saturday mornings in a library's cushioned corner, his little sister not much more than Maisie's age, already done with easy readers, voracious.

Had she been ahead of the curve? Maybe so, if Maisie's progress was a measure.

A hundred memories of Saturdays spent hurrying her to pick books surfaced. Of him huffing when she took forever.

I had zero patience.

"You okay?" Dom asked, gaze lifting to Austin's brow. "You're frowning. Is that . . . Is that still bothering you?"

"Me? No. I'm fine." He looked at the writing again instead of at the man who watched him closely enough to spot shifts in his expression. Too closely. Austin scrambled to switch that focus off him, not sure why it mattered. "You . . . you said she's unpicking sounds?" These were safer waters, the kind Charles filled after work each evening, adding notes and snippets of children's progress to the folders of learning journeys piled on their dining table. "She's on track?"

Dom checked his phone before replying. "She's doing great. The labels her teachers made for us to stick up at home have helped a ton." He shrugged. "Such a simple idea. My dad's gone mad with it. Labels everything for her."

And if Austin had applied labels of his own lately, like *soft* for the stare that caught with his, he'd need to revisit his definition because nothing he'd seen so far matched what he saw next. "Maybe she'll start recognising words on her own soon. Ones that matter. Grampy. Daddy." He touched the M at the start of that shaky *Maisie*, his own voice unsteady. "Mummy too."

"She's . . . Is she away for long?"

"Gemma? Not sure yet." He didn't add more detail, and Austin didn't hound what was none of his business. That didn't stop uneasiness he knew was irrational from curling like mist between them—and it *was* irrational that Dom once being married almost tripped him when Sol was bi. It hadn't ever been a woman who'd come between them—Austin had got in his own way. That didn't stop his mouth from running. "You are bi, right?"

Dom blinked.

Smiled.

Then smiled even wider.

Austin felt those prickles Charles had mentioned rising. "What's so funny?"

"I was just imagining asking Dad to make a label for me so it's nice and clear for you. But I'm not sure exactly what to ask him to print on it. Or where to stick it. On the headboard of my bed maybe? You know, so people can mull it over before getting under the covers with me? Or should I stick it on my belt buckle as an early warning that I'm attracted to all kinds of people? Where do you think would be best, if it matters so much to you?"

He was teasing.

Austin knew it.

That didn't stop him from feeling more rattled than he was used to. "It doesn't matter," he said abruptly. "Not to me. I was just wondering—"

"If I make a habit of marrying women but snogging blokes behind closed doors? Or curtains?" He caught one of Austin's elbows like he had in that shadowed hallway. Here, in the full light of August, nothing hid on his face, humour also right there in his murmur. "You know that the curtain around your cubicle at the hospital was wide open, don't you? Plenty of people walked past. Probably saw us kissing, and I couldn't give a single shit what any of them would think or call me."

His hand moved, rubbing Austin's arm a little, barely any pressure, but Austin found himself edging nearer, a knot unravelling he hadn't known had tied inside him. Dom made its loosening feel easy. Natural. Needed.

"I like the people I like. Had relationships with men and women. I didn't marry Gemma because she was a woman. Would have felt the same about her if she'd been a bloke. We started as friends. Ended up as family, which it turns out is worth more than any amount of bricks and mortar. Losing her as a friend for a while was the worst part of our split, but years on, we're almost back there. Because that's what Maisie needs from us. Looking back, I struggled. We both did. Now I'm choosing to be happy. To look forward not back." He raised eyes that were hard to look into. "Like you, Austin. I'm more grateful than I can *ever* tell you." He squeezed his arm lightly before letting go. "But like I said, I'll find a way to show you."

"You don't have to." Austin studied Maisie's picture one more time before folding it. "This is enough. It's perfect.

Thanks." He took a few steps away, the urge to move coming out of nowhere, dragging him uphill this time instead of to the sea floor. "We should keep going so you can get back home to her."

He led the way, keeping his distance until the art building rose, towering and gothic, its remaining glass panes shimmering.

"Here it is." Austin glanced sideways to see that Dom didn't survey the building. He watched him instead, studying him much as Maisie had done during his first weeks at Glynn Harber, her frank interest disarming. Dom's was too, concern there in a line bisecting his brow. Seeing it made spilling the truth easy.

"I do keep waking up thinking I'm still underwater. Can't get to the surface. Hearing that she's not sleeping well either . . . Well, I can't say I like the idea of her struggling with that."

He shoved open the art building's front door the same way he'd had to shove down those middle-of-the-night feelings. That took effort. Opening the door did too, its wood swollen. Once inside, his footsteps clicked across the Victorian floor tile, Dom's heavier steps following, the sound louder, echoing once they entered the cavernous space Sol had so many plans for.

"Here's why we need a specialist."

Light flooded through a wall of glass that, from the far side of the space, seemed held together by ironwork as delicate as a cobweb. Dom crossed the studio to inspect it, one of those big hands as gentle on the glass as Austin had felt brush his forehead.

"Oh, yeah. This needs preserving." His touch was firmer on the frames, testing "Still sound," he muttered. "Apart from . . ." He probed, pressing. "Hmm. That's not so good." He tested more, muttering more findings, saying, "Go on," just as quietly as he worked his way along a wall of glass showcasing a view Austin barely noticed.

"Go on, what?"

"With what you were saying." Dom checked his phone, then stepped around buckets lined up to catch the water that had found ingress like the ivy that had curled through broken glass panes. "About your dreams." He looked up, scanning what was left of the water-stained ceiling, plaster crumbling. "I'm listening," he said, grabbing a broom one-handed and reaching up, T-shirt rising as he stretched, baring a solid midriff Austin had to drag his gaze from. Dom poked at an exposed beam. "Rotten too," he murmured before asking, "You said you dream you're underwater and . . . ?"

"I can't breathe." Saying that aloud came with a feeling he quickly turned his back on. He pivoted only to be faced with something surprising—Sol had left a painting propped on an easel, a much younger version of Cameron grinning while looking up to . . .

That's me.

Sol had captured what Charles would call a traffic stopper, but had Cameron really ever smiled the same way around him? Surely he'd remember. He pivoted again to find Dom watching. "I know it's only a dream. That it's stupid—"

"It's not." For a big man in heavy work boots, Dom could move quietly when he wanted. His arm settled across Austin's shoulder again, sheltering like this building once had budding artists. "Can't say that I've slept well since either. Keep going in to check on her. Hang on." Maisie must have picked up the phone from where she'd left it, the screen bright again instead of dark. He put their call back on speaker as a little voice sounded.

"Daddy!"

"There you are. You took your time, slow-coach!"

She beamed at them both, curls held back now, her headband glittering. "Grampy found it in the 'stacle course."

"Obstacle course," Dom corrected as if that was a usual place for a little girl to leave belongings. On the screen, Maisie nodded before her face fell. "But I can't find my wings that match it."

Of course she couldn't.

They were lost to what had tried to steal her as well from the man beside him, whose face also fell, smile gone as if the current had won.

Austin made an offer, no idea where it came from. "I've seen someone make fairy wings before. Want me to try to make some new ones with you when I come to tea?"

Maisie squealed loud enough to deafen them both, but Austin didn't notice, too busy soaking up the smile he hadn't known he'd needed to see until Dom shared it with him.

8

Less than an hour later, Austin wished he was still at the top of the hill in a derelict studio smelling of damp instead of in a minibus overwhelmed by the scent of teen spirit.

He wound down the window, fresh air no match for a bus full of students at peak excitement, the noise almost as overwhelming as their combined aroma.

"Christ. How do you stand it?"

Luke glanced his way. "Stand what?"

"The noise. And the stench."

"The noise is them happy to see each other. And stench? This is nothing. It's the smell of boys turning to men. And girls to women. Always comes with enough body spray to knock a hole in the ozone layer. They've started to care about making a good first impression, that's all. Happens every year like clockwork." He next glanced over his shoulder. "Cameron's a good example. Look at the difference in him."

Austin only looked over his shoulder briefly, just long enough to catch a glimpse of hair that wasn't exactly neat and tidy, but definitely had some shape, the cut highlighting cheekbones so like his uncle's. The same haunting eyes too, which caught with his for a second, Cameron smiling at whatever his seatmate was saying.

Austin faced front again, not wanting to witness what he'd seen so often—Cameron turning sullen each time he was around him, no matter what Sol had promised about his attitude shifting.

"See what I mean?" Luke asked. "Not much of a boy left, is there? Or for any of the others, so I'm not going to complain that it smells like an explosion in a deodorant factory in here when all that means is that they're growing up. Plenty of time for them to figure out that less is more. The girls they fancy will soon tell them that they smell too strongly to get close to." He shared a quick wink. "Or the boys."

Austin's fingers rose to his neck without permission. Felt where Dom's mouth had fastened. Could almost feel the brush of Dom's lips against his skin there. Revisiting that sensory moment felt more real than the minibus he sat in rattling over potholes. As concrete, as if Dom sat between him and Luke on this bench seat, leaning in to brush his lips across skin that prickled, a flush rising, sensitive despite this only being a wish, not reality.

Still, desire crackled to life out of nowhere—Austin awake in a way he'd almost forgotten. Now he couldn't stop revisiting those few seconds of Dom's mouth at the crook of his neck and shoulder, wishing they hadn't been interrupted, the ghost of that sensation twisting into a coil of want so pure his breath caught.

Because Dom did want him, no two ways about it.

Meeting him again would only compound it. Would dig a

foundation that he'd never get to build on. Couldn't when he'd move on as soon as the bidding process was over.

But I'd want to.

Want a lot more of . . .

Of what?

He turned as if watching the dark green and gold of gorse flickering past his window, only he didn't see it. Didn't hear the sound of students chatting either. The minibus engine faded along with the music from the radio and Luke's cheerful humming.

Of him.

Of how he makes me feel.

The land started to rise from the road, the shift from field to moorland subtle, gradual, like the internal shift he'd only become aware of since arriving at Glynn Harber. The ground turned rough and windswept, trees showing which way the wind had blown since they were saplings, forced to lean that way for so long they'd stunted.

I don't want to feel like that anymore either.

Forced in the wrong direction.

He sat, no longer overwhelmed by the smell of a bus full of teens or the ruckus of their reunion. Instead he focused on High Tor in the distance, immense and craggy compared to its smaller neighbour, and tuned back into Luke.

"You wait until we drive them back from a rugby match in winter when it's too cold to open a window. Then you'd be right about the smell. Fifteen of them sweaty and steaming? A bit of body spray is nothing."

Austin didn't remind him that he wouldn't be here for that. Didn't have the time to once they got to the car park where Hugo waited with more students who their passengers spilled out to greet them.

Hugo's group were less forthcoming, Austin noticed, hanging back, none of their faces familiar.

"Those are our new joiners. All free-place students, thanks to you." Luke unfastened his seatbelt and reached back for his daypack, checking its contents before asking. "Did you remember to bring your envelope?"

Austin reached for his own bag. Decided not to mention that his envelope was still empty. "Yes."

"Good." Luke met his gaze and held it, and how the hell had he ever seen it as stony? Concerned fit so much better. "I'm glad you came," he said. "Even if we can't convince you to stay, you trusting us to carry something that's weighed you down means the world to me." He opened the minibus door. "Of course, I'm not giving up on you staying for the long haul. You know that, don't you?"

Austin froze, caught between a rock and a hard place, and maybe Luke noticed. He paused before closing the door, shutting them in together. "You know I didn't think I'd ever want to share my desk with you, don't you? Turns out it was okay to change my mind. Only good things happened."

He left then, Austin watching him gather up new students, not letting them keep their distance, herding them to join the others, where he addressed the merged groups, doing what Austin had seen him do so often—leading without domineering, shepherding souls the same way Hugo also made look easy.

Whatever he said must have resonated with Cameron, who straightened. He stood taller, listening, Austin certain he'd have pretended not to hear him if he'd been the one to lead the conversation.

Despite what Luke had just said, getting out of the minibus to join them then didn't seem too appealing.

Making himself dig in his daypack for his empty envelope was tough too. He did it, closing his eyes for a moment trying to do what Luke had asked, thinking of what he'd let go, if he could.

My target.

Constantly needing to chase a big bonus to try to hit it.

What could symbolise that weight on his shoulders?

He made his choice then while laughter rose outside, Luke working his magic.

Austin unfastened a watch he'd been given instead of the cash bonus he'd expected. At least if the worst came to the worst, it would have some resale value.

But not nearly enough.

He slid it into the envelope and sealed it, sure it would be safe in Luke's possession.

He left the minibus to stand at the rear of a crowd of kids, most taller than him, not able to see Luke, but he heard him clearly.

"Has everyone brought their gift exchange with them?" He waited until the sound of agreement dissipated. "Then let's go. We're heading for Whisper Tor. Watch out for the quarry at its base. Don't want anyone to fall in, although we do have our very own life-saving hero with us today who usually shares my office, who is fresh from fishing one of Glynn Harber's youngest students out of the sea at Porthper-rin. Say hello to Austin Russell, everyone. He's not only my right-hand man, he's a real-life hero for all of you to aspire to."

Hugo must have circled the group. He clapped from behind Austin, students turning at his applause, the crowd parting to show something surprising—Luke clapped,

Cameron beside him, who hesitated at first, but then slowly but surely joined in.

THEY GATHERED at the foot of a Tor much smaller than its nearest neighbour, this one's base a solid rock face curved by years of weather. The white of the envelope Luke unpacked was stark against its granite, signalling a rush of movement—daypacks dropped from shoulders, students digging inside their own to retrieve what they'd brought to swap with strangers who would become friends through trusting and sharing.

Again two groups formed, Austin keeping his distance, but this time Luke didn't try to merge them. "Okay," he called out, the sound somehow carrying as clearly as a bell, chiming, despite the distance.

For a second time, Hugo stood behind Austin. "Amazing how the sound travels at Whisper Tor, isn't it? Has to do with the curvature of the stone. That's why he always stands there to give this talk. Gives the new students space when they're still nervy, but ensures they don't miss hearing the heart of the message."

Luke's voice did carry. "Remember, old hands, you can share what's in your envelope, but no asking what's in the one you're entrusted to carry. New hands?" He waited until Glynn Harber's newest sixth-form students nodded. "You only need to share what's in your envelope if you want to, when you're ready, or never. No judgement. Just let go of whatever it is you brought with you for a while, okay? Let us carry it for you."

He worked through a list, matching old students with new

until only Cameron and a new boy, equally tall and surly, stood at the base of the tor with him.

Students milled, clutching the envelopes they'd been gifted, each one listening to the old hand they'd been paired with, but Luke's voice still carried. "Now I'd like to share what I've brought with my partner."

That'll be me.

Austin drifted closer, wondering why Luke bothered with this story. He'd already shown him that knight-in-tarnished-armour picture. There was no need to explain it to him again.

Luke continued regardless, but first he moved away from the rockface, making this part of his conversation private. He slipped the picture out of his envelope to show the new student. "Teo? Can you tell who this is?"

The student held it, gaze flicking between the knight's face and Luke's before nodding, saying nothing.

Luke took it back, sliding it into his envelope, which he then sealed. "I used to think that protecting something I loved as much as Glynn Harber was only down to me. It killed me that I couldn't do it on my own. I imagine that's how you might have felt before your sister came here."

Austin grasped then why Luke spoke more quietly, remembering a tearful tutorial he'd once witnessed in Luke's study.

Luke asked, "How is Leonie doing now?"

The student muttered, "Okay."

"Good." Luke held the envelope out, Austin almost step-ping forward to take it before grasping that Luke wanted Teo to have it, not him. "I know you wanted to fight for your sister, Teo. Felt frustrated that you couldn't so you fought other people instead. Learning that I didn't have to fight on my own was my hardest lesson. Communicating didn't come easy but it made all the difference. That's why I think you're the right person to carry this for me."

He put the envelope in Teo's hands.

"Put your sword and shield down for a while, yes? No more getting into fights now you're here at Glynn Harber. Leonie doesn't need you getting a criminal record. She's on track to becoming a doctor. She wants you to have a bright future as well, so hold onto this every time you feel the urge to lash out. If you can try to do that, I'll carry whatever it is that's been too heavy for you."

Austin watched Teo hand over an envelope to Luke, realisation dawning at the same time it must have dawned for Cameron.

Or maybe that wasn't realisation on Cameron's face.

Horror would fit better.

We're each other's partner.

Austin saw the boy who'd come to live with him and Sol take a step back as if he'd shoved him, and he couldn't blame him. But yet again, Cameron surprised him.

His jaw clenched but he steadied.

Stopped retreating.

Took a step closer at the same time Hugo murmured, "Good man."

"Here." Cameron thrust what he held at Austin, who almost dropped it, envelope contents nearly falling onto rock, a perfume bottle that would have shattered.

"It's my gran's," Cameron grunted. "*Was* my gran's," he added before flashing a look Luke's way, a dog begging its master not to kick it.

All Luke did was nod encouragement, his eyebrows raised as if to say *you can do it*.

Cameron's shoulders slumped before straightening. "It's

called Happy," he said, grittily. "That's what she wanted for me when she was alive. Took me a while to let myself be happy after she . . ."

Austin couldn't translate the look Cameron flashed at him.

"After she . . ." He stopped. Looked away as if seeking an escape route. Finally swung a grudging gaze back to Austin. "Uncle Sol used to spray it on my pillow when I moved in with him. Didn't realise he'd done that until the bottle was almost empty."

There were only a few drops left in it, Austin noticed.

Luke murmured, "She'd be so proud of the man you're becoming, Cameron. Seeing things through from start to finish instead of running away like you used to."

Cameron stilled then.

Rallied.

Must have dug deep because he lifted eyes as stormy now as when Austin had left his uncle. As defiant. But something else familiar lurked there, a hint of Sol who did the right thing no matter what it cost him.

"Gran would tell me that happy wasn't only the name of her favourite perfume. It's what I should let myself feel even though she's gone now. That the only way I could ever disappoint her was by not grabbing every chance I got to be it." His gaze dropped, voice wavering, not quite breaking but close, so close, until he looked up and it deepened. Levelled. Strengthened. "I'm allowed to remember good things about someone I miss. It hurts, but moving on is better than staying sad forever. I'm allowed to be happy. It's what she would have wanted."

He lurched forward, snatching back his envelope from Austin.

Of course he doesn't trust me with it.

But Cameron delving inside to hold the bottle to his nose one last time forced a small sound from him that Whisper Tor must have carried.

Hugo squeezed Austin's shoulder. Squeezed it again as Cameron slipped the bottle back and sealed it away, shoving the envelope into Austin's hands while whipping away the one Austin had carried, stalking off with it before he could tell him to be careful with a watch worth thousands.

Thousands?

Austin watched him leave, knowing there was nothing matched about their giving. Nothing at all. Not even close.

What Cameron had given was worth far more.

Austin carried that realisation all the way to the top of the tor while students milled below in pairs, friendships forming. He also carried Cameron's message every step of the way up a climb that left him panting.

The view from the tor's summit was stunning.

Austin barely saw it. Could only focus on the sight of Cameron, who continued walking away from the others, Austin's envelope dangling from his hand. For a moment, he wondered if the only thing he had left of value was destined for the bottom of the quarry, hurled by a kid he'd once let down.

Letting down someone else also struck him.

If he does, how the fuck will I tell Mum I've raised zero cash this year?

Somehow, what Cameron had said at the base of the tor rang louder than that worry.

Austin heard him again.

I'm allowed to be happy.

He wanted that for Cameron. Wanted it so fiercely, he

couldn't keep standing. Needed to sit. Settled for lying flat on his back, ignoring the stones digging into his back, too intent on remembering what Dom had also told him.

Now I'm choosing to be happy. To look forward not back.

Austin stared up at an arc of faded denim sky, wanting the same.

He pulled out his phone, dialling before he could change his mind.

"Mum?" he asked. "Yes, I'm still coming home in a few weeks. No, I won't cancel this time." He winced. "We'll talk about this year's fundraising then, Mum," he said, hoping to God he'd come up with a bigger number than zero by then. "But first . . ." He closed his eyes and saw Dom's smile again after Austin had made Maisie a promise, happiness aimed right at him. "Mum, do you remember when you made fairy wings for Tamsin?"

He listened to silence for what felt like forever, something else Cameron had said echoing.

It hurts, but moving on is better than staying sad forever.

He heard her swallow then, her "yes" quiet and cautious.

"I was wondering . . ."

His own swallow felt as rough as granite.

"Can you tell me how you made them?"

9

A few hours before the renovation bid deadline, Austin almost regretted asking for his mum's help. Admittedly reading her emailed instructions was a good distraction from the last few bids arriving. Like he'd thought, even an increased budget didn't come close to what local builders wanted.

Cutting corners it is then.

Which ones though?

He prowled up and down the wall covered in designs amounting to a wish list. Or to a set of dominoes arranged one after the other.

Which domino could he remove without toppling the rest of Sol's plans for his building?

He left the study rather than think about it, rationalising on his way downstairs that surely anything was an upgrade compared to the poky classroom Sol had put up with for years. He paused outside its door, studying another wish list, this time of fairy-wing supplies sent by his mother that

Charles had promised to help with. It held more items than he'd expected.

Would he want to cut out any of the hot glue, ribbons, and rhinestones his mum suggested?

No.

Not when his phone also held a photo Dom had sent that morning of Maisie beaming, her glittery headband a twin of one worn by the doll she cuddled.

Dom: *Guess who's so excited about you coming to tea they got the whole house up at dawn?*

Dom: *Might need matchsticks to prop my eyes open later.*

Austin's reply hadn't yet been answered.

He stared at what he'd typed, wondering if trusting his gut like Luke had suggested had been a mistake, the words *can't wait* now seeming over enthusiastic. Too full on for someone Dom had only . . .

Kissed, his brain provided. *Twice now*

Stress justified the first, sparks flaring due to high emotion. And the second could have been . . .

What?

Dom checking if that first had been a fluke between them?

"I clung to him like a fucking limpet," he muttered to an empty hallway. That had been too much, surely? He returned to the list of supplies. Was this too much as well?

A sound inside the classroom stopped him from second guessing.

Paint cans knocking together.

He peered through a gap in a classroom door that showed the reason.

Teo watched Cameron unpacking spray-paint cans for the new school year that would soon start, one of the last deliveries destined for this space, if a last-minute bid miraculously came closer to the budget.

He also overheard Cameron paint a verbally brutal picture.

"Yeah," he said. "This room's a shithole, but Uncle Sol won't have to put up with it much longer. That's if his ex hasn't fucked up the finance. Wouldn't put it past him."

"*Him*?" Teo asked, the first time Austin had heard him speak. "His ex is a bloke? That's—"

"Gay?" Cameron's back was to the door, but Austin saw him square his shoulders. "You got a problem with that? Might want to find someone else to show you the ropes here in case it runs in our family."

Austin hovered, not sure if he should stay or go, this conversation both private and also potentially explosive if what Luke had mentioned about Teo fighting was true.

"Does it?" Teo asked.

Protectiveness came out of nowhere.

Austin pushed the door open wider, maybe years too late but unable to walk away this time.

"Cameron?"

"Yeah."

He had no idea what else to say next, especially when, now that he could see more, Teo looked the opposite of combative. He did back away from Cameron though, hands raised as if Austin had come in swinging.

Austin's mind blanked. "I ... um ..."

Cameron pointed to a backpack. "It's in there."

"What is?"

"Your envelope, so you don't have to follow me around checking if I've still got it." He pressed his lips together, another family likeness Austin recognised all too well, Sol stopping himself from asking Austin to ease up at bringing work home or networking at corporate parties, desperate for the next rung up that ladder.

Like back then, he could also guess what Cameron now wanted to ask him.

He put him out of his misery.

"I've got your envelope somewhere safe. I promise. Up in my desk drawer, if you ever need it and I'm not . . ."

Still here.

His phone buzzed, reprieve perfectly timed. "Got to go." He waggled his phone. "I'll leave you two to it."

He left, crossing the hallway to the classroom where Charles waited for him. The moment he saw Austin, he backed into his supply cupboard. "At last. Thought I'd have to send Hugo off without me."

"Off?" Austin followed him in.

Charles frowned, a rare enough sight to stop him. "Are you okay?" He tapped his temple. "Head isn't still playing you up, is it?"

"Playing me up?" Austin touched his brow. "No. Why?"

"Because I told you at breakfast that we're sneaking off for a bit of leave before school starts. Wedding planning, remember?" he added, smile back again, beaming. "Only a year later than I expected, but the Church is a devil of a taskmaster. Keeps finding extra jobs for Hugo, all meant to inch him closer to being a certified God botherer, but"—the high-beam of his smile dimmed—"I can't help thinking someone waits until we set a date before coming up with yet another hoop he needs to jump through. It's happened twice now, so setting a third date's got to be the charm, right? He's got another interview as well. Third time lucky for that too, maybe." He pulled a face. "Can't say I'm looking forward to it."

"Interview?"

"For a parish of his own. Wouldn't start until next year when the current vicar retires, but every process in the church takes forever." He fixed Austin with another probing look. "I said you could have the Defender, remember, if you gave us a lift to the station. You might need it to carry everything I've found for you and little Maisie." And just like that, any clouds were gone, Charles back to sunny. "Right. You need some of this, and these, and some of—"

"Stop."

Charles did not.

He added more to a growing stack of crafting supplies that Austin tried to keep balanced. "These beads would be good for her hand-eye coordination. Get her to thread them. Nice and sensory for her. Don't want her to slip behind over the summer."

The only thing about to slip right then were the craft supplies that mounted. "Seriously, stop. That's enough. I don't need beads. It's one set of fairy wings for a little girl, not for a fleet of Boeing 747s. Besides, I've got a list."

"Enough?" Charles eyed the shelves. "I'm just getting started."

The shelves towered, bulging. "Reminds me of home," Austin said without meaning to share that.

"How?"

"Just that Mum's got a cupboard crammed with craft stuff."

"Your mother's arty?"

"My sister was when she was little. Don't know why Mum still keeps it. Crap falls out each time I open the door."

"Oh, a cupboard of doom," Charles said. "I used to live with someone who had one of those. Gave up trying to rush him to empty it. He cleared it out when he was ready, and I'm ready right now to let go of some of this, so show me your list." Charles took his phone, squinting before coming to a verdict. "That's nowhere near enough glitter to—"

"To what? Make her visible from the moon?"

"No. To impress her daddy. The one you haven't stopped thinking about since . . ." He mimed diving, his tone gently reproving, reminding him of Hugo. "Don't even try to pretend you haven't. You've barely argued with Luke about not working lately, and you sat with Hugo in the garden for ages yesterday, nodding away like you were listening to him. You didn't hear a word he said, did you?"

"Of course I . . ."

Actually, no.

No, he hadn't.

"I was actually thinking about—"

"Climbing Maisie Dymond's father?" Thankfully Charles didn't notice Austin's mouth open then close, unable to deny that had been on his mind for days now. For nights too, which at least beat dreaming of deep water. "To be fair," Charles said, "I zone out sometimes too when Hugo gets going." He sighed. "He's so smart. No idea what he sees in me."

Charles rooted in a box, oblivious, Austin decided, to the fact that him taking this time to help was exactly what Hugo appreciated, kindness a thread knotting his housemates together. He almost said so until Charles stopped him with what he said next. "But at least Hugo has you now."

"Now?" Austin held in a sigh. "Charles, you know I'm—"

"Leaving?" He found a sheaf of shiny stickers. "Does that mean you've heard from Heligan?"

"Heligan?" That name rang a bell, though it took a moment to pinpoint. "Your ex?"

Charles clapped a hand on Austin's shoulder. "Goodness, no. He was a bloody good shag, not a boyfriend, but did he ring you? I asked him to."

Austin shook his head.

"I'll give him a nudge. You'll like him. Smart as a whip, like you. Filthy in bed and filthy rich too, or he will be when he inherits. But until then, keep making Hugo happy by listening to him. Even if you zone out sometimes, I know he loves having you there to listen."

Austin's voice came out scratchy. "He'll be fine when I leave." He cleared his throat. "You two talk plenty."

"Only because I've learned to keep a question up my sleeve to deflect him in case he checks I'm listening."

Austin couldn't help smiling. "Like what?" He took the box of supplies before Charles could ram in any more glittery supplies, carrying it out to the classroom.

"Like, which of the disciples is his favourite," Charles said, following. "That one keeps him going for ages. Or I'll ask if he thinks dogs will get raptured as well as the faithful." He lowered his voice as if sharing a secret. "Just in case you're wondering, Hugo thinks that yes, all dogs go to heaven. The verdict's out on cats, but I think that's only because he's allergic."

Charles reached out. Pushed a strand of hair back from Austin's brow—fussing that he would have shrugged off if his hands hadn't been full. "I was going to suggest you think of some questions to keep up your sleeve in case you and Maisie's dad run out of conversation, but I don't think that'll be a problem."

"Why?"

"Because, didn't you say you were going to his place at teatime?"

Austin nodded.

"He must be impatient. It's not even noon, but he's here already."

Dom's here?

His surprise must have shown on his face, or maybe Charles saw something else. "Oh. You don't just want to climb him like a tree, do you?" His gaze skipped to the window. "And it's mutual."

Austin slipped past him without answering, only to see what Charles had described—Dom did walk past the outdoor classroom. He stopped, lifting one of those big hands Austin remembered pulling him closer so Maisie could see them both on his phone screen. The ghost of that sensation drew him closer again as Dom lifted it to shield his eyes.

He's looking up at the study window.

For me.

Austin almost knocked on the classroom window, hand stilling at the last moment.

Shit.

He's come to cancel.

Dom held something in his other hand that he tapped against his lips. An envelope? Some paper? Then he moved off, disappearing from view.

Austin didn't think.

He took off across the classroom, part of him conscious he wasn't alone—Charles witness to him stumbling over a chair. Over his own feet too. Even worse, witness to Austin pushing a door he needed to pull to open, almost falling outside once that mistake computed.

Laughter followed him into the outdoor classroom. He drowned it out by shouting.

"Hey!"

Dom turned, almost at the school's front door, hand outstretched for the handle. It dropped as a grin rose. "Hey, yourself." He jogged back, that smile spreading, and something tight inside Austin loosened.

Christ, Charles is right.

He would have raised a shield then, like the one in Luke's framed photo, if he'd had one. Instead, he felt bare—a hermit crab well and truly out of its shell—exposed as he asked a question that came out sounding doubtful.

"Are you here for me?"

He didn't have to turn around to know Charles had heard him—another chuff of laughter told him. He also heard the doors to the classroom close, glancing back to check, seeing Charles making a heart shape with his fingers.

He turned back just as quickly, but Dom must have moved fast too, almost back at the fence. Then he was right there, pressed to it like Austin, only wood and wire between them.

"Who else would I be here for?" Dom asked, low enough that even if Charles had left the classroom doors open, no one could have overheard him, that question for Austin's ears only.

"Y-you're hours early." And what the fuck was up with that stutter, a red flag that would have signalled weakness if he still worked for Supernus? Part of Austin fired off an internal memo to pull himself together. The rest of him stood on tiptoe and planted a kiss on a cheek freckled with tiny paint dots. He reeled back just as quickly, covering embarrassment with abruptness. "And you're covered in paint."

In a move that was starting to feel familiar, Dom caught hold of his elbow. He didn't pull Austin closer again, exactly, more supportive than controlling, but Austin leaned in instead of away, eyes closing the moment Dom's lips brushed his cheek too.

"Hi to you too. And yes," Dom rumbled. "That's what happens when I try to finish a job in a hurry." He hadn't let go, maintaining their connection. "Painting masonry isn't my skill set, but even I don't usually slap it on so fast I get this covered."

"What was the rush?"

"This." Dom finally let go of his elbow to pull what Austin had seen him tap against his lips from the back pocket of his jeans. He passed it over the fence, taking a step back as soon as Austin took it from him. "Didn't want to miss the deadline. Would have given this to you last week, but I needed to check someone's availability first. Clear my own too." A tooth dug into his lip. "It's for you."

"Deadline?" Austin held what it looked as if Dom now almost regretted handing over, his arms crossing as if he too wished for a shield.

Austin unfolded the paper. Read the few lines written on it.

Checked a column of figures.

Turned it over to find no more detail.

Flipped it over and read it again.

"This . . ." Austin raised his head to find Dom had uncrossed his arms now, expression as naked as Austin had felt moments before. "This is a bid for the renovation."

Dom nodded, tooth digging again. "Hope it'll win."

"Win?" Austin shook his head. "Not sure how it could lose." He pointed to the total column. "Did you realise this is—"

"A big fat zero?" And there was that smile again, but smaller this time. "It's not a mistake."

"You're offering to renovate the art building for free?"

Dom nodded.

"From top to bottom?"

He nodded again.

"But how . . . ?" He didn't finish asking how a two-man family firm could make that happen, or afford to throw cash at what all those other bids suggested would be a money pit with no bottom. He settled on another question. "Why?"

"Because I promised I'd repay you."

Dom came back to the fence, freckles of paint as clear as what he added.

"This is me just getting started."

10

Somehow, Austin found the gate in the classroom fence. Managed to let himself out and to shut the gate behind him. But that was where his body quit cooperating—he couldn't let go of the latch, his other hand also clenching around that sheet of paper.

His mouth didn't share the same problem. It took over. "You can't."

"Can't what?"

Austin opened his mouth. Closed it just as swiftly, not sure where to start dismantling this offer because, yes, it was likely made with the best of intentions, but there was no way in hell he could submit to the backers. Not when it was unrealistic—a top-to-bottom rebuild for nothing?

It would look like a joke.

He couldn't present it. Not when all those other bids showed just how badly Dom had miscalculated. He tried to find a way to phrase that, but struggled, and that was another sign that it was time to get back to corporate finance. Hesitation had no place in decision-making. Not in any of the companies he'd worked for before, or where he'd next be headed. But that's what he heard loud and clear: reluctance to hurt Dom's feelings.

"You . . . you can't be serious?"

Dom stifled a chuckle. Couldn't do the same to his smile or stop his gaze from straying, dropping lower. He gave up holding back, laughter escaping. "Not sure someone wearing that sticker gets to question whether I'm the one who's serious, but yes. Yes, I am serious about this. Completely."

Austin looked down. Saw a sticker Charles must have pressed onto his shirt without his knowing. He read *I've been a very good boy* and muttered, "Fucking Heppel," before adding, "I mean you can't be serious about—"

"Listening to someone who's been a very good boy again like when you saved my daughter?" Dom reached for him, his tug gentle, drawing Austin away from the gate and closer to him. "Or, I can't be serious about offering to take on the project for nothing? You should check the small print. It's the labour that's free. The cost of materials depends on how much we recycle."

"No. I mean, yes." Austin took a breath and started over. "I mean, you can't offer to start something there's no possible way you can finish."

Dom's eyebrows climbed.

Austin stuck to his guns because, hurt feelings or not, there was also no way to avoid that the project was monumental. Way beyond the work Dom had described to him. "You told me what you do. That you can turn your hand to most trades. Brickwork. Plastering. A bit of painting." He snatched back a hand that had lifted without permission, drawn to those dots of masonry paint, shoving it into his trouser pocket. "None of that's even close to what the project entails. The planning permissions alone could take months. I mentioned the red tape involved in getting them, didn't I?"

Dom nodded, smile not quite gone, which only drove Austin to come closer, needing to hammer home this message.

"And I said how I think that's why all the bids have come in over budget?" In the distance, glass glinted above the tree line. He pointed at it. "I wasn't kidding. The issues I showed you were only the tip of a massive iceberg." One topped with antique glass only an expert could deal with. "None of it will be a quick fix."

"I'm not afraid of long hauls," Dom told him, that smile almost gone now. "Or of complex projects. To be honest, I prefer them." He squared his shoulders. "Commitment doesn't scare me."

"Committing to this should. It's a massive mess. Fragile too. You saw that. I saw you notice that even parts of the iron-work are—" He almost added the word *brittle* to a list of defects until he remembered both Sol and Charles calling him the same thing lately.

He shook that off, pushing on with what felt like a demolition, only of Dom's well-meaning kindness instead of the art building. "It all needs a specialist not an . . ."

The sun caught on something in the car park before he could add the word *amateur*. Dom's van, he realised, its windscreen the only shiny part of a vehicle that had seen better days.

"I'm sorry," he said, because he was. Beyond sorry to state bald facts that couldn't be avoided. "This feels . . ." His fist clenched around Dom's bid, a single folded sheet of paper that had done something to him, no other way to explain why his voice softened instead of firming. No better way to describe his shift in tone either, because this offer did touch him somewhere missing a shell. "I actually don't know how to describe how it feels."

The bid was essentially worthless.

Why did it feel worth more than *anything* he'd ever been given?

He smoothed out the creases in a debt repayment Dom didn't owe him, not when *he* was the sole reason Austin could stand here, inhaling the scent of fresh paint and sawdust, drenched by sunshine instead of seawater.

That loosened an explanation.

"You know, I phoned my mum this morning, which is usually an ordeal, but I've done it more since you kept me afloat than in the whole year before it. I spoke to her last night too. She's helped me plan how to make Maisie's new wings. Keeps emailing me more suggestions. Talking to her so much . . ." And here were words he never thought he'd put in the same sentence. ". . . has been good. Now I can't stop thinking about all the times I've put off calling her. You never know . . . You never know when it'll be the last time you get to do it, do you?"

Dom slowly nodded. Then nodded faster as though Austin's segue made sense to him.

"You didn't need to do this," Austin promised. "Offer your time for nothing, I mean. You've already given me something I didn't know I needed. That's paid me back plenty. You're really not the one who owes . . ."

Dom watched him try to wrestle the right words into order, his head tilted, listening.

"Thank you," Austin finally managed. "But I can't accept this or give it to the backers."

Dom surveyed him for a long moment before asking, "You can't, or you won't?"

"Won't," Austin admitted. "It's a nice idea. More than nice. And I appreciate the thought behind it."

He really did.

"It means more than I can say."

That only made voicing the rest harder.

"But the fact is that no amount of free labour makes up for experience in this kind of renovation, so . . ." He held out the bid.

Dom didn't take it from him.

He crossed his forearms, his head still tilted. "You think I don't have experience? Because I have. Decades of it now, starting with Dad as soon as I could hold a saw. Then for myself, upcountry, before I came back for Maisie. There's not much I can't handle. I—"

Austin had to stop him. "I'm saying this project needs specialists." And that was yet another example of his going soft—the old version of him would have been much more dismissive. Would have told Dom that a bit of painting and plastering was laughable in the face of what was needed.

Maybe some of that showed, Dom's eyebrows rising again.

"So you think I'd make an offer I couldn't see through?"

"I . . . I think you'd *want* to see it through."

The sun glinted off the windscreen of that old van again, and maybe Dom noticed Austin's gaze flick to it. He looked over his shoulder before facing him and asking a different question. "Or is it that you think I can't *afford* to keep it?" That smile was back, not only at the edges of his mouth but in his eyes, twinkling. "I can afford the cost of the labour. I promise."

Austin didn't only see that twinkle. He noticed laugh lines

too that had only been faint impressions so far. Now they deepened, Austin having no idea why Dom was pushing back so hard or finding an awkward conversation funny, unless pride was his driver.

He tried again. "Listen, you saw one of the bids. You know the numbers other firms are coming in with. And I know plenty of small family firms make a decent living, but this bid means you'll effectively stop yourself from earning. For months, Dom. Because this can't be something you'd fit in around other jobs or do in the evenings and weekends. It's a full-time project."

It needed to be if Sol's building was going to be the new jewel in Glynn Harber's crown sooner rather than later.

Dom still smiled and nodded. "Yep. Full-time project for months. Got it. No problem."

No problem?

Austin pivoted from business to personal to hammer home his message. "I also know Maisie's school fees are about to increase once she moves up a year group and Charles isn't her teacher." He touched the fence around the outdoor classroom. "There's a lot less play in her next class and more structured teaching, so it's more expensive." Austin couldn't help eyeing a van that looked one pothole away from a big bill in Dom's future. "It's actually quite a jump between pre-prep fees and the junior school. You might want to start saving." He made a quiet offer. "You know there are payment plans, don't you?"

He hadn't expected laughter.

Dom's rang out to fill the valley. "I'll bear that in mind. Thanks." And there was that head tilt again. "You know, you could try something for me if you wanted?"

"What?"

"Trusting."

And yes, it really was time Austin put distance between himself and Cornwall because he wanted to, right then. Wanted to trust more than anything while standing beside a school he'd been sent to shut down but had ended up fighting tooth and claw for.

Fuck it. He wanted to do much more than trust.

He wanted to see this man smile again with him as his sole focus.

He broke eye contact, aiming for the tone that used to get him through bruising meetings.

Finding even a fraction of it was a struggle.

"And you'll just have to trust me when I say that you haven't seen the real extent of the work. I've got a surveyor's report that would make you go grey. Greyer," he snapped, and God, why did him losing his cool only make Dom's smile widen?

"Greyer," Dom echoed. "You make me sound like I'm in my eighties when I'm not even thirty-eight yet. But let me see if I got this straight. You won't accept my bid because you think I don't have experience, I'll end up putting my family in the poor house, and I'm too over the hill for you to spend months working closely with me?"

"Me?"

"You," Dom agreed. "That'll be in the small print when I win the contract. Someone's got to manage the project, right? I choose you."

"No." Austin stopped, rubbing his brow even while knowing he couldn't blame a scrape that was long-healed for tripping over his words. He started over, speaking slower. "No. You're not too over the hill for me."

"Good to know." Dom backed away before he could reiterate the other factors that were still a problem, Austin taking a few steps after him before he made himself stop.

"Where are you going?"

"Back up to the art building. See what this hopeless amateur missed so I can add a few more zeros to my bid, if that makes you happy."

"I didn't say you were an amateur. Or hopeless."

Only he kind of had. Several times already.

Austin started over. "But I know what the backers want. Someone who doesn't only know their way through red tape, but who will stay sympathetic to the bones of the building. Make it something really special *and* inclusive, like I showed you upstairs." He ducked his head. "And it's not only the backers. It's me. *I* want it to be good."

He lifted it to find Dom's smile not gone but fading.

"For your ex. For Sol?"

"Yes," he admitted. "Not because I . . . because Sol and I . . ." He huffed, exasperated. "I already said there's nothing like that between us, but weren't you the one who said caring isn't like a switch? One you couldn't turn on or off at will?"

Dom nodded.

"I can't turn off wanting the best for him either. So that means finding specialists like the surveyor's report suggests." He pictured the report pages he and Luke had pored over, detailing every single fault and blemish. "It'll be a challenge for whoever gets the job."

Dom inhaled deeply. Exhaled slowly. Nodded again, decisive. "I'm still up for it if you are."

Fuck.

He still isn't comprehending that he's way out of his depth.

Austin knew how that felt. Dom hurling himself in head first all over again wrenched at something inside him. It came out in his tone. "Right," he snapped. "You don't believe me. Maybe you'll believe the surveyor's report. I've got it over at the stables."

He turned on his heel, heading that way before realising Dom hadn't followed.

Austin turned back.

Dom watched him, eyebrows higher than ever.

He waited without speaking, nodding when Austin came back and said, "Sorry." Nodded again after Austin added, "I snapped because this matters. Really matters. And not only to me." He filled Dom's silence. "I was stressing about it before you got here. Been getting wound up about it for weeks now." He made another confession, touching a bare spot on his wrist. "Can almost hear a clock ticking the closer it gets to the deadline."

"That's something you do? Stress about things? About deadlines?"

"Doesn't everyone?" Austin shared another secret. "Been stressing about making those fairy wings for Maisie too. Don't even know what made me say I'd help her make some."

That wasn't entirely truthful. He knew the real reason. It was right there in the start of a smile his snappiness had almost driven from Dom's face. A smile he wanted to prolong, not shorten.

"But I did offer, and the wings will probably turn out to be shit even if I follow the instructions Mum gave me, and I hate asking for help, but here you are making an offer to do something that's way beyond your skill set too, and I—" His throat chose that moment to tighten out of nowhere. "—I'm *really* not good at being grateful."

Dom uncrossed his arms and Austin walked into where they'd opened, no idea why it was easier to get wrapped in an embrace and speak into the crook of his neck rather than face him. "But I am," he said as one of Dom's hands swept up and down the back Austin hadn't known was rigid until it melted. "Really grateful for the offer, even if I can't put your bid forward. I mean that. And even though I hate asking for help, I absolutely would ask you for yours, if . . ."

If things were different.

Dom gave him a squeeze like he'd heard that. A hug that was over before he had time to appreciate it, but Austin wasn't ready to let go and maybe Dom felt that too. His arms closed around Austin again, making it easier to say what had been on his mind all week—what had made him snatch up his phone each time Dom had messaged. What had also made him run across a classroom while Charles laughed at him, tripping over his own feet to see him.

No, Austin had to admit. *Charles hadn't laughed at me.*

He was happy for me.

Happy seemed too small a word to describe what stirred inside him as Dom's arms slowly loosened as if moving any faster might start a deadline clock that had, for once, quit ticking, this moment between them frozen.

Fraught too, because being banned from working for a while had left so much time for thinking.

For accepting what he wanted.

More of this, not less.

I wish I could have it.

Still in the shelter of his arms, Austin admitted that, and it was easy. "If things were different, I'd say yes to you in a heartbeat."

Dom looked down at him then.

At Austin's mouth.

His eyes.

His mouth again before saying, "Show me," from so close Austin felt it as well as heard it.

He almost did—nearly reached up to show Dom how much he'd been thinking about him. Got ready to do it, wetting dry lips just as Dom said, "The report."

Austin blinked. "What report?"

And there was a smile like the one Charles had worn while making a heart shape with his fingers. "The one from the surveyor?" Dom said. "I've got to get home. Promised Maisie we'd have lunch together with Dad. Her mum's joining us too."

"She's back?"

"Video call, so I can't miss it or Dad will only press the wrong button. Cut off the call without realising. Then there'd be tears because family time is everything to Maisie. Has been even more so since . . ."

Austin nodded.

"Bring it with you later, yeah? The report?" Dom reminded, backing away. "Then maybe I can convince you that my bid's still worth submitting."

Austin heard what he didn't say aloud.

Trust me?

Dom doubled back as quickly as he'd retreated, his kiss quick—too quick—before he jogged back to his van and drove off, much slower than usual, no gravel skittering.

Trust me.

Austin watched, still in the same spot minutes later, wanting so much to do so.

11

A fter dropping Charles and Hugo at the station,
Austin got to Dom's place late, unable to find a
parking spot first, then lost while on foot in a
rabbit warren of Porthperrin's narrow alleys.

The surveyor's report almost slipping from the top of the
box he carried was no excuse for the uptick in his heart rate,
but it kicked even faster as he turned a corner.

Dom stood on the sunny side of the street, waiting
for him.

He leaned against the front door of a quaint, if tiny,
cottage cheek by jowl with others, his head down, checking
his phone. He looked up frowning from its screen, Austin
catching a glimpse of the man who used to roll up late for his
daughter. Now he knew him better, those drawn brows told a
different story.

That's him worried instead of pissed off.

He was never annoyed at having to collect her.

He also got to see another difference. Yes, the sun made
the cottage windows dazzle, but that had nothing on how

Dom lit up the moment he saw him. He pushed away from the door, sliding his phone into his pocket. "There you are."

And that confirmed it.

He was worried I wasn't coming.

Dom added more proof that his first impression had been so wrong, eyes the same shade as the ribbon of sky above them, warming. "Haven't been stood up since I was sixteen. Was starting to get flashbacks." He crossed his arms. "Thought you'd changed your mind too, and I'd scrubbed all that paint off for nothing."

"Sorry, sorry," Austin said to what he had to admit was a much cleaner version of Dom, his face free of that morning's speckles. His shirt too, scruffy Dymond and Son T-shirt replaced with a button-down, cool linen so much smarter.

For me.

Dom reached for the box loaded with crafting items, surveyor's report almost slipping again. He caught it before it could fall. "Come on in." He opened the door, a vanilla scent of baking greeting Austin. He breathed it in, also taking in a typical cottage hallway, age-darkened oak beams crossing its low ceiling.

Dom placed the box and report on a hallway table. "Good thing Maisie can't tell the time or she would have been climbing the walls even more than she has been since breakfast."

"Sorry," Austin repeated. "Couldn't find a spot in the car park." It had only been weeks since his last visit to Porthperrin, but the village had stepped up a gear, rammed with end-of-summer tourists. "Had to leave the car up the hill and walk down."

"You're here now. Come in." Dom stood to one side to let Austin pass, only to stop him, the front door still wide open.

Light streamed in as they faced each other. The sound of voices too, a family of holidaymakers pointing out the bunting strung between each building, fluttering like something did inside Austin at this sudden closeness. At Dom's murmur too, quiet and somehow private, for his ears only.

"Aren't you forgetting something?"

Austin had barely jogged down the hill, no excuse to sound this breathless, but he heard it when he said, "Me? Forgetting what?"

Dom must have heard it as well. His smile, which had been a shocking surprise once, was starting to feel familiar. Wanted. It spread before Dom said, "Did I dream it, or did you kiss me hello earlier?" That questioning tilt to his head was also habitual, Austin realised, as was that tooth digging into a lip he knew could feel surprisingly soft. "Because I'm pretty sure you planted one on me." Dom squinted. "Although I'm not sure another one will have the same impact without you wearing an *I've been a very good boy* sticker. I could always ask Maisie to make you a new one."

Austin shut up Dom's teasing by repeating what he'd done in the outdoor classroom, only this time there wasn't a fence between them, or Charles watching him replay the same greeting.

Or almost the same.

Dom must have tilted his head another fraction. Instead of his cheek, Austin's lips met the corner of a smile. He stepped back. Or meant to, only Dom rocked forward, arms coming around him like they'd done earlier as well, and this time, Austin met his mouth and kissed him.

More voices floated in from the street outside.

Austin couldn't make himself care. Couldn't make himself let go either, not while Dom did what he'd done several times already, gathering him up, solid everywhere he and Austin connected.

They kissed hello, voices outside fading as the tourists meandered downhill.

A different voice came from much closer.

"What are you doing with Austin Russell, Daddy?"

Austin stumbled backward, or would have done if Dom hadn't grabbed him. Steadied him again. Somehow answered his daughter's question without dying, sounding matter-of-fact. "Hugging him hello."

"Why?" Maisie asked, hopping from one foot to the other, wobbling.

"Because I'm happy to see him."

"Me too!" She skipped back through a hallway door that had been closed when Austin had got there. Now the sound of a TV somewhere deeper in the house drifted. Her voice too, yelling, "Daddy's cuddling Austin Russell because he's happy."

"What?" a man's deep voice boomed.

Austin did back off then. Dom's eye-roll stopped him from following those holidaymakers like he was sorely tempted, and he couldn't help mirroring his smile at what Maisie said next.

"I saw Daddy kissing—"

"Santa Claus?" that big voice boomed, teasing tone maybe genetic. "In August?" it boomed next. "Are you sure, Maisie? Has he come all the way to Porthperrin from the North Pole to see if you'll make it off the naughty list by Christmas?"

The man filling the doorway was as tall as his son but leaner. Greyer. Still handsome. A walking representation of how Dom would look in the future. "I've been a good boy all year," he said loud enough that any holidaymakers left outside must hear him. "Does that mean I get a kiss too?" He puckered up and Maisie giggled.

"Dad," Dom said, long-suffering. "Where are your aids?"

"What?"

"Your hearing aids. You're shouting. Never mind. Come and meet Austin. Austin, this is my dad, Kenneth."

"Ken Dymond." His father advanced, suddenly much less room in the hallway, a hand outstretched. It wrapped Austin's, work-rough grip another link between father and son. "You must be Austin," he said despite Dom already making that introduction. "Good to see you. Now maybe Dominic will stop flapping, thinking you weren't coming."

He didn't let go, using his hold to reel Austin into a hug he hadn't expected.

He froze, thawing just as quickly because Ken Dymond might have thought he whispered but the whole street could have heard him.

"Thank you," he said. "So much. For what you did for Maisie." He still didn't let go entirely, only pulling back far enough to hold Austin by the shoulders. "For what you did for us all. Thank you," he repeated.

Austin nodded, mute in the face of the reminder of what driving back into this village had brought back all too clearly, water in the harbour glinting jade between buildings on his way downhill, each glimpse somehow shocking.

"Already got thanking him covered, Dad." Dom picked up the surveyor's report. "Just need to go through this before hammering out the details and scheduling a start date," he said as if that was a foregone conclusion. He craned his neck next. "Maisie? You coming to say a proper hello?"

"Yes!" She hopscotched across flagstones the same way

Austin had seen at school, ending by standing on one leg, little arms windmilling.

It was a small thing.

A way to stay balanced, that was all.

He still lurched to catch her like he hadn't managed down at the harbour.

"Steady."

She grabbed hold of his hands, clinging, still balancing on one foot but grinning. "I'm the best at hopscotch." She twirled away, shouting, "I've got chalk!" for some reason.

Dom's dad called, "Maisie, where are you off to?" He followed his granddaughter, hallway door closing behind them. Dom closed the front door as well, shutting out the sound of seagulls shrieking.

"I would say it's not usually as noisy and chaotic here, but . . ."

"You'd be lying?"

Dom nodded, but Austin also saw something flicker, that report now rolled in one hand, which Dom tapped against the open palm of his other.

Austin eyed that motion. "Well, chaotic or not, spanking me with that report won't make me change my mind about not putting your bid forward."

"Spanking you? Oh." Dom let the report unfurl. A smile too. "Don't give me any ideas. Having enough of them lately without that visual. Besides, Maisie would only walk in again at the wrong moment." Perhaps that reminded him of what his daughter had interrupted—a kiss that felt like unfinished business.

Dom shifted closer, then hesitated, humour turning careful, serious now instead of joking. "Listen." He focused on the report he held instead of Austin, his voice turning gruffer. "Can I tell you something? A few things, actually. They've been on my mind." He lifted his head, his gaze guarded.

Worried, now I know what that looks like on him.

Once Austin nodded, Dom continued. "Dad was right, I had got myself into a proper tiz-woz when you were late. I thought you weren't coming."

"I'm sorry—"

"No. Don't be. It's . . . it's been an intense few weeks. Stressful. Starting with . . ." He gestured, Austin almost turning to see where he pointed, not needing to when he realised it was downhill, in the sea's direction. Dom wet lips Austin guessed salt must have lingered on like it had for him. "No," Dom admitted. "That's not actually true. It's been more than a few weeks, starting long before she fell in. We . . . uh . . . Both Gemma and I have been distracted. Not saying that's an excuse for Maisie slipping out without being noticed. For the miscommunication that let it happen. But maybe it was the warning shot we needed to stop burying our heads in the sand about some news."

"News?"

Dom nodded. Seemed about to add more before Austin watched him shutter, closing off as he said, "It's not life or death." So why did he look bleak before he recovered? "God knows we know the difference now after her dunking. Gemma and I will work through it when she gets back. Until then, my number one priority is making sure Maisie's safe in future. So the last few weeks have been all about making some changes around here. Being present. Which is why I've been slower than I would have liked to see more of you. Not because I didn't want to."

It was cool in the hallway, cottage walls built with thick

stone, but Austin still warmed, his chest and cheeks heating. "I know. You said."

"Want you to believe it, that's all." A hand stole to the back of Dom's neck, rubbing while he made a quiet confession. "You know I haven't been able to stop thinking about you, right? And I don't only mean thinking of ways to thank you. I've been thinking about *you*. About how you were doing after getting concussed. About whether you were sleeping, when neither me nor Maisie could." His brow furrowed. "Gemma, either. But when I saw you again, it sounded as if you'd been dealing with stresses at home too. And at work. I mean, you said you're leaving but you're still working hard on securing the best for your . . ."

"Ex."

Dom nodded. "Yeah, but that's what I keep coming back to every time I get a minute to think, which to be honest isn't a whole lot lately." He scrubbed a hand over a cheek next. It had been paint spotted that morning. Now it was freshly shaven, bare like his gaze, which didn't waver, no longer shuttered. "You know I fancy the pants off you, right?"

Austin had guessed that. Felt the same attraction. Hadn't expected to hear it out loud and so plainly stated. Hadn't expected what Dom asked next either.

"Is it set in stone that you're leaving?" He didn't wait for Austin's answer. "Because if there's a chance you'll stay, I'd want to get to know you better. A lot better. See you again even if you're not staying long-term, just as long as that isn't a conflict of interest with the project. If it is a conflict, pretend I didn't just kiss you, yeah? Now, or before."

He blinked as if reliving the same moment in a hospital cubicle Austin had a thousand times already. The other times they'd kissed too. "Set all of that aside, even though I think we'd be good together." There was that bare look again, raw and honest. "Got a feeling we'd be much better than good, but go ahead and forget any of that happened if that means the project gets to happen."

"You know that there are other—"

"Bidders?" Dom nodded. "Doesn't matter if there are. There's no way they can undercut me, and it doesn't matter what that report says about the renovation needing a specialist to wrangle the permissions because I wasn't kidding. I said I'd get the job done for the cost of materials only, and I will with one of the best specialists in the country. I've already squared it with him."

He must have seen Austin about to argue.

"Don't believe me? I'll put it in writing on headed paper before you go, if that helps you trust me. That's as good as me swearing on Maisie's life, I promise."

His head cocked then as if he heard something, and Austin did too, Maisie's laughter filtering from the other side of a door.

Dom said the rest fast. Emphatic. No room left to argue, the words ripped from him.

"I'll swear to it because you're the reason I still get to hear her laughing. *You.* What you did made me look at the news Gemma and I got from a whole new perspective." Dom closed his eyes as if reliving a tough moment. "But watching your kid drown and not be able to reach her?" His eyes reopened, gleaming. "That's the actual end of the world. Anything else doesn't compare. Doesn't come close. Is just a minor bump in the road."

His chest expanded, Austin mirroring an inhale that felt soul-deep, leaning in as Dom exhaled a whisper. "I get to hear her laugh because of you. There's nothing I won't do for you for giving me that. *Nothing*. That's personal, Austin. And me wanting to take you out no matter how long you're in Cornwall?" His gaze left Austin's face and travelled.

Down.

Up.

Turned hungry enough that Austin's breath caught. Maybe Dom's did too, because he sounded husky. "That's personal too." He closed the distance left between them, and maybe hungry had been the wrong word. From this close, Dom watched as if Austin was a different kind of sustaining to him—something he both wanted and needed—and Austin felt the same pull as he last had underwater, dragged out of his depth.

This time, he didn't fight it.

Didn't want to, and almost said so.

Dom beat him to it.

"Because once with you wouldn't be enough. Not for me. So yeah, that's all personal. Very." He surprised Austin by raising the surveyor's report between them. "This, on the other hand, is business. If I can only have one part of you, that's the part I'll take—the business side, so that we get this project agreed before you move on." He squared his shoulders. "I can be professional around you if that means I get to repay you properly. Just know that given a choice, I'd want both."

"Both," Austin echoed.

Dom nodded, something solemn about that slow movement. Something steady and confirming. A promise. He hesitated before adding, "But it's your choice. I know your clock's ticking." He scrubbed a hand through his hair. "I *do* know that . . ."

He met Austin's eyes again, helpless, a look Austin hadn't

known would be attractive on this man who backed off instead of advancing when that was clearly what he wanted. "I don't know why I'm so attracted to you when all you did for months was give me a hard time." He tapped the face of his watch like Austin had done so often when he was late for Maisie. "But tick-tock, right? So—"

"Personal," Austin blurted. "Business too. I mean, I'd choose both if . . ."

"Yeah?" And like that ribbon of sky above the narrow street outside, Dom brightened. He backed away, pressing against the hallway door between them and his family. "Really?" He stood there, waiting, Austin realised, making good on that *your choice* promise.

Austin took one step, then two. His third closed the gap between them, his face raised as Dom's lowered.

They kissed again, Dom's arms coming around him, slow and testing until Austin realised that too was on purpose, Dom holding himself back until Austin crowded closer. Then Dom's arms wrapped him. Held him. Pulled him against a solid torso, and every clock in the world could have stopped and he wouldn't have noticed.

His mouth opened to Dom's tongue, and nothing else mattered.

How was the sensation more intense each time he felt it?

More perfect?

Austin pushed himself up to kiss him deeper, wanting however much he would give him, and Dom reciprocated, grasping him tighter, their mouths still connected as he clasped Austin by the back of the thighs and lifted.

Austin wrapped his legs around Dom, and at any other time, that would have been a first step in sex. Would have led to getting pressed against a wall, maybe, or bent over that hallway table. He could almost picture the frantic scramble of belts and buttons, and he broke off, chest heaving as Dom's mouth found his throat, sensation devastating.

Austin clutched his shoulders, gaze lighting on the table by the doorway. It did look sturdy—

The sound of footsteps cut through the haze, Dom breaking off, his hair ruffled from Austin's fingers through it, his face flushed, lips so well kissed that something inside Austin puffed with pride. Preened. Circled before settling in a patch of sunshine.

"Daddy?" The door muffled Maisie's voice. "Is Austin Russell coming?"

"Soon," Dom quietly promised, gaze locked with Austin's. "We both will."

12

The kitchen Dom led him into a few minutes later was a surprise, taking a moment to process.

"This is . . ." Austin took in a huge space flooded with light, yet rustic, a more recent extension, blending older aspects of the cottage with a modern addition, the room stretching wider than the narrow front of the cottage suggested. The oak beams across the whitewashed ceiling in here were paler than those in the hallway. Only the flooring was the same patchwork of ancient flagstones. "This is really . . ."

He jumped when Dom's father answered.

"Big?" He rose from where he'd crouched behind a kitchen island, adding a biscuit tin to a tray of mugs. He carried it to an open set of French doors and backed out. "Wasn't like this when Dominic was born here, I can tell you. But my son's always had a thing about size."

"You sure you couldn't say that any louder, Dad? Not sure all of Porthperrin heard you." Dom had to work at stifling a smile.

Austin could tell. Could see it plain as day in a face he couldn't drag his eyes from until Dom's dad said, "Fill the pot when the kettle boils, will you?" the doors to the outside closing behind him, shutting out the sound of seagulls and Maisie singing.

"But yeah," Dom admitted, looking around as if seeing the space they stood in through Austin's eyes instead of his own. "Size did matter in here. Fuck knows how Mum used to manage in the old kitchen."

"It was small?"

"Nothing wrong with some small things," Dom said, looking him up and down like he had in the hallway, smile hovering. "But calling it compact would be generous." He pointed to the right where an open-plan kitchen was covered with evidence of the baking he'd smelled on the way in. Flour dusted every surface, cake pans empty on top of an Aga the same rich cream as the cupboards. "Up until we had Maisie, getting to buy the cottage next door for Mum and Dad and knock through to build her dream kitchen felt like I'd peaked, you know? Reached the top of the tree. Like nothing could be better. Told her I'd build her a dream kitchen when the business took off. She was so happy when I made good on that promise."

He answered a question Austin wasn't sure how to phrase, his smile not gone, but slipping. "Ten years now. Since we lost her, I mean. Glad she got to enjoy it."

"I'm sorry." That didn't seem enough. Adding a quiet, "Bereavement's tough," didn't sound much better, but he saw that slide reverse, Dom's smile returning when he added, "My mum would love this kitchen."

"Yeah?"

"Yes. She used to stalk kitchen showrooms when we were

kids. Was always weighing up what would be better." He slid a hand along a counter. "Wood like this or something tough like granite."

Dom ran a hand along the same length. "Granite's easier to look after. Wood's a bugger to maintain, but Mum preferred it, so . . ." He shrugged as if to say *what can you do?* "What did she choose?"

For a moment, Austin didn't answer. Couldn't. It had been so long since all those showroom visits he hadn't even known had lodged in his subconscious. Now a hundred mundane moments of entertaining his little sister while his mum had priced up worktops washed in, not stopping until Dom broke the moment by repeating his question. "What did she settle on? Wood or granite?"

"Settle on? Oh, neither. That was before she set up the charity she runs now. Don't think she could justify the cost to herself once her focus was on raising funds not spending money." He scanned a room that once would have been her idea of perfect. "The kitchen at home could still do with an upgrade. To be honest, the whole house could. It's in a pretty suburb. Well-kept. Think it's letting our street down."

"Quiet place?"

"Should be, but it's on the outskirts of Exeter. Commuters use it as a cut through. Bit of a rat run, to be honest, but like I said, it's pretty. Apart from our place." He recalled his latest phone call, his mum letting more slip than the usual statistics they shared. "I . . . I missed a couple of visits home, so I've promised to catch up by cutting back the cherry tree in the front garden when I'm next there. It's dislodging the gutter-ing. Maybe you could give me some pointers."

"Maybe I can. When are you going?"

"End of next week. I always go home for my sister's birth

day. She's—" The kettle whistled, a shriek from outside rivalling it for loudness, and Austin picked up the box of craft supplies Dom had set down on the counter, glancing at the door his dad had left through.

"You can go on out," he said. "I'll only be a minute." And there was a head tilt that was increasingly familiar, Dom paying more attention than Austin was used to. "Or if you're not sure you're ready to be deafened by an inquisition the whole village will hear, you could take a look around at the rest of what my size complex made me rebuild." He pointed to the left, gesturing at skylights flooding the rest of the space with light.

Austin took him up on that offer, walking around a long dining table as sturdy as the hallway table, made by the same craftsman maybe, sunlight painting its surface mellow. Board games covered one end, an incomplete jigsaw the other, along with a roll of labels. They were everywhere he looked, spelling out what each one was stuck to. Austin turned away from a framed photo labelled *my family* before he moved on to where couches were arranged around a wall-mounted TV, a Disney movie paused on its massive flatscreen.

Maybe that modern touch should seem out of place in a fisherman's cottage, but it fit, everything here in proportion down to the screen's placement between those exposed beams.

Austin turned back, "You did all this?"

Dom nodded while dropping teabags into a pot.

Austin looked again at the room's proportions, squinting. "Was this end of the house another cottage once as well?"

"Yes. Got lucky after a big storm made a lot of villagers sell up." He grabbed the kettle, shaking his head. "Fuck me, that sounds ghoulish. What I mean is that I'd been waiting for years to buy the cottage next door so Mum and Dad could have three in a row. Would have been happy enough to wait for longer once Mum died. Didn't seem as important. But the big storm happened at the same time we moved back to Cornwall. I needed to keep busy, so . . ."

He poured water in the teapot, steam obscuring his expression. "Someone else would have snapped it up like all the other cottages that flooded the market that winter. I bought a few. Already had one along the coast I'd renovated years before with Dad. Doing up a few more with him kept my mind busy. Still does. Nothing like a project for that. But I'm particularly glad I got to buy the cottage next door or it would have got cramped when I moved back in when we realised that's what Maisie needed. At least she's got a nice big bedroom."

Austin's gaze flicked to that family photo, Maisie a toddler between Dom and a woman with Maisie's curls. Dom must have noticed. "Yeah, that was the winter we split for good. Gemma lives nearby."

"So you live here—"

Maisie had tired of waiting. She burst in, twirling. And holding up a fat stick of chalk that she brandished at Austin. "I need you to do my numbers!"

"Aren't you forgetting something, Maisie?" Dom asked.

"Please?"

At some point Austin would look into eyes so like her daddy's and be able to say no, but today wasn't it. The rest of the afternoon didn't look too likely either, because he started to follow her out before Dom said, "And then come upstairs to take a look at my numbers while I read through that report?"

"Aren't you forgetting something?" Austin said without

thinking, teasing coming naturally in a house as warm as the gaze that met his.

"Please?" Dom asked. "I've got a brand-new bid for you. Listened to what you said and typed it up as soon as I got back."

"So the total is more than zero this time?"

"The total doesn't matter to me."

"Might matter if you want to impress the school's backers."

This time when Dom tilted his head, Austin came back, pulled by a slight movement that was turning into a signal. A clue that Dom was about to get honest.

"The only person I want to impress is you."

He'd already done that. Had more than turned Austin's first impression on its head, but he wasn't done adding more proof.

"And nothing in that report will scare me. I can't be put off, Aus. I'm already one-hundred percent committed to giving you whatever you want."

That struck like an arrow, Dom also scoring a bullseye with what he added.

"Don't even care that it's for an ex of yours. I'd move mountains for my ex too. Some relationships are worth preserving, like old buildings, yeah? Like a family home. You'll go home to maintain yours for your mum. I'll do pretty much anything to keep mine standing too, so I get it."

Austin nodded, box of supplies clutched to his chest as though that might stop his ribs swinging open, Dom cutting through bone and gristle to the heart of what drove him.

"It doesn't matter who it's for, Aus." And didn't him short-ening Austin's name sound different to when anyone else said it that way? Feel different too, like a curl of an arm around him even though they weren't touching, although they were closer to that now Austin had drifted even nearer with just the box and a steaming pot of tea between them.

"Doesn't matter who it's for, or if you move on before it's finished. If a renovated building's all I end up with, it'll still be worth it to me." Dom straightened. "All you have to do is put my bid forward. I promise I'll see it through from start to finish."

Austin almost said yes, even without Dom reading through exactly what he would be getting into. Nearly nodded despite knowing that if he'd presented a proposal based on trust instead of hard, cold cash at his last job, he would have been laughed out of the boardroom. He held back, and again Dom noticed.

His gaze slanted upward at oak beams that would one day turn the same shade as those in the hallway. "Does getting to see that I'm not afraid of renovations help?" It slid next to the kitchen. "Or seeing that I'm not afraid of mixing modern touches with heritage features—"

They both turned at the sound of something bumping the glass doors, Maisie's nose pressed against it. She turned away, yelling, "No, they're not kissing again," and Dom chuckled.

"Let's get this done, and then I'll try harder to convince you."

THE COURTYARD behind the cottage was another surprise. A sun trap shaded by a rose-covered pergola. Terraces came next, steps cut into Porthperrin's steep hillside, each level covered with what looked like rubber matting holding hand-built play equipment.

"My 'stacle course," Maisie told him, chalk in hand, so Austin could add numbers to the shaky squares she'd drawn on the matting.

"Obstacle course," Dom said on the way past with the teapot.

"Makes me stronger." She flexed puny biceps. "Show Austin Russell your big ones, Daddy!"

Dom did, flexing once he'd reached the highest terrace where his father flexed too, laughing.

Maisie hopscotched, clutching Austin's hand, her arms around his neck a surprise once she'd finished. Her mouth close to his ear another. "We made cakes for you." She whispered about as quietly as her grandfather. "They're a secret."

"Maisie." Ken boomed a warning that she danced away from, giggling, tripping over her feet, giggling harder as Austin caught her.

Austin laughed too. Couldn't help it. Couldn't help nodding when Maisie used her please and thank yous to ask him to help her keep her balance again, hopping over and over until Dom said the tea would get cold. She demonstrated the rest of her play equipment on the way up to the table, stopping on each level, everything she showed him mimicking what Charles had mentioned.

Hand-eye coordination and sensory input being supported. More chances to balance. He looked back at that rubber matting. *Safe places to fall over and over as well.* Then he reached the top of the garden, the view distracting him from anything else. Would have stripped away the last of his breath if Dom hadn't already done that, the afternoon sun choosing that moment to light him while he looked at his daughter. To paint him, but not with speckles this time, but with something Austin didn't have words for.

He built all this for her.

With his own hands.

Austin watched those hands stroke his daughter's hair from her eyes as she dug craft supplies out of the box Austin had set down, gentle, so, so gentle while adjusting her headband. They kept catching Austin's eye as tea gave way to fairy-wing construction.

Maybe it shouldn't have needed three adults to piece them together, but the next time she hopscotched across the bottom terrace, heading for her bath and bedtime, they glittered, flapping as if she'd take off once her game was over.

As if she'd fly.

Something inside Austin almost did too when Dom drew him into the shade of the pergola instead of following his family inside.

"She loves the wings," Dom promised while scrolling through photos he'd taken of them. "Genius idea doing it in the garden. No glitter to hoover out of the carpet. Can't remember the last time I did something like this outside."

"I can remember when I last did."

Dom stopped scrolling. Looked up. Waited. Interested, and why that was all it took the floodgates to open, Austin couldn't have explained, no formula to apply here like he would to his spreadsheet columns. No reason that Dom's pleasure at seeing his daughter happy unlocked a door Austin had pressed his shoulder against for years now. But Dom made space beside him, and maybe sitting in the pergola's shade helped, because words that had been hard to shape before slipped from him as soft as the petals the breeze scattered.

"It was just before we lost my sister."

Dom's lips parted.

Closed.

Parted again.

Finally he asked, "Lost?"

Austin shrugged. Nodded. Shook his head, lump in his throat still enormous considering it had been years.

"I'm so sorry."

Austin was too. Sorry that he hadn't been half as patient back then as he'd managed for Maisie today. He rested his elbows on his knees, paint-streaked hands clasped together. "You make being patient look easy."

"Patient?"

Austin nodded, voiceless, focusing on glitter stuck to his fingers instead of speaking, aware that Dom had repositioned, one arm resting along the back of the bench they shared—there if he wanted to lean back but not demanding.

How did I ever see him as uncaring?

I really did get him all wrong.

Or maybe he'd spent too long seeing the world through a lens blurred by a hundred moments of his own where he could have been more attentive. "Maisie reminds me of her. Of Tamsin. Always has," he admitted.

"How?"

"How?" Austin sat up straighter. Crossed his arms. Faced forward so Dom was out of his line of vision. "Tamsin used to..."

Bounce.

Dance.

Shout when she should be quiet, also sharing Maisie's struggle with keeping secrets. "She loved wearing wings. Had a fairy party for her sixth birthday. That's how Mum knew how to make them."

Dom let out a breath as if Austin had punched him some-where tender. "Christ, and we just spent the last few hours—"

"It's fine." He shrugged, unable to hold in something surprising. "It was actually good."

Dom touched him then, his hand light on Austin's shoulder. "I am sorry though. For your loss. What—"

Austin stiffened. "Happened to her?"

"I was going to ask what was she like. Your Tamsin."

Rose petals fell and seagulls cried before Austin could answer, because nobody asked that. *Nobody.* And yet once he started, this list was easy.

"Silly. Smart. Seven."

He sniffed.

Blinked.

Felt the sweep of Dom's hand leave his shoulder only to rub his back. He fought to keep it straight instead of crumpling. "Anyway," Austin tried to say briskly. "We should go take a look at your figures before I leave."

"Figures?"

And didn't it say something that for a long, transparent moment, Austin could tell Dom had forgotten the real purpose of his visit. "For your bid?" He got to his feet, Dom's hand falling away as if he could see through him. Saw that moving on would be kinder than letting him sit here bleeding.

"We could do that, although—" The sound of crying seeped from an open window, seagulls on the roof of the cottage shrieking in answer. "It sounds like Maisie's kicking off about bath time again, so maybe tomorrow?"

Austin nodded. Sat again as abruptly as he'd just stood. "I get it, that's all. Why you're grateful, I mean." He stifled the urge to downplay. Made himself face this man who kept listening. Met eyes that searched his and tried not to hide how much he meant this. "I would have been grateful too if things had been different. If . . . If I hadn't lost my sister. But don't let gratitude or"—he didn't need to stretch far for this word—"guilt nail you to a cross you can't get off."

"By putting in the bid? Why would it?"

Austin blinked, the answer was so easy. "Because I don't want you to bankrupt yourself to say thank you to me. I owe you too, remember? And if something like guilt is your driver, stop right now." He had to look away, seagulls on the roof watching his struggle. "Don't let guilt be what sinks Dymond and Son. Believe me, you don't want that." And like a compass finding its north, his eyes met with Dom's again. "I don't want that for you *or* your business."

"Good thing it's not my business then."

"Dymond and Son?" Austin said, confused by another of those slow smiles spreading.

"No. It's Dad's."

Maisie's shrieks from the house hit a higher octave. Dom got to his feet this time, taking the report from the box of left-over glitter and glue.

"Pretty sure it'll be his forever because nothing stops him working, but it sounds like he needs me right now."

He leaned down, kiss a brief brush to Austin's temple, soft, like his murmur.

"So how about I read this report later tonight while you go home and look up my business, Dymond and Daughter?"

A ustin didn't wait to get home before googling.

He tried the moment he got back in the Defender only to give up, search lagging on his phone instead of loading, then trying again at the top of the hill out of Porthperrin. He pulled off the road onto a garage forecourt that was closed for the day, only the classic cars that were for sale there keeping him company as he did what Dom had instructed.

The sun lowered, catching the windscreens of vehicles cumulatively worth a small fortune while reading about a business worth another, clicking on the filing history at Companies House linked to Dymond and Daughter.

The set of accounts he opened put Dom's offer into context, Austin's breath catching only to come out as strangled laughter.

Renovate one building?

He could buy the whole school lock, stock, and barrel.

Austin carried that thought back to Glynn Harber, his phone chiming with a message as he got there.

From Dom?

That didn't seem likely when he'd only just left Porthperrin, but for once, Austin caused gravel to scatter, slamming on the Defender's brakes to read it.

He grabbed his phone, a different name on the message preview.

Charles.

Austin put the Defender back into gear, driving around the school, telling himself he wasn't disappointed. Of course he wasn't. More messages pinged as Austin pulled up outside a building where, for once, no one was home to tease him.

That didn't stop Charles from trying.

Austin scrolled through a chain of messages on his way into the stables.

Charles: *I've been thinking about you and Maisie's daddy.*

Charles: *Never seen you move so fast.*

Charles: *I mean, you weren't the only one who moved fast.*

Charles: *Thought he was going to climb the fence to get to you.*

Charles: *Make the most of it before he realises your first language is Excel and making spreadsheets is your idea of foreplay.*

Charles: *Are you sure you want me to nudge Heligan for you?*

Austin stopped, door key almost in the lock lowering.

Do I?

The tail-end of a conversation in Dom's garden replayed, the cross he'd told Dom not to nail himself onto casting a long shadow.

His shoulders bowed and he closed his eyes to see Maisie dancing, wings sparkling, her grandfather bellowing about her manners. But Charles doing it sooner rather than later would give him something constructive to tell his mother while he kept up a job search that felt like hammering more nails into his own palms.

Austin: *Yes.*

Charles: *If you're sure?*

Austin got his key in the lock. Let himself in. But as his back pressed to the door closing behind him, he remembered Dom doing the same in his hallway, shielding them so they could kiss, and he could feel it all over again. Felt Dom hefting him up with no problem. Felt the hardness of his interest as he'd set him down too, Austin sliding down his body until he stood on flagstones as hard as his cock, needing a minute or two of thinking about anything else but the man who'd held the door closed until that heat subsided.

Now his head crowded with everything else that he'd learned since that moment, his phone full of evidence that, yet again, Dom wasn't who he'd expected.

No. He isn't who I assumed.

He pushed away from the door and headed for a sofa he cleared of books before sitting. Austin set aside a bible, gathering an armful of other books, not consciously taking in their titles until a theme jumped out. He slowed down then, like with Dom, and paid more attention.

How to Win Over a New Flock: Tips for Clergy Spouses

The final book he added to his stack looked well thumbed.

How to be a Vicar's Wife without Really Crying

It fell open in his hands on a section Charles had highlighted.

Regardless of the reason for needing a new vicar, parishioners often resent their replacement. Your role is imperative.

Charles had circled that last word, then must have checked its definition, the words *make or break* jotted in the margin, a sad-face drawn next to it. The same scrawl covered a Post-it note he'd used as a bookmark.

Don't tell jokes, Charles had jotted. *Even if I'm nervous. Especially if I'm nervous. Don't laugh too much. Or at all. Be serious like Hugo. Make them like me. For him.*

Austin frowned, muttering, "Make them like him? Who wouldn't?" He closed the book. Set it with the others on the dining table next to a stack of learning journeys, gaze snagged by another Post-it bookmark.

He flipped a learning journey open, passing photos of play in action to read another scrawled suggestion.

Nathan, could we hold Maisie back again?

She's still not ready.

Nathan's answer was brief and much more neatly written.

Yes, I want to keep her.

I'll email her parents again.

Hope they answer this time.

Austin's frown lingered like the paint still drying onto his fingers until his phone interrupted with another message.

Charles: *Message sent. :(*

Charles: *Make the most of Maisie's daddy before Heligan steals you.*

Charles: *Take him out for a Cornish last fling. Wear some of my aftershave. The Tom Ford one, Fucking Fabulous. Always guarantees a good time. And take some lube.*

Charles: *You'll need it.*

Charles: *You know. What with you being a born-again virgin since coming to Glynn Harber.*

A voice note followed.

Austin saved listening to it for after he'd showered, scrubbing away the last of that paint, but his thoughts swirled like the water down the drain, those how-to book titles hanging like the steam in the air as he dried off.

He's spent weeks checking in on me, making sure I recovered. And ages this morning putting that craft stuff together.

Was he nervous about Hugo's interview this whole time?

Because that was where Charles was headed, Austin remembered. Not only home to plan his wedding, but to a meeting where he'd be under as much scrutiny as his fiancé.

He opened the bathroom cabinet. Sniffed the aftershave Charles had recommended. Dabbed some on while listening to the voice note.

"Listen," Charles said as Austin went to his bedroom about to slip on a shirt, stopping because Charles said, "Hugo says virginity doesn't work that way, but do use plenty of lube, won't you? You're really quite dinky and I'm worried about your poor anus." Another voice rumbled in the background, Austin listening to the kind of good-natured to-and-fro between his housemates that had been the backing track to his last few months. One that reminded him of similar bickering he'd heard while making wings with Maisie.

Like how we used to sound at home too, before Tamsin . . .

He abandoned the shirt to cradle his phone, again feeling a rare urge to call his mother, only Charles continued speaking, perhaps forgetting that he'd been midway through a voice note.

"Of course I'm not being too personal. And of course I'm right to worry. Have you seen the size of that man's hands? If that's a predictor of what he's got in his trousers—"

Hugo rumbled, "Charles," again, sounding long-suffering.

"I know it isn't *always* the case, Hugo, and size absolutely isn't everything, but believe me, my sample group is bigger than average and someone's got to care about his bottom.

Care about him full stop, because if not me—*us*—then who else? He hasn't got anyone, has he? He's all alone in the—"

The message cut off mid-sentence, but Austin could guess how it would have ended, the complete phrase echoing despite Charles not finishing it. Despite it not being true either.

I'm not all alone in the world, for Christ's sake.

He'd been about to call his mum, hadn't he?

That too seemed to echo, sounding hollow.

I will, though. I'll do it right now.

Again, he pictured Maisie, brand-new wings sparkling as she hopscotched. Smelled the vanilla of fresh baking. Saw that photo labelled *my family*, and for a moment he wished . . .

That wishful moment extended, Austin standing still for so long water trickled from his wet hair down his neck. He shivered before wiping it with his towel. Then he scrubbed at his hair fiercely, telling himself to pull himself together.

All families are different.

Mine's perfectly—

A knock at the door interrupted. He ran a hand through his hair on the way there, straightening it as the door swung open to show Dom doing the same thing.

Austin watched a hand that Charles had speculated over drop. Heard Dom say, "Hey," sounding hesitant. But when he asked, "I know we only just said goodbye, but can I take you out for dinner?" Austin quickly nodded.

———

DOM HESITATED in the doorway until Austin found his voice. "Come in." He swiped away another water droplet as Dom stepped in out of the evening sunshine. "Let me just . . ." He backed towards his bedroom. "Sit. I'll be—" He'd meant to say *right back*, but Dom started laughing. "What's so funny?"

"The fact that I spent most of this afternoon wishing my dad would leave us alone for five minutes only to see he got here before me."

"Your dad?" Austin asked, confused. "He's not here."

"But he was." Dom pointed up at an oak beam crossing the ceiling. "See?"

Austin came back. Looked up where he pointed. The initials KD were right there. "He built these stables?"

"Converted them. Must have. This beam's newer than the others." Dom reached up. Knocked on the wood. "Didn't know he'd worked here, but I helped him with similar conversions when I was younger. You ever been to Ed's place?"

Austin shook his head.

"His mum used to let out their house to holiday makers. We converted her stables into living accommodation the summer before I left home. If you look up at his place, you'd see my initials on his beams too."

"On his beams?" Austin backed off, grip on the towel he'd dried his hair with tightening like his voice did, brittle out of nowhere. "The ones across his bedroom ceiling, I suppose?"

Dom didn't let him go far, snagging the towel to halt his progress. "That was a long time ago, and I meant you'd find my initials next to my dad's." He glanced up again. "I like spotting where he's worked. His dad before him too. Didn't exactly appreciate it before Maisie. One day she might look up . . ." He shrugged. Fixed his gaze on the towel he hadn't let go of yet. Tugged on it until Austin stood closer.

Much closer.

"I didn't come here to talk about Ed. Can't actually say I'm hungry for dinner either after all that cake."

"Why'd you come then?" Austin's chest rose and fell, another water droplet meandering, slow as syrup, and maybe Dom watched it. Must have. He stopped its passage, wiping it away with the pad of a thumb, his voice lowering.

"Because I wanted to see you. To check in with you. You had time to look me up yet?"

Austin nodded, watching Dom find another bead of water and wipe it away, his touch lingering.

"Then we can talk about what you found out, if you want," Dom murmured before finding one more droplet at the base of his throat. He kissed it away, lips skimming, brief touch electric. "Or we can talk about you smelling really fucking good."

"It's Fucking Fabulous." Austin said, and Dom must have taken him lifting his chin as an offer. He leaned in, sniffing what Charles had promised would guarantee a good time. He hadn't lied, Austin decided, because Dom's lips skimmed again, higher now, sensation bright as a struck match, bold and flaring.

"You are, aren't you?" Dom said. "Really fucking fabulous. Guessed you were a while ago. Knew it this afternoon. You're so good with Maisie."

Dom dropped his end of the towel.

Now he stood empty-handed under an oak beam his father must have shouldered decades before, and waited. Watched. Wanted too, if Austin could trust what he read in his expression.

He waited some more, both hands open, and why that made Austin unclenching his fingers easy, he'd think about later, busy now dropping his end of the towel. His guard too, stepping into Dom's space and looping his arms around his neck, pulling him down into a kiss that somehow felt like breaking the surface.

Their mouths met, yet Austin breathed easier for what felt the first time since they'd both gone under.

But we've already done this.

Why does it feel like a first time?

Those questions would have to wait now that their mouths were busy, lips parting and tongues meeting, slick and devastating.

Dom's hold tightened, palms skimming his back, exploring, and Austin did the same, only mapping a chest Dom's shirt still covered.

He tugged at it, wanting to feel bare skin like Dom must, his hands slipping under the waist of Austin's shorts to cup his arse and squeeze it.

He tugged at Dom's shirt again, harder, this time finding a button, but Dom broke off their kiss, his chest rising and falling faster as he covered Austin's hand with one of his own.

Dom had touched him before. Austin already knew his hands were work hardened, yet something quivered at his light hold. At him asking, "There's no one else home?" as well.

"No." Was that Austin's voice so rough and husky? "My housemates are away." And like another match had been struck, what flared between them stayed lit, Dom's grin bright and sudden.

"You want this off?" His hand flexed over Austin's, reminding him that he'd been unfastening shirt buttons. "Because I can . . ." He was close enough that the back of his knuckles brushed the bare skin of Austin's torso, and perhaps that was too much distraction. Dom didn't finish his sentence, hand moving, no longer covering Austin's but exploring what his knuckles had just touched. "Fuck, you're gorgeous, aren't you? What do you want? Tell me. I'll make sure you get it."

What did he want?

He'd take more of what played over Dom's face right now, and he'd get to have it. All of it. Because Dom was a man of his word. He knew it. Had seen it in the strangest of places— in a kitchen he'd promised to rebuild. In keeping a lunch date with his daughter. In a bid that Austin only now let himself believe in, and that would let him leave with a clear conscience.

Maybe Dom took his hand spasming at that thought, gripping his shirt tighter, as a suggestion. He took over what Austin had started, unfastening buttons until his shirt hung open over a chest Austin couldn't keep his hands off. Couldn't stop from pressing palms that had been coated in paint a short while before onto a body that was as solid as the beams above them. Couldn't stop a huff of laughter escaping either because there was some more of that glitter caught in Dom's chest hair, sparkling like the eyes that met his.

"Whatever you want," Dom promised again, and Austin nodded, believing.

Trusting.

Taking.

They kissed again then, chest to chest, Austin's arms a loop around Dom's neck, and it felt right. Dom's mouth did too, kissing him deeper. Wetter. His hold bringing Austin even closer.

That was his cock, Austin realised, hard already under clothing he would have dropped to his knees to free if Dom hadn't chosen that moment to cup his arse again and heft him upward.

This time, he took the few steps to the sofa.

Sank onto it so Austin straddled him, still kissing.

Thank God I moved Hugo's bible.

More laughter almost bubbled.

Dom must have felt it. He broke off again. "That's the second time now. I'd get a complex if I didn't think you liked me as much as I like you."

Austin had been called a lot of things, not all of them complimentary like sharp, brittle, and spiky. A four-letter word stilled him. "You like me?"

That sounded juvenile the moment it popped out, but Dom nodded. "More than like you, to be honest," which was all it took for Austin to shake off that stillness.

Something new roared through him, every match in the world combusting, getting Dom's cock free from his shorts an imperative.

Make or break, Austin remembered, and this *was* a make-or-break moment for whatever coiled tight in his chest like Dom's fist did around Austin's cock, pleasure intense, barely able to breathe let alone kiss.

Their mouths fused together, his groans barely muffled, and he surrendered to pleasure, tipping his head back when Dom's mouth found that place at the base of his throat, drawing up more sensation than he knew what to do with.

"Oh," Dom rumbled. "You like that."

He saw himself in Dom's pupils, his own eyes lidded, and pleasure swept in. Swept out. Washed in again as Dom's mouth met his throat one more time, the slide of Dom's hand on his cock easier, wetter, feeling so good.

"Yeah," Dom said, bringing his hand to his mouth, the web between thumb and forefinger glistening. He sucked it, his cock thick and twitching in Austin's hold. "You *really* like it." For a third time, he mouthed right where Austin's pulse skipped at the base of his neck, forcing out a sound as well as more precome.

He'd bruise. He knew it but couldn't make himself care. Not when he wanted a reminder of straddling this man who got him off like his hands were made to fit him. Whose own cock took all of his concentration to keep holding while pleasure spiralled.

Dom had no trouble coordinating his movements, mouth busy and hands moving at the same time, getting him closer. His teeth grazed, and Austin tilted his head back again, his grip tightening, but Dom didn't complain. He hefted Austin off his lap, making taking his weight seem easy before settling him onto his back, tugging his shorts all the way off, and then kneeling in the cradle of legs he nudged apart.

Dom braced above him, his shirtfront open, curtaining Austin from everything but his gaze, which slid from Austin's eyes down his body to his cock, which he traced, his own flushed and compelling.

Austin couldn't take his eyes off him. Reached for him. Ran fingers along thick veins and spoke with no filter. "Never wanted anything in my mouth more."

"Next time," Dom promised, his cheeks flushed and teeth gritted, face describing determination.

To get me off.

Dom nodded. Wet his lips. Breathed faster, like his fist moved too, and Austin gave in to an orgasm that came as if ordered, his body a long, tight line of tension, turning boneless with Dom watching, soaking up each pulse across his stomach, each hitch of his hips, every squirm of intense feeling.

"Fuck," Dom said, drawing the word out and kneeling

back, finishing what Austin had started, his own cock in hand, fist flying. "Look at you." He repeated the same words slower after licking his palm. "Look at you."

Austin caught his breath. Got himself back together. Pushed himself up on his elbows, eyes fixed on the head of Dom's cock that retreated through a ring of thick fingers.

Austin's gaze locked on them.

I want them in me.

His gaze latched onto the head of Dom's cock as it re-emerged and then retreated.

That too.

"Next time." Dom's promise came out gritty, his brow creasing with climax, which spilled, Dom shuddering. Almost falling. Stopping himself an inch above Austin, his mouth right there, lips parted, breathing harshly.

Austin kissed him.

Pulled him closer.

Lay with their sticky bellies pressed together as they came down together, Dom's head on his shoulder.

He should feel heavy, but Austin breathed easy. Found another fleck of glitter, brushing it away from Dom's eyebrow, fingers shaking but careful. And this time when Dom said, "Think you'll have room for dinner soon?" he didn't nod, he kissed him.

ustin passed the same moorland and coastline for a second time in one day, only this time as a passenger rather than the driver. Sitting beside Dom instead of steering meant he could take in more of the view, but not from the front seat of the dented Transit van he'd seen Dom pull up in so often. No, this was a much more luxurious Range Rover, encasing Austin in a leather front seat, the rear ones scattered with evidence of Dom's usual passenger.

His head had been too full to enjoy the view the last time he'd passed it. Although he wasn't sure *enjoy* would ever be a word he'd associate with the sea since feeling the rip of its currents.

When exactly Dom noticed that Austin would look away each time the coast road threaded close to the cliff edge or that his hand would steal to his seatbelt, Austin couldn't pinpoint. But Dom did more than notice. He shifted gears, slowing, and moved his hand from the gearstick to drop onto Austin's knee, reassuring. "I'm not in any hurry."

"I didn't say you were."

"That death grip on your seatbelt says otherwise, but taking my time isn't a problem." He gestured at the passenger-side window. "Maisie's not a fan of the view along here right now either. Won't step foot near the harbour no matter how often Dad or I take her."

"Can't say I blame her." What she'd been through had been scary enough for an adult. For all three of them, to be honest. "But you want her to go there with you?"

"To the harbour. Well, yeah. It's where . . ."

Austin watched him lift a hand to scrub at the back of his neck, and maybe Dom wasn't the only one learning to read body language. Austin did his best to interpret what he witnessed. "Because it's just down the street from your dad's place and you need her to be safe around the water?"

Dom nodded. Then he shrugged. "It's not just that." He glanced sideways, and now that Austin paid attention to the view inside the vehicle, he saw tension in Dom's shoulders. In his grip on the steering wheel as well. "It's actually where her mum lives. Gemma's place is right on the harbour. Couldn't get much closer to the water."

"Ah, so of course she can't avoid it forever." Another penny dropped. "That's where you thought she was?" He remembered watching Maisie skip. Climb onto the sea wall. Wobble there, with no one to help her keep her balance.

He hadn't seen a woman anywhere close to her, had he? "And that's who you thought she was with? Her mum?"

Dom almost said no. Stopped himself. Austin saw discomfort flicker, so Austin felt around the edges of another question, not quite sure how to phrase it. "There was some kind of a miscommunication about who was responsible for her? You were working, right? Was it your dad? Didn't he hear—"

"It doesn't matter. It was an accident that I've made sure can't happen again. No point casting blame. Dad would never forgive himself, and Gemma—" He stopped himself. Started over. "Well, she blames herself for enough already." He didn't offer more apart from saying, "It could have been me, you know? What's blame gonna do, anyway? Make raising her harder or easier? Make either Gemma or Dad enjoy every moment from now on or constantly relive a once-in-a-life-time nightmare?"

That resonated, Austin's hand stealing to his phone in his pocket, but Dom wasn't finished.

"What I really need to do is find some way of getting Maisie back on track, before her mum comes home."

"Back on track?"

Dom cast a glance his way, and at some point, Austin would stop getting tripped by a shade of blue that should perhaps feel cool. It warmed him instead because all he saw was caring. Worry. A man set on doing his best for his family. He said, "You heard her crying earlier, Aus?"

"About her bath time?"

"It isn't only bath time or going near the harbour that upsets her. It's anything to do with water since . . ." There was more of that worry. "It's been weeks now, but she's getting worse not better. I wish I knew how to fix it. I don't want Gemma upset if Maisie refuses to go home with her. It's the last thing she needs."

He scrubbed a hand through his hair in a way that, for a fleeting moment, reminded him of Cameron next to Whisper Tor's base, caught between a rock and a hard place, not wanting to be Austin's partner but not wanting to let Luke down either.

Dom said, "But I can't force her to like it, can I? Not after what happened. Only I can't have Maisie melting down each time it's Gemma's turn to have her either. She's got enough to deal with."

He winced as if he hadn't meant to say that, turning gruffer.

"Her mum hasn't been herself lately. Nothing life threatening," he quickly added. "But I didn't realise she was struggling. Kids and recuperating don't exactly go together. I had to practically strong-arm her to take a break. That's why she's away. Hoping a bit of time will make all the difference."

"That . . . that all sounds tough."

"Tough?" Dom said shortly. "I've spent the last who knows how many years making tough decisions with no problem. You looked up more than my business name, yeah? Dug a bit deeper into its financials?" His next glance held an edge of worry.

"Yes."

"So you understand I must know how to run a business. What that involves. I don't want you to think—"

"That you were hiding any of that from me?"

Dom's nod was quick. Clipped, like his voice. "I didn't—"

"Lie to me about being able to handle a complex project? I know." He'd already rewound their conversations. Replayed them in light of this new knowledge. Dom had told his truth. *He'd* been the one not listening. "You put in a bid you said you could afford. That you could make it happen. I was the one who assumed that meant you didn't know what you were doing. But that wasn't it, was it?"

Dom shook his head again, the movement slower this time, maybe waiting to see if Austin had come to the right conclusion.

"You meant that you already had experts on tap who could handle it for you. Ones you've worked with before."

"Yeah. Or my friend Jason does anyway. He's a renovation consultant qualified to cut through red tape. Understands how to get permits and permissions. Knows which craftsmen have the right skills for each job. Got contacts all over Europe. All I do is—"

"Put up the money?"

"That was Gemma's skill set. Used to say that the three of us almost made one competent adult." His pause drew out. "Easy to forget how we got started. With sweat equity, you know? Jason finding wrecks to renovate. Me and him getting our hands dirty. Gemma pulling the finance out of thin air to bridge buying the next one. And two, and three. Without her, I would have been like Dad." He met Austin's gaze, a smile there now he knew to look for it, but also a hint of something harder to define. "This last year or so? Not actually seeing being like Dad as a bad thing."

He stopped speaking then.

Swallowed.

Started over.

"Because the way we lived before didn't work for Maisie. Neither of us could ignore that. Kids are meant to flourish, not go backwards, aren't they?"

He stopped again for longer this time.

Finally he changed gear and settled on saying, "Coming home was meant to be temporary. A reset. A slower pace until she was a bit older. More able to handle change instead of melting down and regressing compared to her peer group."

Austin saw that pile of learning journeys then. Could see a Post-it discussion recommending play instead of formal learning. That made more sense in light of this information. "Have you spoken to her teachers? To Nathan and Charles?"

Dom straightened in his seat. Sounded abrupt for a first time. "We're handling it."

Now Austin pictured that anemone Charles had shown him retracting his feelers. "I can see that you are. I . . ." Christ, he was shit at relationships at the best of times. Who was he to offer advice? But he couldn't help saying, "It's just that Charles might have some ideas. He's on your wavelength."

"What do you mean?"

"All that play equipment you built? Her obstacle course. All that sensory stuff? Climbing and balancing? Charles wants more of the same kind of thing for her. Nathan agreed. See? They'd help her . . ." *Catch up* felt like a judgement. "They'd help her learn through playing."

Dom didn't answer right away. Then he nodded. "It was actually Jason's husband who suggested we kit out the garden for her. Vanya said she'd do better outside with more space to master big movements before small ones."

"Sounds like Charles. You should talk to him. I know he'd want to help her."

"Think he'd have any bright ideas about water?"

"Maybe." Or someone else might.

A seed of an idea planted, but Dom had moved on.

"I'll talk to Gemma when she's back. She's . . ." Again Austin waited, Dom finally saying, "I won't do anything without her say so."

Austin sat back. Looked out the window, view of white-tipped waves crashing against cliffs preferable to examining why that comment prickled for no reason. Dom's hand landing on his knee again surprised him into meeting his eyes for a fleeting moment, long enough to see they were as soft as ever.

"When it comes to Maisie, I mean." He put both hands on the wheel. "I loved building the play equipment. Reminded me of what I like best."

"Being hands-on?"

"No. Working with family. Dad helped every step of the way. I'd forgotten how well we worked together. Gemma too. I think it helped her the most." Dom didn't notice that answer prickle as well. He changed gear behind a slow-moving lorry. "Also reminded me of my limits for sure." The only way to describe his tone was pensive. Worried. It was right there in what he said next. "Can't fuck up any more decisions about my daughter. Look at what's already happened."

"Anyone could see you put her first." He'd never forget that look of terror before they'd both dived in to find her, or Dom on his knees in a hospital cubicle to say thank you. *Never.*

"So says Mr-tapped-his-watch every time I was late for her. Fucking hindsight. Should have realised that was only a symptom, not the actual problem." Before Austin could ask what he meant, Dom glanced at his bare wrist. "Not wearing it today? It's a Breitling, right?"

"My watch? No. I mean, yes."

"Thought so. All those dials for different time zones. Jason got one for Vanya. He's Russian. One of his dials is set to Moscow so he doesn't phone his sister too late on a school night." He hesitated. "Yours was a present from Sol?"

"Sol? No. It was a work thing. In lieu of a bonus. It's at home."

At least he assumed Cameron still had it somewhere in Glynn Harber. He shifted in his seat as if that would put some distance between him and a thought that still dogged him.

I got it so wrong with him.

The traffic slowed, stopping at the Porthperrin junction, and Dom glanced sideways as they waited. Rolled his eyes. Huffed at himself as he took the next turn-off, steering his car downhill into the village. "You don't need to hear me prattling on about how hard my life is."

"That's how you think you come across?" They passed the same garage with a showroom full of classic cars where he'd discovered Dom wasn't who he'd presumed. What he actually valued was clearer than ever. "Because I can tell you right now that you don't." He translated what he'd heard on the way here. "It sounds like you're worried, that's all, and that you . . ."

He felt his way around this next part like he had once already, trying to find the edges of what had brought on Dom's frown. "Don't be hard on yourself. If Maisie's mum is away and you haven't wanted your dad to feel responsible, who have you had to lean on lately?"

"Me? No one." His gaze flashed Austin's way. "Huh. Thanks. Hadn't thought about it like that."

Austin faced forwards again, the view stunning, not seeing one bit of it while imagining being that person for him.

CONSIDERING the warmth of the evening, there was a distinct chill in the Anchor's main bar where Dom got drinks before leading him to a table in the snug. Locals had turned their backs, a couple not returning his greeting.

Dom noticed him rubbing his arms after their meal arrived. "Cold?"

"No. Not really. Just getting flashbacks."

Dom turned to the window, twilight harbour in view. "Shit. I didn't think." He picked up his plate. "Swap seats."

"No, it's not that. I just mean that the locals are a bit frosty here, aren't they? Reminded me of where I last worked."

"Not a friendly office?"

Austin shrugged, forking up some pasta. "It was the management style. Give people too-high targets and not enough resources? Sooner or later they'll start backbiting. Even accountants can be cut-throat."

"And that's what you want to go back to? A cut-throat culture?"

Right now, while Dom watched him from across the small table they shared, close enough that their feet touched underneath it, no, he didn't.

He settled for saying, "I've got targets of my own I need to get back to ASAP. And speaking of targets, it seems like you must have one on your back here. Whose chips did you piss in to deserve everyone staring daggers at you?"

Dom snorted mid-bite. Wiped sauce from his lips with a napkin. Grinned, and that was better. He liked it so much he didn't wait for Dom to answer. Instead he made an offer, a seed sown on the way here now germinating. Austin set his spoon and fork down, dinner abandoned.

"Listen. About what you mentioned earlier about Maisie's fear of water getting worse, not better. I could . . ." Second thoughts rushed in so fast Austin almost backtracked. Would have, but Dom leaned forward. "I could ask Cameron for you."

Dom sat back. "Cameron? Sol's . . . ?"

"Nephew? Yes." Although maybe Dom had been more accurate the first time he'd mentioned his name, calling him Sol's son.

Which would have made him mine too, if we'd stayed together as a family.

And that's why leaving them had been safer.

Dom watched, sympathetic. "You were close? Must have been tough when you split up with his uncle."

"Close?" Austin repressed an urge to laugh, aware it wouldn't sound happy. "No. We didn't have that kind of relationship. I'm not cut out for . . ."

For what?

Caring about kids?

He blinked, wondering when his worldview had shifted. "Maisie likes him." Sol had been right about that now that Austin cast his mind back. "I sat with her at lunchtimes quite often, and she always waved if she saw Cameron."

Dom picked up on the wrong part of that sentence. "You sat with her?"

"Well, yes." He picked up his spoon and fork, no reason to feel off balance. Speared a strand of pasta. "Someone had to help her twirl her spaghetti," he said, aiming for offhand but failing if Dom's snort was a measure.

"She's not the fastest," he agreed. "Thank you," he said more quietly. "I didn't know that she needed help." He swallowed. "So she's actually the slowest?"

"Slowest? At lunchtime? No, just finds it tricky." He modelled coordinating his spoon and fork to twirl his own pasta. "But honestly, that table is always like feeding time at the zoo. Food everywhere. I should ask for danger money." It wasn't the speed of her eating that had lodged in his brain. "She brightens each time Cameron passes the table, that's all. Waves and shouts like a complete hussy until he comes over."

Dom's smile returned, he noticed, encouraging him to keep going. "He likes her too. A lot." What had he heard Cameron tell her? "I remember the last time he came over, he said it was okay that she couldn't swim yet. She'd make a great swimmer one day." Cameron had also acted as if Austin was invisible. It hurt less as he remembered. "He drew her a little picture."

"Of a mermaid," Dom said as if slotting a piece into a puzzle. "She keeps it under her pillow."

"Cameron's started teaching at the surf club." He could almost feel the pride roll off Sol all over again then. Felt it touch him too now, remembering those first tough weeks for Cameron, post-bereavement. *Thank fuck he turned that corner.* It was more than he'd managed. "He works with the younger ones at the surf club. Nippers, I think they call it."

"Tiddlers. She had a go at that." Dom rubbed his jaw. "She wasn't quite ready, but I think I remember she was excited about the teacher. He let her take her dolly in the pool with her. That was him?"

"Yes. I could text Sol." Austin pulled out his phone, too late to back out now. "Ask him to pass on a message, if you want. See if Cameron might help her get over her fear of water, maybe?"

"The signal's pretty spotty here."

He tried anyway, and maybe luck was on his side for once because his phone pinged only minutes later.

"Okay," Austin said after reading. "The good news is that Cameron's agreed to talk to me."

"And the bad news?"

Austin grimaced. Mimed tying a noose. Yanked it tight and said, "That means I'll have to talk to him too." But for once, the thought made him happy because Dom burst out laughing.

15

The same group at the main bar who'd gone quiet when they'd arrived were still there when they settled the bill, watching them in silence. Only one person spoke, a man who arrived as they were leaving, his single-word greeting of "Dominic" almost cheery in comparison.

Dom caught Austin casting a glance back on the way out. The sky had started to darken, not only with dusk. Clouds had gathered after a day of unbroken sunshine, heavy like Dom's expression.

"They aren't always like that."

Austin checked over his shoulder again as the door closed, aware as Dom must have been too that the noise had picked up the moment he'd left, previously silent observers chatting.

"Rude, you mean?" Because apart from that one greeting, that was what he'd just witnessed: multiple counts of them being made outright unwelcome. "Or prejudiced because we were a same-sex couple?" He stopped only a few steps from the pub while Dom continued walking. "I didn't mean that *we're* a couple."

"I knew what you meant." Dom came back, feet scuffing the cobbles as if each step was weighted. "And no, I don't think that's their problem with me." He stared at the door as if he could see through it. "Not when the owners have a gay son and partner who I know everyone accepts here. Fuck it, the whole village loves Rob and Jude, so it's not that." His gaze swung Austin's way like his arm did over Austin's shoulder. "And even if it was, they'll have to take me as I am because I'm not changing. But I am starting to get the feeling that being part of a couple with a kid is a problem for you. Is it?" he asked without preamble.

"I . . ." Austin was glad the night had started to draw in, hopefully hiding a momentary freezing. "I'm not against the concept."

"But?"

"I just don't have . . ." *the best track record* might be overstating the one time he'd been half of a long-term couple. "I haven't . . ." *met the right person* felt wrong while Dom switched sides as they walked, putting himself between Austin and the water, not making a big deal out of a small but thoughtful action. He settled for saying, "It's not the right time, not when I need to . . ."

"Move on?"

Austin nodded.

"But not for a while, right?" Dom dropped his arm from around him and stopped at the mouth of an alley. "You'll see the project through, yeah?"

Austin hadn't intended to.

His mental deadline had been to leave much sooner.

But like this alley where shadows softened its stone walls, that timeline blurred too.

Dom, on the other hand, was crystal-clear. "Because even the planning stages will take months before the on-site work starts, and the thought of having all that time to see more of you?" He ducked in, lips brushing Austin's. "Well, it makes being made unwelcome on my own doorstep like that worth it. Or easier to put up with, at least."

"Why do you have to put up with it at all?"

Dom tipped his head uphill. "Because of Dad." Then he tipped it back towards the pub. "A lot of the same people that just kept their backs turned are his friends. People he's known or worked with for years."

"Friends? They didn't act like—"

Behind them, a gruff voice called out. "Dominic?"

They both turned to see a couple of men had left the pub, heading for them, and yet again he saw Dom do something that must be second nature, hands curling, putting himself a step ahead as if Austin needed shielding.

He didn't.

In fact, the urge to put himself in front of Dom before these men could get any closer surged in. Instead, he stood beside him.

"How's little Maisie doing?" Now that he was closer, Austin saw a face that rang bells, chiming even louder after the man added, "Susan's been asking."

"You're Luke's dad," Austin blurted.

A steady gaze met his. "I am. Carl Lawson."

"I've seen your picture in his study. We work together. I'm—"

"Austin." Carl's handshake was quick. Firm. Came with a small smile that must be a family likeness, reminding him of

Luke so strongly. "Heard a lot about you." He gestured at the harbour mouth. "Looks like my son had you pegged right when he first met you."

"Me?" Austin looked where water frothed, whipped by a breeze that rose like those clouds did in the distance.

"Yes. Luke said you were like a dog with a bone. Wouldn't ever let go. Good thing for Maisie you wouldn't let go of her either. Brave," he added quietly, and like praise from Luke, it poked Austin somewhere tender. Carl addressed Dom next. "Been up to your dad's a few times but haven't caught you or Ken in. How's Maisie?"

"Good." But maybe Carl also shared Luke's way of winkling out the truth by saying little because, after a few beats, Dom gave a more truthful answer. "She's having a few ups and downs. Bit scared of water." He turned his attention to the taller of the two men. "Can I help you with something, Simon?"

"Yes. Didn't know you were in the Anchor tonight. I was in the office. Would have come into the snug to chat otherwise. Wanted to know the same as Carl. About Maisie. Kept thinking I'd see her, you know?" He gestured at a house at the far end of the harbour, set higher than the smaller cottages, its view uninterrupted across the water. "I normally see her in and out of her mother's. Gemma's—"

That's where his ex lives?

Austin took in a building as strong and stony as Dom's answer.

"She's away." Unlike his response to Carl, he didn't offer more information. Or at least, he didn't until the second man made a confession.

"Aged me about a decade the first time Jude fell in the harbour. He wasn't much bigger than your Maisie." Simon hesitated before clasping Dom briefly on the shoulder. "Every parent's worst nightmare." Then he echoed what they'd discussed while eating. "Sooner you can get her back in the water the better, only maybe start someplace shallow before you build up to throwing her back in. Because that's what you need to do if she's gonna be safe here. Get her used to being submerged and to know not to panic, but first pick somewhere like—"

Austin recognised him then. "The rock pools. I . . . I saw you there a few weeks back."

"That's right," Simon said. "Not a bad place to start building confidence. Anywhere shallow, if she's nervous. Just don't leave it, yeah? The sooner the better." He backed off, giving Austin a quick nod.

Carl stayed a few moments longer, just as gruff, reminding Austin more than ever of Luke. "Maisie's struggling?"

Dom nodded.

"Having bad dreams?"

Dom nodded again.

"Susan wondered if she might be. Picked out some story-books for her. Ones about kids facing fears." He turned back to the pub but called a last offer over his shoulder, "I'll drop them round."

"Thanks," Dom said, sounding as gruff as Carl. "Tell her thank you, will you?"

Carl stopped. Came back. And there was another echo of Luke. "Thanks? No need for that. You're one of ours, Dominic. You having a bit of time away doesn't change that. Coming back with enough money to buy half the village doesn't either. But some of us have noticed what you've been doing lately." He glanced back the way they'd come. "Won't take long before the rest notice as well."

Austin saw Dom's curled fists loosen as the two men went back into the pub. Curl again before loosening one more time as though he wasn't sure what to do with what had just happened. With what Luke's dad had just said either, those fists may have been a signal it was something he'd hold onto, if he could trust it. Austin gave him something else to hold onto, sliding a hand through his.

Dom held it, squeezing after Austin asked, "You bought half the village?"

"No," he chuffed. "Nowhere near half." His gaze slid sideways, meeting with his. "Maybe a third."

Austin got as far as saying, "Of the whole village—" before catching sight of a twinkle that had gone missing in the pub. "No, you did not. Don't lie about numbers to an accountant."

"Okay, okay. Not half or a third, but yeah, I bought a few more cottages than the one's next to Mum and Dad's place. I mentioned the big storm, yeah, and locals selling up. Moving for work when it dried up here?"

Austin nodded.

"Someone was always going to buy up their houses." Dom pointed at the cottages at each side of the alley. "Like these. Seemed a no-brainer to start converting them to holiday lets once the village turned a corner. Got famous for Rob and Jude's food. I kind of got the blame for there being no cheap properties left until I sold them back to locals, but I swear to God, no one wanted them after that storm. Looks like another one's building now."

The sky had darkened, evening shifting to night helped by more of those clouds banking, and for the first time in weeks, Austin felt rain coming, a heaviness in the air that came with a rumble.

That thunder was faint, still a long way off, but Dom's arm found his shoulder as if he needed shelter. He also drew him into the mouth of the alley, but Austin wasn't done asking questions.

He stopped, shadowed by houses he now knew Dom owned. "So that accounts for what he said about you owning half the village, but what did he mean, that he's noticed what you've been doing?"

"No idea." Dom made to move off but Austin didn't follow, and maybe there was enough light left for Dom to see his raised eyebrows. He capitulated, grumbling. "Okay, so there's still a lot of storm damage in the village."

"What do you mean?"

"To fishermen's cottages. They're hard to insure. Especially the ones fronting the water. It wasn't a big deal for me and Dad to make a few minor repairs between paying projects."

"You mean, you've been fixing up places for free?"

Dom's tone could have matched Carl's. "I'm not quite ready for sainthood."

At some point they'd drifted closer. Close enough that darkening sky or not, Austin thought he saw colour rising. Lifted a hand, Dom ducking away from Austin's quick touch, but not before he'd felt what he'd suspected. "You're blushing."

"I am fucking not."

And there—*there*—was one of those Dymond smiles he couldn't pinpoint when he'd first noticed. Had no idea that he'd learned to copy, unable not to.

"It was a bit of carpentry, that's all," Dom insisted.

"Replacing a few roof slates. Slapping on some paint I had left over. I didn't give anyone a kidney, so you can hold off putting my name down for the Queen's birthday honours."

"You're a massive softie."

"Says the only cut-throat accountant I know with time to help a little girl twirl spaghetti. *My* little girl." His voice couldn't have gone any lower. "Seems like we're as bad as each other."

"Or more evenly matched?"

Dom looked like he wanted to argue. Gave up just as quickly. His kiss as good as agreement.

16

If anyone else left the pub and passed the mouth of the alley while they kissed, Austin didn't notice. Couldn't. Too busy taking in how Dom's mouth felt on his, his tongue seeking and finding, their hands both skimming and grasping.

He didn't hear anything either, other than a rumble that wasn't thunder. Pleasure, he decided, coming from this man pressing his mouth to Austin's throat, finding a still tender spot that forced the same sound from him.

Fuck, why do I like that?

Dom acted as if he heard that question. Held him closer and sucked some more as if that was an answer. Rumbled again at how Austin responded, hands clutching Dom's shoulders. His hair. His shoulders again, tighter this time, fingers digging in to keep Dom where it felt good.

His mouth did eventually move on, roaming, lips skimming, his breath warm across Austin's ear, like his hand, which found a way under his shirt to pull Austin against him.

"We're matched like this too." He rubbed where Austin's cock had hardened, and it didn't matter that the light had dropped too low to make out every detail, Austin could picture enough. Could guess the blue of Dom's eyes was swamped by black, pupils expanding, greedy, as if he'd starved for what he stared at.

Austin gave him back the same sensation, he hoped, Dom's cock hard under the heel of his palm. He pressed, pushing along its length until Dom broke their kiss, jostling him into deeper shadows, granite rough against Austin's back where his shirt had lifted.

He sucked again, but not at the base of Austin's throat. This time, the lobe of his ear got some attention, and he melted. Would have staggered if Dom didn't wedge a thigh between his legs to keep him upright.

He'd suck my cock too.

Right here.

Drop to his knees where anyone could walk past, that's how much he wants me.

Dom kissed him again, sucking his tongue too, a hand on his fly, as if about to start that process, but going still as a car door slammed close by.

They breathed then, in sync.

Inhaled, their mouths still close together.

Exhaled and got back to kissing, Dom's hand on his belt again, rougher now and yanking it loose, stopping as abruptly at another door slam.

His head swung in the car park's direction, and Austin's eyes must have adjusted because he saw more detail when Dom looked back, his lips kissed fuller and gleaming. His eyes too, glinting with stars or magic. Austin didn't care which as long as this evening wasn't over.

"Come here." Dom hooked a finger through a belt loop, pulling, Austin following him further up the alley.

He stopped then. Fumbled with keys that jingled. Swore before a gate swung open.

Dom herded him into complete darkness.

Gravel crunched underfoot followed by the hollower thud of decking, lights blinking on, brilliant, detecting their motion.

Austin froze then in a courtyard garden.

Looked up at darkened windows.

"Yours, right? It's empty?"

Dom nodded, one hand finding where Austin was harder than ever, the other pushing the gate closed behind them, and Austin had been right—Dom did look every bit as hungry as he'd pictured.

The lights clicked off, but this new dark wasn't complete. A few solar lanterns lent a soft glow, Dom soaking up what they showed him, and Austin could only guess what he looked like—his hair a mess instead of tidy, his belt hanging open, erection straining against a half-lowered zipper.

Dom looked back at the gate, perhaps replaying how fast he'd steered Austin inside, huffing out something close to laughter as he turned back. "Fuck me, I'm out of practice," he muttered. "I promise I can be smoother than this. Don't usually shove dates into alleys, hump them against walls, and then drag them into a back yard to rip their clothes off."

"I'm not complaining."

"No?" His lips brushed Austin's then like his hand did his hard-on, slow, feather-light, teasing. "Don't tell my dad," he said quietly, "but I'm finding it hard to remember my manners around you."

"Can we not talk about him?"

"He brought me up right, is all I'm saying. Would expect me to wine and dine you on a first date."

"Wining. Dining. What are his views on sixty-nining?"

Dom laughed. "Don't know about him, but it's my favourite."

Austin barely listened, already down on his knees unfastening Dom's belt and zipper. He couldn't have shoved his hand inside his underwear any faster, pulling his cock free, not caring that Dom laughed again, muffled by his hand but delighted.

The groan he let out next did register.

Austin felt it rock through him as he touched Dom. Licked him. Sucked him. Liked causing more of that low, rough sound. Pulled off and wet his lips before trying to take him deeper, having to close eyes that watered, Dom's cock a lot to handle. Almost too much to swallow. But size was only a number and big ones had never scared him.

He pulled off again. Got Dom's cock wetter. Slicker. Ran his tongue from its base where pubes tickled and musk thickened, to his crown, saliva flooding as Dom watched him, now a million miles from laughing.

His eyes had been dark before. Now they closed as Austin blew him, intent once they reopened, shining, catching his attention.

So did the sound of footsteps.

Austin froze.

The steps came closer, echoing in the alley, only a gate between him on his knees and a stranger.

Dom touched his shoulder, Austin's swallow pure instinct, not deliberate, but Dom reflexively shuddered, eyes closing again for a second like he couldn't help it. Then he widened his stance, that hand on Austin's shoulder more a suggestion than an order, but Austin complied, staying where he was while Dom shifted position, shielding him should the gate swing open.

Austin could breathe again then.

Could swallow too, knowing no one would get past Dom.

Could suck, slow and almost silent, and really like it.

He held Dom's shaft, lips meeting the ring of his fingers, quiet as his head bobbed, eyes on Dom's the whole time.

The night did something to the way sound travelled, or maybe it was the narrowness of the alley, those footsteps both close and also distant. The grit of soles on cobbles loud yet also fading. No way to tell the direction they travelled.

Austin gave up trying to guess if they approached or distanced. He only felt the pulse of a thick vein against his tongue, the grooves in the decking he knelt on, and his cock aching, all far more concrete than the world outside this courtyard, until something jingled.

A set of keys must have struck stone outside the gate, dropped as if by someone about to use them.

Austin stilled again, but only for a moment, looking up into eyes that didn't hint at panic. That smiled even though Dom's hand covered his mouth. That he trusted. Because Austin did, he decided as he licked around the crown of Dom's cock oh-so slowly, finding the slit and probing, feeling a tremor run through him.

It didn't matter who was out there. Dom hadn't lied to him yet—if he said this was his place; that he had every right to be here—Austin would believe him. Besides, no one would get through him. Dom was solid in a way that Austin couldn't keep from touching, one hand splayed over Dom's stomach as the other fed his cock back into his mouth, which flooded, more than wet enough to make bobbing his head faster easy.

Dom's own head fell back, the dull thud of it striking the gate thankfully muffled by another jingle of keys, whoever had been on its other side moving off towards the car park.

Their footsteps faded, as did the rest of the world, Austin lost in scent and touch and sensation. The brine of the harbour and that musk scent he wanted more of; the slap of water against boat hulls; the wet sounds of his blowjob.

He added his own gasps to that list each time he pulled off, his chest heaving, the solar lights dimming, just enough light left to show Dom's cock was now glossy, slick with his spit, his balls wet too where Austin mouthed them. And if anyone had walked the alley at that moment, they couldn't have mistaken the deep groan Dom let out for anything other than intensely sexual.

Dom got onto his knees too then. Wrenched Austin's clothes down until the night air kissed what he'd bared. Kissed Austin, tongue sweeping deeply from the outset, as physical as his hand job, pulling out moans that his mouth over Austin's barely muffled.

It was fast and rough and . . .

Magic. Fucking magic.

This is what getting fucked by him will feel like.

The thought made him whimper, balls drawing up, orgasm thundering as fast as his heart. So fast he almost buckled.

Dom's arm came around him.

He held him up, said, "I've got you," and Austin's climax barrelled through him like he'd shot out his soul, not spunk that glistened.

Sensation crackled, aftershocks quaking, nerves still firing as he panted, forehead against Dom's shoulder, but he returned the favour even though his hand shook.

He kissed Dom again, hoping he gave him the same bone-deep pleasure, and maybe sucking on his tongue did something for him as well, because his next groan rivalled the distant thunder. Austin did it again, harder, and Dom spilled, spurting in thick pulses, almost tipping over. Would have if Austin hadn't braced him. Kept him upright. Wouldn't let him fall either.

"Thanks." He kissed Austin again once he'd caught his breath too, softer now. Gentler. Pulled him into what Maisie would no doubt have called a cuddle, two men on their knees coming down together.

Finally, he got to his feet, offering Austin a hand, as well as a tissue he pulled from a pack in his pocket.

"You came prepared."

"Having a kid will do that." Dom cleaned off his hand before refastening his jeans. "Especially Maisie. It's all non-stop messy faces with her, especially after eating. Only you must know that already. You know because you've helped her?" He made a fork twirling gesture. "Makes me . . ."

"Makes you what?" Austin finished wiping himself off. Fastened his belt. Looked up when Dom didn't answer, and maybe that low level of light was a blessing. Seeing as well as hearing this much gratitude would have been hard to handle.

"Makes me feel like she's got someone in her corner when I'm not there with her. Someone taking care. Who takes her as she is instead of comparing her to . . ."

"Compare her?" Austin pictured a child who reminded him so much of his sister it affected his voice, for once its snap well placed. "She's Maisie fucking Dymond. Who wouldn't be in her corner?" That reminded him of their earlier discussion. "You don't actually think her teachers compare her to other kids, do you? I mean, I don't have the first clue about ages and stages, but no one at Glynn Harber thinks like that about any of the kids, and every single one of them is in her corner."

They'd just had what Austin would rank as one of the most intensely sexual moments he could remember, but the hug Dom pulled him into touched someplace deeper. Knotted a loose thread, somehow. Stitched a hole he hadn't known had been there. Brought two frayed edges close together—almost as close as Dom held him for a couple more tripping beats of his heart before allowing a few inches between them.

They stood in a pool of quiet, broken only by soft laps of the harbour water.

Dom's voice was as gentle. "Not sure you can understand what it's like to hope people will treat your kid well. Be kind to them, you know? Especially if they . . ." He pulled that thread tighter. "Because that's what we do, you know? Us parents? Have kids without knowing that handing them over to anyone else is like ripping your heart out of your chest and hurling it into the sea without someone like you there to protect it."

Someone like me?

That rocked him.

Shook him.

Made his usual statement come out shaky.

"I'm no good with kids."

"Liar." Dom kissed his temple. "But that's good to know about the school. Gemma said she had a good feeling about it. Thought it would be the kind of place that wanted to see kids flourish. Help them to grow wings, even if . . ."

His next kiss was quick.

Still soft, like his voice even though his arms around Austin tightened.

"But hearing that you didn't hurry her, like they don't ever rush her either? That you'd come and sit with her at lunchtimes. Help her with her food when I know all the others probably didn't need the same level of attention—"

"It was nothing." He pictured a scene in which Dom had just painted him as some kind of hero. Or as someone with a halo. In truth, he'd had a different, maybe more selfish motivation.

It was his turn to need to clear his throat and be honest. "Helping her reminded me of..."

"Your sister?"

Austin nodded, words beyond him, because that was the truth plain and simple. From her curls to her love of anything that sparkled, it had been easy to let memories he hadn't known lingered slide out from where they'd hidden each time Maisie had needed . . . "A big brother. That's what helping her out reminded me of being." An older brother to someone who'd been as full of life as Maisie, bouncing each time she saw him. "And so what if she can't eat pasta without flicking the whole table with sauce? You just did the same thing at the pub, didn't you? And what does it matter if reading and writing aren't her favourite? One of her teachers is dyslexic, and he's taught a whole class of children how to love the world around them. Besides, she's good at other things, isn't she? Like being a friend."

Dom nodded just as thunder rumbled, lightning painting his face white for one stark second.

"Shit," he said. "I'd hoped that was moving out to sea. Think it's getting closer."

He loosened his hold on Austin. Opened the gate they

hadn't moved far from. Stood aside for Austin to exit, stopping him by saying, "Listen, I don't want to cut this short, but can I drop you home so I'm back before that gets too much closer? She's scared of storms. Dad's great with her, but give it half an hour and that'll be right overhead. I want to be there for her if she wakes up."

"Of course." Austin made to move, but Dom didn't lift the bar of his arm yet.

"Just know that I wouldn't cut this short for any other reason, yeah?"

"This?"

"Tonight. Being with you. Like this. Together. And not just because we . . ." Dom did lower his arm then, a hand grasping Austin's shoulder first, its pressure light as he steered Austin where he wanted, which was closer. Much closer.

Dom embraced him, his murmur low but fervent. "Even if we hadn't got off, it still would have been one of the best nights I've had in a long time." His lips brushed the corner of his jaw. "Afternoon too. Want to do it again sometime soon with me?"

"You mean get to watch all the locals in a pub give you the cold shoulder, then be sent home to bed early? Can't wait."

He saw the glint of Dom's grin. Liked it better than the worry that had banked like those clouds.

"Or did you mean getting me off twice in only a few hours? That sounds like a much better return on my time investment."

"It does." Dom smiled around another quick kiss before backing away, but aspects of their conversation must have lingered like it had for Austin. Dom brought it up again after driving him back to Glynn Harbor.

He pulled up outside the stables next to the Defender. "Listen, what I said about comparing Maisie—"

Lightning lit the sky for much longer than down by the harbour, and Austin stopped him.

"Can it wait?"

Dom nodded.

"Then go. Get back to her. That storm's definitely heading in Porthperrin's direction."

"Okay." Relief was a good look on him. "Sorry to cut the evening short though." He turned on the interior light, nothing hidden. "Because this feels like us heading in the same direction as well. At least it does to me. How about you?"

Austin's nod was instinctive.

Dom let out a held breath. "Good. Great." He leaned across, hooking a hand around Austin's neck, and once again that pressure was light. Subtle. Would be easy to break away from if he wanted.

He didn't.

Not even a bit.

Would have shifted across to climb onto his lap if the steering wheel hadn't been in the way, and if Dom didn't have a little girl scared of storms who might need him.

He settled for leaning into a kiss that came once. Twice. Three times, before Dom drew in a long, slow breath and pulled back, his tone rough all over again. "I'm taking Maisie to see her mum tomorrow. Staying overnight so they get some decent time together. Can I see you when we get home?"

Austin gave him a last nod.

Watched him drive away.

Let himself in the empty stables where he sent an email

outlining Dom's bid, more than certain he had the means to see the job through from start to finish.

Then he lay in bed and counted Mississippis between each flash of lightning through the gaps in his curtains.

His phone *pinged* an interruption.

Dom had sent a photo.

He was too big for the bed he lay in, but at least it looked strong, crafted like everything else in his father's cottage, built to last and sturdy. But that sturdiness also had a soft touch, a nightlight revealing fairies carved into the headboard.

A string of messages followed.

Dom: *Made it home just before she woke up.*

Dom: *She didn't cry for too long.*

Dom: *Think she's out for the count now.*

Another message pinged in before Austin could type a reply.

Dom: *Sorry again about cutting short our evening.*

Austin wasn't.

Couldn't be as he scrolled back to that photo, not when the soft light didn't only show fairies carved with care.

Another reason nestled against Dom's chest, Maisie fast asleep with her dolly, safe with her daddy's arms around her.

ustin woke the next morning with a jolt, saved from another dream of swirling currents by the *ping* of his phone.

Dom had sent another photo, this one taken inside his father's hallway. Maisie stood with her back to the camera in the open doorway, hands on her hips, wings catching the light and glinting.

Dom: *Someone can't wait to show her mum her new wings.*

Dom: *And tell your mum thanks for the instructions, yeah?*

He quickly typed a reply, still a little bleary.

Austin: *Travel safely.*

He lay back, aware suddenly of how quiet it was in the stables without Charles bringing tea uninvited into his bedroom.

As if he had the same thought, another photo arrived, Charles naked apart from a strategically placed teacup and saucer. A typed message swiftly followed.

Charles: *How's your bottom this morning?*

Austin dialled instead of texting. "It's in perfect working

order, thank you," he said as soon as Charles picked up. "How's the fam?"

"No idea," Charles replied, far too cheery for this early in the morning. "Haven't made it out of the bedroom yet." He slurped his tea in Austin's ear, followed by the kind of disagreement that had filled almost every morning since Austin had washed up here.

"It is *not* rude, Hugo," Charles insisted. "Slurping shows appreciation. What would you prefer? That I was silent in bed, or that I let you know every single way you made me feel good?" Hugo murmured, Charles answering sounding triumphant. "That's what I thought. How did the wings work out?"

Austin took a moment to parse that the conversation had switched in his direction.

"The wings? Oh, fine. Really good."

"Your mum will be pleased." Charles paused, his voice gentling. "If you haven't told her so already, of course. Maybe you should show her how they turned out? You know, if you took a photo?" And for all his lack of a degree, Charles was smart enough to cut to the core of why Austin should do that. "Do you think she'd like to see them?"

Austin nodded as though he could see him.

"Show her," Charles suggested, using the same gentle encouragement Austin had heard so often when passing his classroom, promising children that he'd help them. He was also as frank at addressing problems. "You're so cagey about her. If it's because of that horrible graph you keep beating yourself up with, I bet she'd rather hear from you about something lovely. You called her for the instructions, didn't you? So she can't actually be an ogre. Or if she is, and you don't want a conversation, send it to me and I'll forward it for you."

"No. She's not an ogre. She's just very driven."

"Well, that accounts for your work ethic. So you'll do it?"

"Yes." Austin went back to the photo Dom had sent, seeing him in his daughter's posture, her feet squarely planted, those hands on her hips spelling determination, wings on her back ready to lift her above any bumps in the road in future.

And he's worried about her future. Why, when he's so successful her life can't possibly be a struggle?

He focused on the wings they'd made together. Dom had tied them on for her, big hands careful with the ribbons, and had called them beautiful.

They were. Just like his sister's had been.

Forwarding it only took a moment.

"Done," he said to Charles, regret already slithering through the crack in a painful door sending it could open. He got out of bed and Charles came with him, his voice strangely reassuring considering he was so often annoying.

"Oh, you are being a good boy following my instructions," he said, echoing that sticker he'd stuck on without Austin noticing. "Now while you're being good, tell me what her daddy's like in bed. And don't leave out a single detail."

The next voice Austin heard was Hugo's. Aghast. Laughing. Resigned, and fonder than Austin could deal with.

He grabbed some clothes, wardrobe mirror reflecting a grin as he selected shorts and a T-shirt, stopping by the window, listening to what sounded like every single morning he'd spent in these stables so far, he could picture his housemates so clearly.

Hugo must have taken the phone. He said, "Austin?

Charles will call you back later when he's had a chance to reflect on the rudeness of invading the sanctity of another person's sex life, okay?"

Austin could still hear Charles, somehow both aggrieved and laughing. His voice carried. "But he's not another person, is he? He's *our* person."

Austin saw his own smile widen. "No problem," he told Hugo. "Enjoy your break, and . . ." He pictured those books crammed with *make them like me* Post-its. "Good luck for later, but whoever you're interviewing with will be lucky to have you both."

He ended the call, about to slide his phone into a pocket, but his hand stilled because he could also remember so many other mornings where he'd started the day without the noise of Charles and Hugo, the silence of the empty stable somehow louder, and out of nowhere, the familiarity struck him.

This is what it was like at home after I—

Movement in the courtyard outside saved him from finishing that thought.

Sol and his partner carried easels, Jace calling out to a few of the new sixth-form students settling in before September.

Austin turned away, but only to throw on his clothes because he'd gone to sleep just fine, despite the storm, but had still woken gasping. Maisie going through anything similar meant he needed to do as he'd promised, like Simon had said, sooner rather than later.

He slipped on shoes and let himself out, jogging, calling out, "Sol?" when he'd almost caught up. "Where's Cameron this morning?"

"Good morning to you too." Sol set down his easel. "Why? What's up?"

Austin's phone pinged.

He glanced at it before answering. Then he stared at it for longer, transfixed by a brand-new photo.

"You okay, Aus?" Sol had closed the distance. "What is it? Bad news?"

Austin tore his gaze from the picture filling his screen. It slid back just as quickly.

Dom hadn't sent this one to him.

The wings on the screen were smaller than the one's he'd made for Maisie. Speckled with less sparkles, but lovely. So lovely because his sister wore them.

"No," he finally forced out. "It's not bad news. It's good. From Mum."

Sol blinked, maybe recalling Austin's more usual reaction to messages from home. "So, she's doing better?"

"Better? What do you mean?" Austin glanced at his phone again, strangely hard to look away. Strange too how it was easier to remember laughter he'd forgotten now he saw Tamsin wear them. "Better at what?"

"Never mind." Sol backed up before changing his mind. He cut the distance between them. "I mean, so she's doing better at dealing with this time of year, Aus. You know, with Tamsin's birthday coming up so soon."

Austin did look up again then, but not at Sol. He focused on the trees instead, leaves alive with shades of emerald before sinking to drifts of last year's, skeletons fragile, only lifting his head as Sol said, "I know it's a really rough time of year for your mum." He chewed at his lip before blurting, "But it always seemed like double whammy for you, Aus. You had to cope with it *and* with your mum's way of dealing with it. Still do." His squeeze to Austin's shoulder was brief but supportive in a way he hadn't known he'd missed. Not until Dom had reminded him lately.

"I'm fine."

"But you don't have to be, you know?" Sol said. He mentioned a word they'd never mentioned. "Like you don't have to keep tracking grief on that spreadsheet you two fixate over."

"I don't fixate—"

"Aus . . ." This time, Sol's pause extended. "All I'm saying is that I'm pretty sure it doesn't help either of you. Grief isn't meant to keep trending upward. It should fade, shouldn't it? I'm not saying I didn't sketch my own grief for the first year or two after I lost Mum. Painted it too, over and over. She's right there on each canvas I worked on. Now I can look at them and see her in every brushstroke, but as a reminder of something good, yeah, not a burden. Not a target I have to track daily, like you do."

Austin's hand flexed around his phone. "I don't track it daily." Or he hadn't lately, at least.

Sol surveyed him, sympathetic. "Good, because I never knew her, but I'm pretty sure that isn't what any sister wants for her brother."

Austin would have answered if a lump in his throat hadn't blocked it.

Sol took advantage, and how the hell had Austin ever thought he'd been the quieter half of their pairing? "She'd want you to be happy, Aus."

That was a reminder of the perfume Cameron had entrusted to him.

Austin cleared his throat, which took some doing. Said, "I just need to talk to Cameron." Asked, "Do you know where he is?" and this time Sol told him.

18

It was only a ten-minute walk to where Sol said he'd find his nephew, but Austin covered the distance in less, dodging puddles left by last night's storm to get this conversation over.

Over?

I don't even know how to start it.

The Haven care home shared the same woods as the school, neat vegetable gardens taking over from its wildness, some of the Haven's residents busy with weeding. One of them stood as he approached, a trowel in hand that caught the sunlight. "Austin? I was about to email you."

Austin shielded his eyes. "Mr Brodie?" He squinted, and yes, it was the legal counsel for the school's backers. Like Austin, he was minus his business suit this morning, his T-shirt grubby with soil. "You got mine?"

"Keir, please." He dug his trowel back into the raised bed he'd been weeding. "And yes. That's why you're here? Got to say, I wasn't expecting someone to offer to take on the project for virtually nothing."

"Me either, but no, that's not why I'm here." At least this was a chance to practice how to phrase his request. "I'm here to find Cameron Trebeck."

"Cameron? What for?"

"To ask his help with the little girl that I—"

"Saved? How is she?" Keir sat on a railway sleeper edging the vegetable bed. "You know that you jumping in like that meant a hell of a lot to Tom and Nick, don't you? It would be good to give them an update if you know more." He patted the sleeper beside him.

Austin didn't sit down. Couldn't relax before speaking with Cameron, tense because until he got an answer, he couldn't reply to a photo that had opened a door both he and his mum had kept closed for longer than was healthy. Sol had only confirmed that, even if the thought of discussing anything other than figures with his mother made him uneasy. Dom and Maisie had started that ball rolling. He needed to return the favour, so he pushed on, hoping it would lead to finding Cameron so he could do that.

"Physically, she's the same as ever. But emotionally?" He dug the toe of his shoe into the soft mulch of the pathway. Studied a beetle that ran across it, its carapace a dark rainbow. "Her dad says she's very up and down. Gets upset quickly. Is fearful too, especially close to water."

"Ah. The sea?"

"Any water, right now. Even struggles with bath time." He met Keir's eyes then, none of the steeliness in them that he'd faced across a table outside the Anchor. Now they were soft, like the overripe strawberry one of the Haven residents surprised him with, offering it to Austin perhaps as consolation.

Keir said, "That's kind of you, Justin, but you can keep

your berry. Austin's okay. He's just worried about someone else, that's all. You know, like how you get worried when your friend Mary's upset? That's why we're talking. Sharing worries makes them lighter to carry, right? That's all Austin's doing now. Sharing a worry."

The resident sat next to him, strawberry carefully cradled, and although Austin didn't catch his whisper, Keir must have. "Yes, save the berry for Mitch. He does love anything juicy." He returned to their conversation. "So she's afraid of all water now?"

Austin nodded. "That's particularly tough on Maisie, which is why I need Cameron's help to—"

The soft mulch on the path meant he didn't hear Cameron's arrival, jumping as he spoke from behind him.

"Maisie Dymond? What's so tough on her that you need me?"

Austin faced Cameron, surprised all over again by the height he'd gained this summer. "Um . . . With the fact that her mum's house is by the water."

"By it?"

"Right on the harbour. Couldn't be much closer. If she looks through any of the windows, she can see where she—"

"Fell in?" Cameron's stance changed, arms uncrossing, although he didn't sound any warmer. "What's that got to do with me?"

"Her mum's . . ." *Away* sounded too much like a vacation. What had Dom mentioned? It came back as clearly as the scent of herbs here in this sheltered spot where people dealing with trauma stayed long-term. "She's recuperating from something, but she's coming home soon. Very soon. And Maisie's dad . . . Dom's . . ."

The right word was harder to capture. *Desperate* seemed

wrong, but he'd definitely do anything to see his daughter happy. "It would mean a lot to him if Maisie could get over her fear as soon as possible. That way she can stay with her mum whenever it's her turn to have her."

"Her turn? Her mum and dad don't live together?" Cameron asked. His eyes narrowed. "They both came with her to my Tiddler swimming group. Stayed to watch, then left together."

"They're divorced." Voicing this wasn't easy. "I don't know how to help her."

"Who is it you want to help? Her mum or Maisie?" Cameron's voice might have deepened, but there was no change to its abruptness.

And maybe Keir heard that sharp edge. He stood. "Almost time for your next activity, Justin. Let's go get ready." He guided the resident away, looking back to say, "Austin, I'll reply to your email properly later, but you trust the renovation bid is serious?"

"Yes." He had no doubt about that now.

"Then I'll look it over as soon as I can. Draft a provisional contract if I agree with your figures, and email it to you." His focus switched to Cameron. "You almost ready for us?"

Cameron nodded.

Keir left them after saying, "I'll go gather the troops. They'll be with you in a minute."

Cameron nodded again, but his dark gaze hadn't left Austin, waiting for an answer to his *who do you want to help* question.

"It would help both of them," Austin admitted, not entirely sure why helping a woman he hadn't met mattered so much, but it did to Dom, who wasn't that dissimilar to the young man barring his way, arms crossed over a chest that was yet to fill out, but who was just as family-focused.

Christ, he's grown up so fast.

Sol's done such a good job with him.

Another thought swiftly followed.

Could I ever have been part of that if things had been different?

"Why is sorting out her fear of water up to you?" Cameron repeated, once Keir and Justin were out of earshot.

"It's not up to me, exactly."

"So why are you here?"

That was easier to answer. "Because I want to help him too."

"Her dad? What's he got to do with you?" Cameron's frown was out of place in this space filled with sunshine where laughter came from the gardens around them, but that's what Austin had always provoked from him.

That painting of them happy together up in the art building had to be Sol's wishful thinking. Cameron had never smiled like that at him, had he? This scowling version was more familiar, even though it had been years since Austin had done what he'd thought would be best for Cameron and Sol. Now his frown drew down further, Cameron coming to his own conclusions.

"You're seeing him, aren't you? Her dad, I mean. Must be. It's the only reason you'd act like you care about her." He turned on his heel then, stalking between raised beds, putting distance between them.

"Wait!" Austin brushed past something pungent, herbal scent exploding like Cameron did as soon as Austin grabbed his elbow.

"Let go of me, and stay away from Maisie. She's a good kid."

Austin lurched back. "I know she is. That's why—"

"That's why you should leave her the fuck alone."

For a split second, Austin saw the same conflict Sol had often worn once Cameron had moved in with them, desperate to do the right thing for a newly bereaved kid.

But he'd also known Austin had been unhappy with their new living situation. That had put him in a tough spot. One that Austin had assumed his leaving would ease.

In hindsight, it had hurt all three of them.

Cameron confirmed that. "Don't convince her you care about her, not if you're just going to up and leave her dad too."

That struck like a spear, skewering him in public before Cameron stalked away, leaving Austin bleeding.

He made himself move, catching up with Cameron at the door of an outbuilding.

If that door closed between them, would it also close on his best chance to help Maisie?

That outcome felt certain, a lock snapping closed forever.

He scrambled to stop it, mouth opening before he thought through what spilled out.

"I gave you my watch."

"What?" Cameron didn't sound any closer to believing, but at least he'd lowered his hand, enough of an incentive for Austin to keep going.

"On the moor. In my envelope. It's a Breitling."

"Breitling?" Cameron shrugged. "Doesn't mean anything to me."

"It means it's expensive."

"You want it back then." Cameron grasped the handle again, this time pulling it open a fraction that made Austin desperate.

"No, I don't fucking want it back. Never wanted it in the first place. I was promised a cash bonus."

Cameron's face twisted. "You think I care about how much you earn?"

Austin almost shouted, "No! Listen. Please." He drew in a sharp breath as Cameron's lips pressed tight together. "The cash wasn't for me. It was for my sister."

"Sister?" That blank look meant Sol hadn't told him. For a moment, Austin didn't know if that was worse or better, but he nodded. Had to clear his strangled throat for the second time that morning, but maybe that change in his voice made a difference. Cameron's hand dropped as Austin added to his confession.

"She died when I was thirteen." The same age Cameron had been when he'd moved in with him and Sol. Funny how he'd seen Cameron as a child. In comparison, at the same age, Austin had stood beside a small grave feeling ancient. "Ever since then, we've raised money for a charity in her name. That's what I was promised in my last job with Supernus—a bonus plus extra corporate sponsorship. It's the only reason I took the job in the first place. They'd match my giving and give even more if I hit my targets. But my boss—"

"Was a wanker?"

"Yeah. A wanker who switched the goalposts. Gave me a watch that won't have anywhere near the resale value I need to—" He tried again to clear his clogged throat. "It won't be enough."

"Why'd you give it to me then?"

Austin hadn't anticipated ever saying this to his ex's nephew. Hadn't verbalised it at all, not even once, but like a key turning in a lock, another door swung open, this time deep inside him. "Because no amount of cash will bring her back."

That was the truth, plain and simple.

Painful.

He met eyes so like Sol's they fooled him into spilling something Cameron might use against him. "I can't turn back time, no matter how much I want to."

But Cameron didn't attack. His voice softened like his uncle's. "You'd turn back time, even if that meant going back to when we lived together?"

It surprised Austin into answering. "Yeah. You see, you're not my first mistake."

"You think leaving Uncle Sol was a mistake?"

That was harder to answer. "Not explaining why I left was. I didn't . . ." Understand why having Cameron in his care had spooked him? He hadn't had time to unpick why until Luke had made him take this time off. Or maybe that process of realisation had started earlier, when he'd first got to Glynn Harber. "I never meant to hurt either of you. I worried I would if I stayed."

Cameron opened the door, a swimming-pool scent wafting out of the building. "I'm lifeguarding a hydrotherapy session. I need to get the pool ready for it." He held the door open. "I'll give you until the session starts, so if you want my help with Maisie, convince me faster."

———

IF AUSTIN HAD EVER IMAGINED SPILLING his guts to Cameron, this wasn't how he'd pictured. He trailed behind him into some changing rooms that in turn led to the Haven's pool room where he checked dials and picked up a spanner before facing Austin.

"Talk," he said, and Austin had been wrong that he hadn't yet filled out. He was well on the way, his biceps already giving Sol's a run for their money, curving as he hefted it, the head smacking into the palm of his hand. "I wasn't joking," he said, glancing at a clock. "You've got less than ten minutes before I need to do something that isn't exactly your skillset. You know? Like being there for people who need looking after? People who haven't done anything wrong but life took a massive dump on."

Perhaps he saw Austin almost wheel back. Mistook it maybe for a reaction to his actions instead of his words, because he stopped slapping the head of the spanner against his palm and instead knocked it against a piece of equipment that juddered to life. "Tricky pump," he shouted over the initial roar of noise, which quietened. "There's a knack to it."

"To being good with kids too," Austin admitted. "Not sure I'll ever be a natural, but for some reason Maisie likes me."

"You saved her." Cameron stayed as blunt while continuing preparations, scooping out a water sample, which he tested. "Everyone says it. Now they all act like you're a hero." His gaze met Austin's. "Why'd you do it?"

"Why?"

"Yeah. Why'd you put yourself out for her? Get one of your expensive suits all wet. And your watch." That sharp gaze honed in on his bare wrist before lifting. "You didn't put yourself out when Uncle Sol needed you, did you? So you must have had a reason." For a second, he looked conflicted. "I overheard Mr Lawson talking to the padre."

Austin had no idea what Luke could have told Hugo that made Cameron waver, surprised when he continued.

"He said that he couldn't have saved the school without you either." That wavering didn't last long. "You're seeing Maisie's dad, right? Did you already fancy him? Was that why you jumped in? To get his attention?"

"No! I barely knew him." Now, weeks later, Dom and Maisie filled parts of him he hadn't realised Sol and Cameron had left empty. That had been empty long before them. "I did what anyone would do in the same situation, that's all."

Cameron changed the subject.

"I didn't know you had a sister. Or that she died."

"It's not the kind of thing you blurt out to anybody." Seeing Cameron nod instead of slinging back another arrow helped Austin add some more detail. "I wasn't about to tell my boyfriend's kid who'd just been bereaved that I didn't handle death well."

Cameron looked up, his eye as liquid as that beetle's carapace. "No," he accepted. "It's not the easiest thing to talk about."

It really wasn't. "Leaving seemed a safer option."

"Safer?"

"For you."

That was it, nothing hidden, like he'd shared with Sol a short while earlier. And fuck if he knew how both Trebecks could also winkle out more by saying nothing, but more did come as Cameron stayed silent. "It scared the shit out of me that I'd do something wrong. Plus, I needed to keep climbing the ladder, you know? At work to earn those bonuses. Still do, but before I go, I want to help her. Look." He pulled out his phone, scrolling to Maisie's photo. Pressed the phone into Cameron's free hand. "I can't help her, but you might."

The outside door opened and a big voice boomed. "Here comes the Haven's number one swim team. They will not sink. They only float. Born to be in the water, it's Justin half-man, half-tuna Kershaw and the Haven's very own mermaid, M—"

"Mitch?" Cameron called out, voice echoing. "Can you give me a minute?"

A man poked his head around the changing room door. He took what might have been a troubling tableau—Cameron with a spanner in one hand and Austin empty-handed—before nodding. "We'll get changed slowly."

He withdrew, and Austin made to take back his phone and leave, but Cameron wasn't done yet. He'd scrolled onto another photo.

"Hey, that's—"

"Private?"

Dom smiled out of the screen, that gaze as soft as Austin remembered, Maisie clutching her dolly, fast asleep beside him, and somehow that made a difference.

Something shifted for Cameron.

Austin saw it as he handed the phone back gently instead of thrusting. Heard it too in his question, still abrupt but less angry. "Why do you think I can help?"

"Because I know she likes you. I heard you were good with her at her swimming lessons."

"They weren't proper swimming lessons. She wasn't ready, you know? Didn't have the arm and leg coordination. Some kids are late developers, but she was good at the water-confidence parts."

"Confidence?" That was *exactly* what she needed.

"You know, getting used to splashing. It's hard to float when you're thrashing, so we teach them not to panic."

"That's what she needs." More now than ever.

Cameron raised eyes that maybe could be as warm as his uncle's one day. A hint of something like it surfaced.

"Bring her back here the day after tomorrow. Tell her she's invited to a mermaid party, and she should bring her dolly with her."

19

On the day of the pool party, Austin woke with a belly full of nerves.

They wouldn't settle, spurred by a small voice that had started whispering as soon as he'd sent Dom a text invitation. Not even a draft contract arriving from Keir could ease it.

What if doing this today sets Maisie back?

Makes it worse for her, not better.

His guts twisted.

I don't want to scare her.

Those whispers of worry had hours to build, Dom not due back until late afternoon. Him arriving for the party with two passengers instead of one didn't make it any quieter, but Austin plastered on a fake smile as the Range Rover pulled up outside the Haven.

It turned real the moment Maisie clambered over her grandfather to get to him.

"Austin Russell, look at my T-shirt!" She launched from the car, one arm anchoring around his neck like it had once before, in terror. This time she was happy, her other arm clutching the same doll as in the photo.

"Mummy drew on the mermaids." She thrust the doll at him. "On dolly's T-shirt too. She's got gel pens with glitter."

"Careful Maisie." Dom must have got out to stand behind him. Austin felt him there as Maisie chattered, and in another replay of the last time she'd been in his arms, both of Dom's came around them, only this time he encouraged Austin to turn in their circle. He unpeeled Maisie's arms from around Austin's neck, but he smiled as he did it. "Austin won't be able to breathe let alone take you to a mermaid party if you strangle him, will he?" He lowered her to the ground. "Besides, haven't you got something else to show him?"

"Yes!" She hopped, overexcited, almost fell, both Austin and Dom grabbing her before she could topple.

"Both feet on the ground, please." Dom let her go once she'd steadied. "Now go and ask Grampy for your backpack."

She did, rounding the car out of sight, Austin about to follow, but Dom caught hold of him first. "Hey, it's good to see you," he said, smile not gone, exactly, but laced with something different. Concern, Austin realised. "Is there a problem?" Dom glanced at the Haven's front door. "You look worried. I didn't even know there was a pool here. Did they change their mind about letting us use it?"

"No. No, it's fine. Cameron's sorted everything. He helps out here a lot. Sol too because his sister lives here."

"His sister? That's ... ?"

"Cameron's mum?" Austin nodded. "They had everything set up in the pool area before I got here."

And hadn't that surprised him after a sleepless night full of what-its? Touched him as well to see the work Cameron had put in, considering how their discussion about using the pool had started with him plainly still harbouring resentment.

Because me leaving hurt more than it ever helped him.

He saw that portrait Sol had started up in the old art building in a different light then.

That had been a younger version of his nephew. The kid who used to come and visit them for birthdays and Christmas.

We used to have fun when he visited.

I wish I'd remembered that instead of running.

"I'm not worried about using the pool." Austin checked before continuing, seeing Maisie had wandered away with her grandfather. They examined the same raised beds full of berries where Keir had told a Haven resident about sharing worries. Now Austin looked into the eyes that bedtime photo hadn't done justice to and did the same. Honesty rose along with something else in his chest, no room left for everything he usually kept in. "It's just been a bit of an eye-opener, you know?"

"An eye-opener? What has?" Dom tilted his head, listening.

"Asking Cameron for help. We, uh . . . We didn't exactly get along when he came to live with me and Sol."

"You mentioned something about that over dinner."

Austin didn't remember. Whatever he'd mentioned could have only skimmed the surface, but more must have lurked, waiting to rise since Luke had forced him to face a kid he'd once turned his back on.

Him pairing them hadn't been accidental. Luke must have done it to make Austin face his past instead of avoiding it. Not only face it, he realised, but confront it, like he did now. Admitting this was rough.

"Cameron arriving freaked me out, to be honest. I couldn't leave fast enough. Hit up all my contacts. Networked my arse off and took the first job that came up outside of London. All to get out of looking after a kid who had problems."

Dom's eyebrows shot up, and he pulled back, letting go of the drawstring at the front of Austin's board shorts he hadn't realised Dom had used to tug him closer. By comparison, Dom's step back was abrupt, like his tone.

"Cameron having problems was a dealbreaker for you?"

"No!"

Austin closed the distance. And wasn't that a sign that something else inside him had shifted, another tide slowly but surely turning, because stopping Dom's frown was more important than keeping his old shield hoisted.

"Him having problems wasn't an issue for me. Causing him *more* was. I used to . . ."

Lie awake thinking of all the ways I might let him down too.

Come home to walk on eggshells, afraid I'd fuck up another family.

"He'd lost his gran. Virtually lost his mum. Needed so much it scared me shitless. You wouldn't know it to look at him now, but Cameron was so bloody fragile." Which was awfully close to his own brittle descriptor, he recognised, tucking that away while clearing up something more urgent. "Now here I am all over again, just as shit scared as back then that doing this is going to set another kid back."

"You're worried about Maisie?"

Austin almost shouted. Couldn't help it, emotion a cork shooting from a bottle shaken by days of worry. "Of course I am!"

Ken's head shot up, looking their way.

Austin lowered his voice just as quickly.

"What if doing this scares her instead of helps her? Stops her from wanting to stay at her mum's?" His nails dug into the meat of his palms, fists clenching out of nowhere. "I'd be responsible for that too."

"Come here."

Dom's brief kiss wasn't enough to reassure him. Wasn't enough full stop. But his answer helped his stomach to settle as well as an ache in his chest he hadn't known was there until Dom eased it.

"First of all, you aren't responsible for Maisie. I am. If I think this will put her back, I'll say so. But . . ."

"But what?"

"But I can't help thinking that she'll at least try to dip a toe in for you. For Cameron too." Dom didn't kiss Austin again, but he kept him close, a hand skimming up Austin's arm, stopping at his shoulder. He squeezed it in confirmation. "Even if she doesn't touch the water today, getting to see that more people want to help her isn't the worst outcome, is it?"

This was a different man to the one who'd pulled back abruptly only minutes before. Different to the one who had pounded along Porthperrin's harbour wearing work boots and abject terror as well. A very different man to the one who'd dropped to his knees in a hospital cubicle, struck by relief that felled him.

This version seemed easier in his skin now.

Relaxed, considering even the thought of going near water had freaked out his daughter.

Maybe that was down to whoever had drawn sparkling mermaids on his T-shirt too, he now noticed. A spell cast by someone who'd waved a wand over Maisie as well, back to her old gleeful self. "Balloons!" she shouted, skipping ahead to where Cameron had tied some either side of a homemade banner spanning the pool-house entrance.

"That's my name!" she shouted next, twirling and caught by her grandfather. Then she circled back, jumping to a stop in front of Austin. "I like your shorts! You've got . . ." She made pincers with her fingers.

Austin looked down at board shorts he'd borrowed. "Crabs?"

"Yes!" Maisie skipped ahead again. "Charles Heppel loves them!"

"That explains a lot. I borrowed them from him."

"Go on in, Dad," Dom called out. "We'll be right behind you." The moment the door closed behind his father, he found that drawstring again. Didn't let go this time, tugging. "So Charles gave you crabs while I was gone? I didn't realise you were seeing other people."

Austin met eyes that gleamed today. That danced with amusement like his daughter's. That warmed even more the moment Austin said, "I'm not seeing anyone else." And at some point, he'd learn to quit while he was ahead. More slipped out than he'd intended. "I don't want to."

Dom's hand stole around Austin, pulling him closer. Close enough that kissing him again was easy, Dom only breaking off to murmur, "Me either." He kissed him one more time, any last trace of shadows under his eyes faded.

"You . . ." Austin wasn't sure how to phrase this. "You had a good time? Your ex is . . ."

"Better," Dom said, dropping one last kiss onto his lips before heading for the entrance. "So much. She'll be back home where she belongs in no time. And if this works, Maisie might be there to meet—" He held the door open for Austin, but the swimming-pool scent wasn't all that met them. The sound of panic also carried, Maisie not quite crying yet, but close to it, and in a blink, Austin recognised today's difference in Dom.

Hope.

That's what had buoyed him.

Now he watched it slip and rushed to stop it.

"Maisie?" Austin's call echoed, both Maisie and her grandfather turning his way at the changing room doorway.

Ken was on his knees holding out a pair of inflatable armbands that Maisie backed away from, her dolly in a death grip.

"There you are." Austin stayed in the doorway so not to crowd her, doing his best to sound casual. "That's a pretty swimsuit, but there's something missing." He tapped a finger to his lips as if thinking. "It would look even better with wings."

"Fairy wings?" she asked, dubious but distracted at least from panic.

"Nearly." He pulled off his T-shirt before reaching into a crate of swimming aides designed for the adults the Haven sheltered. He rooted through it. "Fairy wings might get too wet in the pool."

"Or get lost," she said, sniffing, the faded denim of her eyes red-rimmed.

"See how these water wings are stronger. That's because they're for mermaids and mermen." He slid on a pair similar to the child-size ones Ken held, no time to feel foolish while Maisie watched him. "Maybe you could show dolly how you put on your mermaid wings too?"

She nodded again, still sniffing, but almost smiling.

"Right," Austin said, holding out a hand. "Let's go and see if we can find Cameron, shall we?"

More balloons had been tied to the pool hoist. On the railings leading down the slope into the water as well, which was shallower now than before. Much shallower.

Cameron must have borrowed a wand. Cast a few spells himself, like that visit to Maisie's mum must have done to make Dom easier in his skin now. In Cameron's case, that magic had transformed the pool into a seaside haven, pebbles bordering a pathway leading to a sign, lifelike mermaids painted on it showing talent like his uncle's.

Maisie attempted to read what he'd written.

"Stuh," she sounded out. "Op," she finished before her eyes widened and she held up both hands, barring the way, almost dropping her doll in the process. "Stop!" she said, excited. Delighted. And why the hell piecing one word together seemed worth celebrating when his sister had known hundreds at the same age, thousands maybe, he didn't have time to unravel, not while Dom and Ken cheered.

Maisie squirmed with pleasure, pride leaving her beaming, and that ache in his chest slammed back, only different. He rubbed his sternum as she asked, "What else does it say?"

Austin crouched, reading for her. "Only mermaid dollies allowed and their mermaid and mermen helpers."

"But you don't have a dolly." She clutched hers even tighter. Then she did something that caused Dom to let out a soft sound.

Maisie kissed her most precious possession before handing it over. "Don't worry, dolly," she promised, little voice echoing. "Austin Russell won't let you sink."

"That's okay, Maisie," Cameron said from behind them. "We've got some more dolls here who need helpers." A resident cradled one of her own, Austin recognising dark Trebeck eyes.

Cameron's mum led the way down the slope and sat at the edge of the water, holding her doll with care that Maisie must have noticed, dipping its toes in shallow water.

That lured Maisie closer, her toes almost at the water's edge too. Or perhaps it was Cameron's ease with his mum, modelling the same movements with a doll of his own, only he sat in the water to face them. Either way, when he asked, "Want to play with us?" Maisie inched closer.

"My mum likes it when I put her dolly on a pool float and push it to her." He did that. "Want a float for your dolly too?"

Maisie splashed through ankle-deep water to fetch the one he offered.

Cameron edged out deeper, taking it slow, sailing another pool float her way, Maisie reaching for it, slipping, both Dom and Austin lurching for her. Ken too, but Maisie didn't need any of them to catch her.

Cameron was there, and she laughed in his arms, her hair jewelled with water.

Dom's eyes were damper.

He caught Austin staring at them.

"Should have brought my phone in," he said, his voice thick. "Videoed this for Gemma. Be a hell of a weight off her mind."

"Go ahead and get it."

Dom almost did before sinking back down into the water, worry also rippling, eyes fixed on Maisie, still only ankle deep, but splashing with more enthusiasm, pushing her float to her grandfather.

She kicked, diamond droplets flying, splashing Austin, who brushed them off. "Or I can grab it for you?"

"Would you?" Dom reached for the doll Austin held. "Thanks." His hands covered Austin's before he glanced at his daughter. "I know nothing's going to happen to her here. I mean, Cameron's a lifeguard for fuck sake," he murmured. "Dad's right there too, but . . ."

He didn't need to finish that sentence. Austin could guess that like Maisie, it would take a while before the hooks of this particular fear loosened. "I'll go." He got up, sharing a quick smile with Cameron who, for once, returned it.

Then he looked back, glad he had because Dom had finally stopped watching Maisie like a hawk, his gaze fixed on him as if he was also worth his keeping a close eye on, warm and grateful.

Austin carried that with him into the changing room, the mirror reflecting happiness that he couldn't contain. That refused to subside. That kept rising, a tide showing no sign of turning. It stretched so wide his cheeks ached.

A traffic stopper, Charles had called it.

He grabbed his own phone first, taking a quick selfie to send him, finger hovering over his contacts after doing that to send it to one more person. He typed a quick message to his mother.

Austin: *At the pool with Maisie. Think those fairy wings worked real magic. She's back in the water.*

A reply pinged in, Charles the first to answer.

Charles: *WOW. You know you should marry the man who makes you smile like that don't you?*

A hearts-in-eyes emoji followed.

Austin typed a hurried answer while heading for the lockers.

Austin: *Calm down. No one's proposing marriage.*

Charles replied just as quickly.

Charles: *Let yourself fall for him a little.*

Charles: *What's the worst that could happen?*

Charles: *But I'm sending that pic to Heligan too. Bet it makes him call you back in a hurry.*

His mother also replied.

Her sending the same hearts-in-eyes emoji as Charles was surprising.

It turned his smile watery. His eyes too as he grabbed Dom's jeans to retrieve his phone. It lit in his hand, not with an emoji but with a message he read without thinking.

Gemma: *Tell him about me*

His hold on the phone tightened.

Tell me what about you?

Another message arrived, the phone vibrating, the urge to read it almost overwhelming. He must have fought it for too long. The door to the pool area opened, Dom there, dripping too and in a hurry. "Hey, couldn't you find—"

He saw Austin holding both phones.

"There's a message," Austin held Dom's phone out. "From your wife."

Dom slowed then, hurry forgotten, standing half-in and half-out of the doorway.

He looked over his shoulder.

Maisie's voice echoed from behind him, but not melting down now. She sounded . . .

Happy.

Really happy.

Might be even happier with her mum home and no distractions. He did say they're still close—

Dom swung back as if he'd heard that thought, something rippling across his face Austin wasn't sure how to label. Indecision, maybe?

Dom demonstrated the opposite, taking one step closer, the door swinging closed behind him. He held out a hand

and Austin passed him the phone. Or tried to. Dom didn't take it. He clasped Austin's wrist instead and didn't let go. "She's my ex, remember?"

Maisie must have splashed him. His hair was wet, dripping, rivulets running from his shoulders. Austin fixed on their slow trickle rather than look up at what Dom next said, speaking slow and careful.

"The last time someone looked at me like you just did, they'd got bad news they thought I'd . . . I don't know. Blame them for? Or walk away from? No idea why you'd think I'd walk away from you in a hurry, so let me tell you what I'm thinking real quick, okay?"

Austin wanted to nod. Made himself say, "You should get back to—"

"Maisie's fine." Dom's hold hadn't loosened. He used it to bring Austin closer, his voice lowering but still emphatic. "Because of you, Austin. She's fine because of you."

He took the phone then. Scanned it while another trickle of water meandered, beading on his chest hair. "Okay. I can see how this reads." He looked up. Met Austin's gaze. Held it, his own rock steady. "Yes, I'm close with my ex. Closer now maybe than when we were married, but there's a bloody good reason for that, and it's splashing away in that pool, as happy as Larry. Because of you," he reminded. "Do you know who I couldn't stop talking about on my visit?" He answered before Austin could ask. "Maisie's favourite person."

Austin hauled up old defences, aiming for offhand, but failing.

"Her dolly? Oh, I know. Tor Trelawney."

His brittleness couldn't have rung true—Dom's laugh echoed.

"Good try at deflection, but nope." The gap closed

between them. Austin shivered as Dom said, "You, Aus. *You.* That's something both Gemma and I are grateful for, okay? I can think of a few other things Gemma might want me to tell you about her. But until I check with her, I'll stick to saying this: She's my ex *and* she's more grateful for the man who jumped in for her daughter than I know how to tell you. Believe me?"

Austin tried to speak. Settled for nodding, his own phone buzzing.

He read a message from a number Charles must have loaded into his phone, the name making him blink.

"Problem?"

Austin looked up. "What?"

Dom nodded at Austin's phone. "Is there a problem? You're frowning. Thought I was the only person who made you glare. Or I used to, at least." He glanced at the phone again. "Can I . . . Can I help?"

"No. It isn't a problem." Austin read the message one more time. "It's an invitation."

"Ah. For your sister's birthday? You mentioned that's soon, yeah?" Sympathy shouldn't be so attractive—was something he usually avoided. Coming from Dom, it made him turn his phone without hesitation.

He watched Dom scan the screen, a frown of his own emerging as he read under his breath. "'Hello, friend of Charles. Might have an opening for you if you can be in London later tomorrow?'" Dom met his gaze. "Who's Heligan?"

"Someone Charles went to school with. Works for a private bank in the city. He put in a good word for me." Another message arrived.

Heligan: *Would have been in touch before if I'd seen your photo sooner.*

"Charles put in a good photo too?" Dom said dryly.

The air was cooler in here compared to the poolside. Austin shivered again. "It probably won't come to anything."

"Good. I'm not . . ." Suddenly, Dom was closer. "I'm not ready for you to leave yet."

"I wouldn't. Not right away. I'd need to give notice." One Luke couldn't refuse, this time. Or maybe it was the sound of Maisie's laughter, bright and sparkling along with Cameron's, a much rarer treasure, that added a layer of want that must have sounded authentic. "I'm not ready either."

Dom repeated what he'd just said. "Good." Then he added what they both knew already. "I mean, you always said you would. Go, I mean. Next rung up, right?"

Austin nodded.

"Thought we'd have longer, that's all. So . . . We should make the most of every minute?"

Austin nodded again, agreeing with what felt like every cell in his body.

Dom said, "Good," for a third time, turning a simple agreement into something complex. Warming. A promise made before another shiver racked him.

Dom rubbed his arms, stopped by water wings from chasing away his goosebumps. "Because that's why I brought Dad with me. So he could take Maisie home if everything went okay here. And it has. So well. Because of you, again." That rub to Austin's arm slowed. Turned into a hold he stepped into. "Let me take you home?" Dom rumbled. "Start making the most of it somewhere more private?"

Austin let his kiss answer for him.

20

Austin had thought he'd walked fast to the Haven the first time. Today's walk back was even faster.

He swung a backpack holding damp shorts and towel over his shoulder, wanting to leave that *might have an opening for you* message behind—stupid perhaps when it was exactly what he'd wanted.

What I still need.

The last of the afternoon light filtered through leaves, but all he saw was that fucking graph trending downward.

There's no way to reverse it if I stay here.

But with a city banking firm's pay and bonus package . . .

He walked faster, wanting to leave that dose of reality behind, only slowing when Dom called out from behind him.

"Hey. Where's the fire?"

"Fire?" Austin turned, still walking, to see Dom strafed with beams of mellow sunshine, gorgeous.

So gorgeous.

I'll miss . . .

Austin stopped. Managed to say, "What do you mean, fire?"

"Just that I know I said we should make the most of every minute, but I didn't expect you to take off running." Sunlight striped the hand he held out. "It's a beautiful evening. Don't know how often we'll get to do this." Dom shrugged. Smiled, although it wasn't quite as easy as the others since returning from a family visit that seemed to have made a real difference. "What if making the most of it while you're still here means neither of us rushing?"

"You want to hold my hand while we walk at a snail's pace through the woods? I had no idea that you could be . . ."

"What?" Dom didn't only extend his hand. He wiggled his fingers. His eyebrows too, lightening a moment that could have felt too heavy. "Romantic?" A real smile emerged then.

Fuck, he's the real traffic stopper.

Austin reversed direction even though getting back to the privacy of the stables felt more pressing, more vital than lingering here where the lowering light gilded the man who waited, his hand still extended. He walked first, breaking into a jog that ended with something else Charles would have been proud off, Dom catching Austin after he jumped, hoisting him upward, braced and steady.

"Romantic?" Austin grumbled into the side of his throat, arms locked around his neck, doing his best to sound scathing. "More like a massive sap."

"Sap?" Dom grasped him, no chance of Austin slipping, but he sounded winded. "Only lately."

It was a simple reply, like the kiss he gave him, no reason for parts of Austin to stir like the leaves did in the breeze above them. No accounting for an unfurling feeling either, but as Dom's lips parted and their tongues met, warmth also filtered like the lowering sunlight did through the boughs, and how the fuck was Austin going to make it back to the stables, let alone leave here long-term? How, when Dom pulled back to look at him like he was the one wielding magic? Or when he walked slowly instead of quickly, asking a hundred questions.

The woods listened to his answers, Dom soaking them up too and nodding, holding his hand the whole way back until the trees thinned, Glynn Harber ahead, silent, the car park empty.

"They're all off camping tonight."

"Everyone?"

"Pretty much. This is the last week before everything starts to rev up for the new school year. Last chance for leave. Luke and Nathan have taken the new sixth-form students off tonight with their kids. Will keep them busy all week so everyone else can go home one last time if they want to."

"Good timing for you then?" And here was proof Dom had listened for longer than this leisurely walk Austin was now glad they'd taken their time over. His hold on his hand tightened. "Although going home must be tough if it's your sister's birthday."

It was. Tougher each year. "Feels like it should get easier, not—" He stopped at the fence around the outdoor class-room used by children a similar age to Tamsin, unable to keep this in. "Should have been her twenty-first this year."

He focused on the balance beam, picturing another little girl who'd been a gift, he now saw. A second chance. Or a third, given how he'd messed up with Cameron.

Again, they shared a wavelength. Dom pointed to the

same balance beam. "This is where I first noticed you. Almost crashed Dad's van at seeing some stranger holding Maisie's hand. Then you gave me a telling off for being too late for her. You did that a lot?" he asked. "Before I got to know you?"

"What, give you bollockings for being late?"

"No." Dom caught hold of his hand again. "Stopped my daughter from falling."

Austin nodded, the text Charles had sent floating across his field of vision.

Let yourself fall.

Too late, he thought as they moved on, taking the path around the main school building, both of them hurrying now, perhaps hearing the same clock ticking.

Way too late.

I fell for him already.

———

THEIR THREADED FINGERS only loosened for one reason— Austin needing to get his door key from his backpack once they got to the stables.

He slid it off, digging through board shorts and a damp towel to find it, his hand shaking. Then the key skidded across the lock instead of finding the keyhole, Dom crowding behind him. His mouth latching where Austin's neck met his shoulder didn't help to steady his hand.

Austin tried again, but Dom gained entry faster, sliding a hand under his T-shirt. He pulled Austin back the last inch so they connected, all that solidness his to lean on.

Austin let himself have that, shifting, and heard Dom's breath catch. Felt him start to harden, and Austin's breath seized too. It came out shaky, his exhale stuttering like his key did across the key plate, nowhere close to finding where it should slot in.

Annoyance at himself blossomed. "For fuck sake."

Behind him, Dom let out an almost-silent gust of laughter.

"You always have this much trouble getting it in?" Then his breath coasted across the shell of Austin's ear, pitched low, a lit match thrown on petrol. "Or is this your way of saying that you want me to do it for you?"

"Do it for me?"

"Or *to* you, maybe?" Dom took the key, and perhaps Austin should have felt caged there with a locked door ahead and Dom behind him, but another mental image made his knees weak. Not of a text message, this time, but of blowing Dom behind a closed gate in Porthperrin, with only this man between Austin and whoever had walked the alley.

Remembering that sent his blood south, had him wanting to turn to kiss Dom instead of answering, but Dom wasn't done yet with his questions.

He nuzzled the side of Austin's throat, and maybe if staying at Glynn Harber for longer had been an option he'd learn to stop dissolving each time Dom kissed him where he was tender, but for now it still got to him somewhere funda-mental. Somewhere that meant he needed Dom to brace him. To support him. To kiss his throat again and grind against him.

Thank fuck the school is empty.

Dom rumbled against his throat, a barely tamed big cat purring, and some of the blood that had rushed south rose to where Austin knew a bruise would also blossom.

He wanted it.

Wanted whatever marks Dom left on him to ache tomorrow and each day after as a reminder of what meeting his match felt like.

Because that was what he was, Austin knew as Dom rubbed his cock, flare of arousal spotlighting what he couldn't ignore any longer.

I thought he was my opposite.

But he's . . .

Dom murmured, his voice full of opposites too, both rough and gentle. "Or do you want to be the key in my lock instead?" He dotted kisses that had Austin tilting his head back, eyes closing against the sight of nests in the eaves above them. Against the sight of the birds that had built them too, swooping black against a shade of blue so familiar he ached to see it.

He also ached for everything else Dom suggested in a hoarse, low whisper.

"Because I want in you like you wouldn't believe. But if you want in me? You got it. Today you get *anything* you want, Aus. Your chances look pretty good for tomorrow as well. Given a choice, I'd want you for—"

Had he been about to say the word *longer?*

Austin didn't get to find out.

Dom had stilled behind him. His hand too, that slow, delicious rub stuttering to a stop before he heard Dom swallow. Then it restarted, Dom holding him closer as he made an offer. "I'll switch if you want because I'm starting to think you weren't the only one who hit your head on the rocks outside the harbour."

"You hit your head too?" That took a moment to process,

desire clouding his senses. "Shit, are you okay?" Austin tried to turn. Couldn't move while Dom muffled a quiet laugh against his shoulder.

"I'm fine, but a knock to the head might explain why I'm up for anything with you. *Everything* with you Aus. But I'm pretty sure that out of the two of us, I'm the best at manual labour, so if you tell me to slide my key into your lock—"

Austin laughed too.

Couldn't help it.

"Will you shut the fuck up and open the door?"

Dom did, the key sliding home with no problem, his hand steady as ever, and the door swung open.

Austin kicked it closed behind them.

ONE BENEFIT of coming straight from the pool in only shorts and a T-shirt was how quickly Austin could get naked.

His T-shirt flew.

He didn't care where it landed, too busy shoving down his shorts, which puddled at his ankles almost as fast as want escalated, rocketing inside him. Dom didn't move much slower, but impatience had Austin wrenching at the front of his shorts, getting a hand inside before Dom could shrug them off completely. And there was his laughter again, loud in the confines of the stable entranceway, deep and delighted.

"What's the rush now? Got somewhere better to be this evening?"

Austin didn't answer. Made himself ignore that fucking ticking that he couldn't even blame on a watch now that Cameron was its keeper.

Austin made himself ignore the sound. Had to because

tracing the thickening outline of Dom's erection would be a crime to rush through. He'd take his time to map every ridge and contour. Engage all his senses. Feel the cling of cotton jersey that hid it from him. Touch it to remember later along with the faint scent of the pool and shower gel, musk only a vague hint, thickening like Dom's cock did the moment Austin fell to his knees and pressed his mouth to it.

The cotton would have wicked away any trace of moisture if his mouth hadn't dried already at Dom watching him so closely, another role reversal of when cubicle curtains had been open behind him, a hospital bustling while Dom had thanked him.

He'd hidden nothing then.

Didn't now, gaze making the same promise as then.

He still looks like he'd do anything for me.

He's already given me everything I wanted.

Yes, Austin would leave, but Sol's building would be resurrected. An old wrong finally righted.

He couldn't think about not being here to see it happen.

He gripped strong quads instead, which trembled under his touch as if that strength was deceptive, only sheer will holding Dom upright. He trembled harder when Austin peeled his underwear away to find Dom's cock flushed and thickened for him.

Austin grasped it, licking, and Dom quaked, having to brace a hand either side of the entranceway, but that barely registered. Austin's mouth flooded with reminders of an afternoon he'd never forget.

There was more of that faint pool scent. Pine too from a shower both Dom and his daughter had sung through, no sign of tears from Maisie, only giggles at her dad's falsetto.

And there was more of Dom too, the essence of him filling his mouth.

Pubic hair crinkled under the hand Austin ringed around its base, and he sucked, his mouth as full as his hand, not enough room in his chest for his heart to beat, to pump, to ache at the same time as he blew him, taking his time until Dom let out a rough sounding, "Want you too."

Dom's colour had heightened when Austin got up, the blue of his eyes a startling contrast. He almost stumbled, saved by Dom hauling him close.

He buried his face against Austin's throat, sucking harder this time, and Austin saw heaven. Felt it too as Dom found his cock, wrapping fingers around it that wrung pleasure from him.

Dom only let go to grasp him by the back of the thighs and heft him up one more time, their mouths connecting briefly but deeply, Dom breaking off to ask, "Which way?"

"You," Austin decided. "In me."

"Sweet," Dom said, eyes dancing, laugh lines crinkling. "But I meant which way to your room."

Dom carried him across the right threshold, only loosening his hold to drop him onto his mattress.

Austin lay there, stretched out, naked, and wanting, stripped bare of so much more than his clothes, nothing buttoned-up left about him as Dom's gaze drifted down his body only to dart away to a framed picture on his bedside table.

Dom recognised its artist, laughing again. "Sixty-nine and a fuckton of glitter? That's got to be by Maisie. Fuck, I'd forgotten she told me your favourite number." Then his gaze met Austin's, more heat there than ever. "I told you it's mine too, right?"

He showed him, bending over the bed to get his mouth on Austin's cock, then manoeuvring so he lay beside him, his own right there, and Austin mouthed it. Got it wet like Dom did to him too, mirroring actions that had him close to coming far sooner than he wanted—that edged him even closer when Dom found his hole and touched it.

He pressed. Must have wet his finger. It circled, easy, and a whole new current swirled, dragged Austin under, drowning him in pleasure.

Dom shifted, his cock slipping from Austin's mouth, out of reach for a moment, and Austin let out a sound that he'd deny making if anyone but Dom had heard it, then let out another, deeper this time and loud enough he was glad the stables were empty. Glad the school was too, because Dom didn't only shift position, he paid Austin's balls attention, his mouth hot, so hot, as he sucked them one after the other.

Austin almost rolled onto his back, but Dom held him in place. Lifted his upper leg to make more space, no word for what his tongue felt like on that stretch of skin between his balls and his—

Austin shouted, or at least his mouth opened, but if he'd made a sound, Dom didn't react or respond, his mouth busy.

Now his tongue probed, and Austin had to grab hold of the base of his own cock, it felt so much better than good. So much closer to perfect. So good surely nothing could be better, but Dom didn't stop there, and Austin groaned so loud that Dom's hold on his leg eased. He moved away long enough to check in. "That's a good sound, right?"

He must have taken whatever he saw on Austin's flushed face as an answer because he rolled him over onto his front. At least one set of synapses in Austin's brain still fired—he got onto his knees, just barely.

The evening sun spilled through the window, painting the wall bright white, apart from a cross left by the shadow of the window frame, and Austin could have prayed then, he felt so close to heaven. Instead, he fell forward, bracing on both hands because Dom didn't pray either, like a man might say grace before his dinner. He spread Austin's cheeks and feasted.

Must tell Charles it's not only dogs that get raptured.

Accountants get to see the face of God too.

Austin slumped, face mashed into his pillows, fingers clutching handfuls of his sheets as if that might save him, which only lasted until Dom got a finger inside him. He found where pressing made Austin's cock leak, a drip turning into a drizzle that maybe Dom noticed and used because his second finger should have been harder to take, not slicker, surely? Or maybe Austin's brain had shorted, blanking out that Dom must have rummaged in his bedside drawer because that much slickness had to be lube.

He felt a cool spill of it then, trickling. Tickling. Saw his bedside drawer hanging open, strip of condoms now next to his death grip on the sheets as Dom fingered him open, a slow and steady torture that lit nerve endings Austin had forgotten existed.

Have I always had this many?

He'd had good sex before. Plenty of it, but Dom did something to him. In him. On him. Generous in ways maybe he should have predicted.

I'd give him more too, if I was—

Dom added another finger, Austin choking on the immenseness of what he wanted, and Dom stopped. Went still behind him. Checked in again, rubbing the small of his back as he did so.

"Too much, Aus?"

Austin somehow got his head up from the pillows.

Managed to look over his shoulder, blinking through a fog of both pain and pleasure.

Found two words to sum up what he needed.

"Not enough."

He followed with two more.

"Fuck me."

Dom watched him, still checking, resuming what he'd started, fingers twisting, and there was no kidding himself anymore—Austin would never want this to end, if he had the option.

Let yourself fall.

He closed his eyes to stop seeing a different future where feeling this much was normal. Where sex came with this much caring, proof right there in that hand rubbing his back. In a squeeze to his hip too, along with a rumbling question.

"Ready?"

He answered by blindly nodding, that strip of condoms gone when Dom lined up his cock and pushed in, and Austin's eyes shot open.

There was no evading this tide. No gentle receding, even though Dom must have pulled back, because he filled him again, even deeper, realigning everything Austin had known before coming to Glynn Harber.

Dom wasn't silent. His first full thrust had come with a low groan. His next with swearing. With the sweetest look of worry too when Austin looked over his shoulder. "It's good?" he asked. "Not hurting?"

Oh, this would hurt plenty.

Would be agony in the near future.

Austin buried his face in the pillows again to save seeing

another sunless, soulless office. Another never-ending spreadsheet. A life he hated needing.

"More," he managed to get out, hoping it came out as a demand instead of edged with desperation. "Don't hold back. Do it."

Dom did, but Austin hadn't known that him taking him at his word wouldn't only put his arse under pressure. His heart was instantly in trouble.

His cock surely reached his ribcage, no room left inside it, and no sight left either, each thrust blurring his vision.

"Like that?" Dom asked, and if his voice had come out hoarse before, now something rougher edged it.

Austin must have reached back. Couldn't let go of Dom's thigh now even if he'd wanted. Didn't have the brainpower to compute that bracing on two hands might have helped him withstand what Dom next served him, fucking him like he meant it, the slap of skin against skin only slowing for the seconds it took for Dom to pour more lube where they connected.

Austin felt its trickle. Dropped his head to see a thread of it join the precome that each deep thrust encouraged. And had he ever given up this much during sex, his body overflowing in every way it could show him?

No.

A clear strand swung from his cock, which ached until Dom reached around, his grasp as desperate as his gasping. "Fuck. Fuck. I can't—"

Hearing Dom so close to the edge slid another key into a lock—Austin came in throbbing pulses, Dom's grip on his hips two-handed now, unrelenting. His race towards the finish meant deep grinds instead of long thrusts, but they still shunted Austin face first again into the pillows.

He couldn't care about that.

Couldn't care that Dom collapsed over his back either, hot and heavy, his chest heaving.

All Austin had headspace left for was doing this again before their time was over.

21

L ater that evening, Austin heard the shower shut off while he made tea in the stable's compact kitchen. Heard Dom's footsteps next, followed by him crowding behind him like he had at the front door, saying, "There you are," as if he'd found something he'd lost but badly needed.

His arms caged Austin then, and yes, Austin still liked the feeling. Liked Dom's chest hair tickling the bare skin of his back too. Didn't entirely hate the cool drip of water from Dom's hair onto his shoulder when it came with him kissing those drops away, touch pretty close to nuzzling. But he definitely wasn't a fan of the sound of Dom's phone ringing, because it meant he peeled away to answer.

Austin followed with Dom's tea, pausing with it in the living room doorway, stopped by the sight of a grin that almost made the loss of contact worth it.

Dom's smile touched so much more than his lips now. Like earlier, he saw a distinct difference, studying it as Dom spoke.

"Yeah, Jason. I put the bid in." He gestured for Austin to come closer, who hesitated as Dom added, "I know, I know, you don't have to keep telling me it's no way to run a business. Still can't make myself give a single fuck about not making a profit."

And there was one of those deep laughs Austin could get used to hearing, full and rich instead of hollow, nothing fake about it. He loved seeing it touch eyes that softened as they swung in Austin's direction. He gestured again, Austin complying this time, offering a mug that Dom took a quick sip from. A rumble of appreciation followed, his next sip deeper before setting it down by the learning journeys stacked on the dining table.

He reached out, pulling Austin closer. Close enough to drop a thank-you kiss on his lips, not letting go as he continued his phone conversation. "Yeah," he rumbled again, gaze fixed on Austin. "Don't care if I make a loss on this project. If they say yes, it'll be worth it. I'll let you kn—"

He must have noticed something because that grin widened. "Hang on a mo, Jason." He lowered his phone, eyebrows raising. "Yeah?" he asked quietly. "You heard about the bid? They already made a decision?"

Austin nodded. "Yes. Just before I got to the pool. I should have a draft contract for you to look over in my email. Slipped my mind."

Those eyebrows rose even higher.

"I was distracted." Austin said, flustered. How could he have forgotten to tell him the news?

Because seeing him again felt more important.

Both of them.

Fuck it. All three Dymonds

Dom pulled him closer, eyebrows waggling again. "By the sight of me in board shorts?"

No. By the sight of him sitting in only a few inches of water, patient, so incredibly patient, until Maisie was ready for anything deeper. By the sight of his dad too, who might as well be a glimpse of Dom in the future, a big man holding a doll of his own to entice her. By a family who pulled together, even Maisie's mum from a distance when Austin's own had . . .

We fell apart.

Pretended we were fine.

Focused on the charity instead of talking about what I . . .

He swallowed, gaze drifting to Dom's phone, which he'd lifted again to his ear.

Dom said, "Jason? We got it! The contract? Hang on, I'll find out some more," so transparently happy that Austin found he could meet his smile with one of his own.

Austin said, "I'll forward it to you. That'll be your . . ."

Dom noticed his hesitation. "It'll be my what?"

"Your last chance to come to your senses?" He glanced at Dom's phone. Murmured, "That's your partner?" No that wasn't how Dom had described him. "Your best friend, the consultant? Maybe run it by him? Take the rest of the week to think about it?"

"Nope," Dom said, brushing another kiss to lips that tingled after sex so hot he still felt blistered. "But taking a look at the building ASAP with Jason isn't a bad plan." He kissed Austin before returning to his call. "Can you come down to Cornwall? When? How about tomorrow? Take a first look at the project with me? See what you're getting into. Bring Vanya. I've been meaning to talk to him anyway about Maisie. Yeah, Gemma has too. Think she's finally ready, so both come if you can? Stay at Cliffside and make a holiday of it?" His gaze met Austin's. "Last week of freedom before Vanya has to prepare his classroom for the new school year? Perfect timing then. Okay, go ahead and ask him."

He steered Austin to the sofa. Pushed, his touch gentle but determined. Didn't let up until Austin sat down, the towel around his waist coming loose at the same time, parting.

Dom knelt before Austin could retie it, his phone clamped between his ear and shoulder, freeing both hands which he ran up Austin's thighs, gaze fixed on where he'd started to harden. Then he jolted, his phone almost slipping like he'd forgotten he was mid-conversation, Jason returning to it with an answer.

"He's checking his storytelling schedule?" Dom said, smiling. His voice dropped to a murmur aimed at Austin. "Vanya runs storytelling sessions in the school holidays for families who can't speak English." His attention went back to the call. "Okay, Jason. Just let me know if you can come. No. You'll have Cliffside to yourself. I'm still staying at Dad's with Maisie. Can't see that changing for a while to be honest. Want to stay close when Gemma comes home too."

He wrapped a hand around Austin's cock then. Wet his lips. Met his eyes, that smile changing. Shifting. Flicking a switch that got him hard so fast he felt dizzy. "Maisie?" Dom said as if unaffected while Austin's breathing short-ened. "Yeah, she's doing so much better." He blinked as if whatever he heard next surprised him. "Me?" He re-estab-lished eye contact, nothing hidden. Then he looked down, Austin's gaze following to where the head of his cock emerged from the ring of Dom's fingers. He watched it retreat, Dom's hand teasing out sensation as stunning as his next smile. "Yeah," he said, speaking into his phone but looking directly at Austin. "I'm doing better too. So much better lately."

How did that rope the part of him that was usually restless, constantly searching for that next rung, always climbing?

Now the comment caught him like Dom's gaze did. "Sorry, Jason," he said. "I'm in the middle of something important here that won't wait." He winked. "Yeah, something's come up. How about calling back when you know if Vanya's free?"

His hand was a source of increasing pleasure. A surge that heightened, mounting like Austin's breathlessness, his chest rising and falling, bare toes curling into the carpet, and nipples tightening.

Dom saw that. He leaned in, still listening, his tongue flicking a tightening peak, looking up the whole while, smile still there in the creasing around his eyes.

There was plenty of room between his spread legs, but Austin couldn't help parting them further, drawing up a knee, his heel on the edge of the sofa cushion, almost whimpering as Dom's hand on his cock stopped moving. Let go. Moved to his inner thigh, squeezing.

Then Dom sat back on his heels, head tilted to keep his phone steady, and maybe Austin should feel exposed, but all he wanted was more. More of Dom's eyes on him. His hands and mouth too. His dick—

Austin watched Dom tug free the knot in his own towel as if he'd heard him. Saw him curl a hand around himself, erect already, and his mouth dried.

Maybe Dom's had too, because his voice turned gravelly. Deeper. Rougher in a way that Austin wanted to hear more often, having to grip the base of his cock to ease the ache there. "Jason,"

Dom said, still watching. "Actually, a couple of things have come up that won't wait, mate. Call me back, yeah?" He ended the call then, phone dropped as if he couldn't care less where it landed, and Austin stopped breathing. Almost swallowed his tongue, his heart pounding louder than any clock could tick because Dom lifted his hand to his mouth and wet a finger.

"Yeah, I'm doing so much better" he said as if continuing his conversation while touching where Austin was tender, the tip of his finger both slick and gentle.

"How about you?" That was more a breath than a question, light like his touch to Austin's rim. "Too sore, or . . ." He wet another finger, touched him again, and a starburst of sensation glittered. "Okay," Dom said as if Austin had answered, and maybe his body had done the talking for him, precome shining on his belly.

Austin's eyes closed, blinking open again to see the blue of Dom's almost eclipsed before he bent to suck his cock. A finger sank inside him then, easy, so easy, and Austin whimpered.

Dom's mouth was heaven, his lips a perfect tight ring Austin pushed up into, hips lifting, squirming down next because Dom found where pressing a fingertip meant Austin had to cover his mouth with his forearm to keep from shouting. From almost coming. From grabbing Dom by the head and—

His phone rang.

Dom grabbed it, his cheeks flushed and lips wet. "Shit," he muttered. "Meant to cancel it, not answer." He rolled his eyes, laughing at himself. "Jason? I meant call me much later." He winked again at Austin, but whatever Jason said to him caught his attention. "You want to meet whoever it is who's worth this much money to me?" His gaze had already been warm. Now it melted. "Austin's worth every penny."

Breathing around that took effort. So much that he couldn't answer when Dom included him in the conversation, asking, "Hey, Aus. You free tomorrow?" as if he didn't still rub that place inside him, gaze flicking between Austin's eyes and where his finger eased even deeper, smile not exactly spreading when Austin clenched around him, but intensifying. Deepening. Intent and focused.

Seeing that only made him squirm more, but Austin found the strength to shake his head before closing his eyes. Had to bite the meat of his own bicep to keep quiet while Dom held a phone conversation that, thank fuck, he quickly ended.

"Maybe next time, Jason. Text me tomorrow when you're close, yeah?"

Austin was close right then.

Had he ever been harder?

His cock bobbed, begging, more precome drizzling, which Dom noticed, staring.

Austin dropped his arm, more than precome spilling from him. "It's a cock, not a listed building. Are you planning on doing something with it or just looking at it?"

Dom's bark of laughter echoed, but he pulled out that finger to swipe it through the precome spatters. Smeared it over Austin's hole, pushing back in and searching until Austin's eyes rolled back, his back arching.

"How's that?" Dom asked, conversational, like he'd been on that call. Teasing, as well. "Better? Or I could always call Jason back. Like on *Who Wants to be a Millionaire?* You know, where contestants phone a friend for pointers?"

Austin heard an edge of roughness under that laughter. It

made him lurch up. Grab the back of Dom's neck. Drag their mouths together where he gasped, breathless. "You wouldn't go on that show. You've got to be worth millions already."

"Only on paper. The bank owns most of it. But this? You?" He rubbed where nerves sparked, cupping Austin's face with his free hand as if what he held was precious. "Feeling pretty rich right now."

They kissed, tongues sweeping before Dom finally eased out that finger, desire taking the place of humour. "Stay right there," he ordered. "Don't move a fucking muscle."

Austin did as instructed. Or almost did, sitting up straighter the moment Dom returned with lube and condoms. Then Austin scrambled to get his mouth on Dom's cock before he could wrap it. Saliva flooded his mouth, his chin soon wet, eyes watering, but he couldn't make himself care, almost choking until Dom pulled back to roll on a condom.

He watched Dom pour lube next, then Austin hurried to turn, kneeling on the sofa cushions.

"Like this?" Dom asked, the head of his cock right there where Austin wanted.

"Yeah, just like that."

That was his voice, Austin knew, not a stranger's. Him who let out a sound dragged from somewhere soul deep once Dom breached him, head of his cock almost more than he could deal with. Him too who shoved back, asking for more.

"Like this too?" Dom eased back before thrusting all the way in, and thank God Hugo wasn't here to overhear the groan Austin let out. Or maybe he'd understand that it hadn't been a sex sound.

It had been a revelation.

An undoing and a remaking, because Austin shuddered,

begging without words, no way to say what he needed, but Dom heard him. Fucked him slow at first, then faster, his torso another solid wall behind him, his arms not a cage now but his shelter. His mouth found that spot where his neck joined his shoulder and Austin could have cried. Couldn't stop from groaning, speared with pleasure that turned to disbelief when Dom stopped with no warning.

Austin glared over his shoulder as Dom eased out. "You better not be phoning a friend."

"No," Dom rumbled. "Don't want to hurt you, that's all."

The stream of lube he poured caught the light and Austin had no recollection of getting off the sofa, apart from his legs shaking, or of pushing Dom onto his back on the carpet right there between the sofa and the doorway, but he did hear Dom say, "Fuck, yes," as he sank onto him, the slide down endless, until Austin saw Dom's face flow between pleasure and something close to wonder.

Austin ground himself down and then lifted. Did it again, faster, his head tipped back to see where beams as strong as the man who held his hips crossed the ceiling. And there were initials carved by his father. Long-lasting. Permanent. Chiselled like the way Dom also carved a space deep inside him right now, dovetailed, no way they could be closer until Dom pulled him down to kiss him.

The shift in angle did something to him. *For him.* Austin rocked into each thrust, orgasm, which had eased off, surging the same way Dom had shoved Austin through the water towards a distant sun that shimmered.

This felt like breaking the surface all over again.

Like taking that first breath, gasping.

Like living instead of dying.

His lungs seized, Dom fucking him closer to more than a

simple climax. More than the sum of all the sex he'd had, until now.

Fuck, I don't want to leave this.

Him.

Us.

Not yet.

Not ev—

Austin came, the force of it leaving him weak, dragging him deep, and for a second time, Dom held him until he surfaced.

———

Dom left before Maisie's bedtime but got back in touch earlier than Austin expected.

A text arrived while he was showering the next morning.

Dom: *Breakfast?*

He read it after slicking his hair back with gel for the first time in months, preparing for a day in London where appearances would matter. As the kettle boiled for his first cup of tea, its cloud of steam matched his thought process, muzzy, still hazed by great sex he almost wished hadn't happened because he couldn't help picturing that anemone Charles had shown him, only instead of its feelers retracting, they now caught hold of his finger, clinging, telling him to stay. To ditch today's London meeting.

That was pointless thinking. Irrational like the smile the kettle reflected stretched out of all proportion at a second text's arrival.

Dom: *Or do you need to phone a friend before you answer?*

He still grinned as he carried his tea into the living room, his body also still humming from sex that had taken him apart and had put him back together.

It had been . . .

Good was too small a word to describe what had sent him into a deep sleep and had woken him still aching. *For more,* he thought letting a bit more of that pointless irrationality soak him like the sun did, spilling through the living room window.

He went to text an answer.

Something in the courtyard caught his eye first.

The Defender was outside the window, as usual. Now a second vehicle parked next to it.

Dom was out there too, leaning against his dad's old van, dressed for work in a Dymond and Son T-shirt, phone in his hand, texting.

Austin's phone *pinged* but he didn't read the message, too busy yanking open the front door and soaking up the sight of Dom's smile. The last of his fuzziness cleared, everything inside him coming to attention, alert and ready, as Dom pushed away from the van to meet him.

His kiss was quick, his hug lasting longer, Austin enveloped, and this—*this*—was what he hadn't known he'd missed or needed. Someone this pleased to see him.

The same rock-pool mental image came back, this time, Austin doing all the clinging. He did pull back though. Needed to in case want, which had blown up out of nowhere, bled through.

But that wasn't true, was it?

This hadn't come out of nowhere, he knew as he disentangled. It had simmered like the water in his kettle. Had done since his arrival at this school that would soon fill with children ready for a new year full of learning.

How the hell had he ever spent months looking out of his study window and seen someone lacking?

Dom was a lesson in learning to look closer. At himself too, even if that left him with questions about a career plan that now felt worse than drowning. He asked a different question that felt less like battering himself against rocks. "How's Maisie this morning?"

"Begging to go to sealife school with Simon from the pub. Think her fear of water's well and truly subsiding."

For a third time in only minutes, Austin pictured that part of Porthperrin, and could see Maisie exploring the rock pools, happy. Could picture a whole other future playing out as Dom slid his phone back into his pocket and then tilted his head, as if he too saw what Austin imagined.

I want to see that so much.

And fuck it if seawater soaks my trousers, I want to be there when it happens.

The thought stopped his breathing.

Dom noticed that too. His head tilted again. "You don't really have to phone a friend, you know? Just tell me what you want for breakfast and I'll get it for you." He added a qualification. "As long as the Co-op in the village sells it, because the fridge is empty at home. Go on."

"Because?"

He met Austin's gaze, his own steady. "Because I won't see you for a while, will I? Not if you're going up to London later. I forgot in the heat of the moment yesterday. Remembered this morning when I woke up. Will you come back before your sister's birthday?"

Austin shook his head. "I'll stop in Exeter on the way back. Not sure how long for."

Dom caught Austin's hand then. Hold it in what felt like

consolation. Whatever it was, it touched him like that puddle of sunshine, heating until Dom added, "At least having you home will make your mum happy."

Happy?

As if summoned, Cameron walked past the courtyard with Leonie's brother. Teo, Austin remembered, back from camping on the moor. He was someone else who'd been given a gift from an old hand here. A school family to support him until he found the words to talk instead of fighting. That's what Luke had promised.

Cameron's promise came back to him then too.

Grieving can feel safer, but moving on is what she would have wanted.

He'd been talking about his grandmother. Austin pictured someone younger, so much younger, and had to look away.

"Well?" Dom asked. "Can I at least get to have you for the morning? Make you some breakfast at my place? Maybe you could help me with a few chores. If you're good, I'll—"

Austin's phone interrupted with text confirmation of an interview later that day he should really prepare for. "W-what were you saying?" He dragged his gaze from a text that felt like a punishment, not a reprieve. "If I'm good you'll what?"

"I might let you climb my ladder. I know you've got a thing about them." Dom smiled then laughed at Austin's eye rolling, the sound echoing, rising like Austin's spirits, interview text forgotten.

He'd prepare for it later.

AFTER SHOPPING FOR FOOD, they took the coast road, Austin only clutching his seatbelt once before Dom noticed, easing his foot off the accelerator. The sea sparkling jade to one side also didn't bother Austin so much today, barely aware of waves with white tips in the distance or of the foaming froth where it clashed with the cliffs, too busy watching Dom steer. He tuned back into his surroundings once they passed the Porthperrin turn-off, sunlight gleaming on the windscreens of classic cars in the showroom on its corner.

"We're not going down to your place?"

"We actually are." Dom glanced in his direction, and if he'd ever looked more handsome, Austin didn't know when. Didn't know when he'd started to find seeing him in a frayed T-shirt spattered with paint endearing, but he couldn't stop sneaking glances, taking in that Dom must have left home in a hurry that morning, stubble adding a rough edge to a man who had a core of softness.

Dom caught his eye. "Been wanting to bring you home for a while now."

"Home?" Austin glanced out the window, only the arms of Porthperrin's harbour visible from this part of the coast road. "I've already been there."

"Nope," Dom said, changing gear, tutting at the groan of the Transit's engine. "This is my place. Told you I bought a cottage years ago to stop myself from killing Dad, didn't I?" He slowed the van, which seemed to sigh with relief as Dom pressed a remote, and wooden gates opened. "Welcome to Cliffside. I need to get it ready for Jason and Vanya. Think I mentioned I bought it years ago and used to let it out while I lived upcountry? I moved in once my divorce was final and I thought Maisie was settled in the village. It's my version of perfect." He chuffed out a laugh. "Christ knows the bedroom here makes mine at Dad's look tiny. That's the only room at his place I didn't bother extending. Didn't think I'd need to. If I'd known I'd move back in with him for so long, I would've knocked a few more walls down."

"You think you'll live with your dad long-term?"

"For as long as that's what Maisie needs. Having all of us closer together, I mean, even though this place is hardly far away. You can see it from Dad's and Gemma's. But because . . ." He unfastened his seatbelt, getting out, and Austin joined him, following him around the side of the building where Dom showed him why he'd chosen to live here.

The sea view was breathtaking.

They stopped where the back garden was fenced with clear panels and Austin saw where steps led down the cliff face, the bottom guarded by twin boulders next to a sliver of beach and rock pools. He looked up, Porthperrin just along the coastline. "You moved in with your dad because she didn't settle here?"

Dom shielded his eyes, staring where Austin pointed before agreeing. "She really didn't. Thought all that to-and-froing between us meant she wasn't wanted by either of us. Needed both of us much closer to her for longer. Maybe forever." He met Austin's eyes, his own searching. "Some people might think that's a problem."

That didn't sound as if he was asking a direct question, but Austin turned it over as Dom led the way back to a house that had appeared traditional from the road, but like his father's home, held surprises.

The frontage hadn't hinted at the light flooding through a wall of glass that slid back at the touch of a button. Through skylights too in the kitchen, light catching the glitter of some mineral in its stone counters.

Austin traced a thread of silver across an island where stools jostled. "Quartz," Dom murmured, pulling one of the stools out for him, grazing his lips with a kiss that was gone as soon as it had landed. "Not Mum's cuppa, but I still wish she got to see it." He flicked on the kettle before emptying bags of provisions into the fridge.

"You bought it—"

"After?" Dom cradled eggs and milk and butter, nudging the fridge shut with his hip. "Yeah. The winter she died. Dad and I gutted it together straight after." He found bread in the freezer. Popped slices in the toaster. Lit a flame under a frying pan that he'd lifted from a hook Austin now saw had been set into a beam carved with three sets of initials, a deep JB chiselled between Dom and his father's. "Argued about every fucking detail of how to renovate it until Jason did what I couldn't."

"Which was?"

Dom looked up from the butter he added to the pan. "Drawing what this place could look like if we could stop fighting for five minutes and work together."

"I can't imagine you two arguing."

"Me and Dad?" Dom smiled as he beat eggs next, adding them to the pan, which sizzled. He stirred, scrambling, and maybe this was easier to say while his hands were busy. "We needed to do it. Fight through the grief, I mean. What were the other options? Let it fester? Both of us were angry. She was too young," he said simply.

Austin didn't need to ask for more detail. Dom yielded more like the butter he spread on their toast, his voice soft. "This was more productive. I took out being angry about all the time I spent chasing profits, socking the cash away to pour into the next project. All seemed a bit pointless." His next glance was quick. "I mean, I know it wasn't. Means I get time with Maisie now. Get to have breakfast with a gorgeous view." He plated their eggs. Pushed one towards Austin, along with a mug of tea, and gathered cutlery that he stuck in his back pocket before heading outside again to a table with exactly what he'd promised, the view spectacular, but Dom sat with his back to it.

"You won't get to see much of the view from there."

"Already looking at the best one."

Austin busied himself loading his fork before giving up and setting it down because Dom hadn't quit looking at him. Hadn't quit making it impossible to do anything but return a smile he could only guess at over the rim of the mug Dom drank from, those creases feathering his eyes increasingly familiar.

Increasingly all his.

And maybe that realisation showed, no way to hide it here where the sun left nothing shadowed. Dom nudged his foot under the table, his murmur barely audible over the crash of the sea below the cliff at the end of the garden. "Eat before it gets cold."

Austin did his best, finding it hard to chew and swallow around more of what had hazed him that morning. He changed the subject. "So that's when you met Jason? When he drew up the plans for this place?" He shifted in his seat. Studied the addition to the cottage. But no, turning away hadn't helped, because Dom still watched him, smile broadening as Austin muttered, "Fuck sake," and gave in, leaning across the table, and Dom met him halfway, their kiss tea flavoured.

"Eat up," he finally said, lips tingling from Dom's stubble. "And I mean your breakfast, not me." His hand rose without conscious effort, touching the open neck of his shirt he'd have to noose with a tie later. Dom caught hold of his shirt collar, pulling it aside, his voice gruffer.

"Good thing that doesn't go up any higher. People would think your boyfriend was an animal."

Boyfriend.

Now there was no fucking way he'd be able to eat a single mouthful.

No point even trying.

Austin had to face this. "You know that I'm—"

"Going to see where this goes before deciding there isn't a future in it?" Dom delivered that alternate viewpoint along with a forkful of eggs that Austin chewed fast and swallowed so he could answer.

"I told you that I'm going to—"

"Keep making me wake up every morning so fucking glad we share a favourite number?" Dom scooped up another forkful, eyes threatening laughter that swiftly faded. "Or are you trying to tell me that you've already decided?"

"It's not a matter of deciding. I need—"

"To explain you're leaving to a little girl who thinks you've got a halo hidden somewhere?" His eyes softened, and from this close it didn't matter that his voice did too, teasing abandoned. Austin heard him clear as a bell, the words chiming deep inside him.

"You didn't just swoop in to save her. You rebuilt her wings. Then you doubled down by getting her back into the water, because it isn't only Gemma's house close to it, is it?" He turned slightly, eyeing the sea before facing Austin. "At the moment, both our lives revolve around her, but that's for good reason. I did hope Maisie could live here too one day, with me right here at Cliffside, when we've got a better idea about . . ." He set down his fork, mouthful untouched, studying his plate before his gaze lifted, that clear blue clouded.

Dom was a big man. A strong one. Still, he drew in breath as if he needed fortifying. "You saw that text from Gemma?"

Austin nodded, seeing the words *tell him about me* all over again, and maybe Dom did too, his kiss across the table quick. Sudden. A touch desperate before he asked another question. "And you remember me saying that I needed to check in with her about what she meant exactly?"

Austin nodded, feeling like those anemones must do each time they reached out not knowing if what they touched would help or hurt them. He nodded again when Dom pushed his plate away and asked a final question.

"Want to help me make up a bed for Jason and Vanya while I tell you?"

22

The interior of the house was beautiful. Austin saw that as Dom pointed out where Jason had blended traditional with modern touches, the joins between old and new seamless. That skill was in every room Dom showed him, but his head was too full of what might need an ex-wife's permission to pay much attention.

They made up a bed together in a room with a view that had to make this house priceless. Dom stuffed a pillow into its case, eyes fixed on the view instead of meeting his, and told him. "We didn't mean to have Maisie."

He dropped the pillow to the mattress. Dropped himself as well to sit on its edge facing away. "Kids weren't ever in our plan," he said, shrugging broad shoulders. "Maybe we both already knew we were better business partners than personal."

He joined Dom then, rounding the end of the bed to sit beside him, listening while he spoke, staring out of a floor-to-ceiling window where the sea went on forever, Austin not sure if Dom saw it

"We were drifting and we both knew it. I was over flipping houses, and that was the strongest glue between us. I wanted to do more of what I do with Jason. Architectural renovations. Rescuing buildings with a bit of history from ruin, not slapping two-up, two-downs with white paint and grey carpet for first-time buyers."

Austin saw those storm-damaged cottages in Porthperrin in a new light—not a money-making venture like he'd assumed, but exactly what Dom had just said, a rescue mission.

That's what he's really built for, but not only with houses. He does the same for people.

Like me.

I'd be dead without him. What the hell would that have done to Mum?

Dom kept going, unaware Austin had to blink fast a few times.

"Gemma was always more in tune with the figures. She's like you—brilliant with them. With leveraging the equity into new projects. We needed each other at the start to make that happen. I had the tools and construction know-how. The muscle," he said with a small smile. "But she was always the brains behind our operation." That smile faltered. "Long story short, we stopped needing each other." He shifted to face Austin. "Funny that it took Maisie for both of us to need each other more than ever."

He stood then and went to the bedroom window, facing Porthperrin while saying, "Took us coming home to a village where treating homes like spreadsheets entries would get us on the wrong side of the locals to see it. Getting the time to put that right feels so much better. Time we wouldn't have had without our daughter."

Austin stood too and joined him, seeing the house Maisie needed to feel safe in on the far end of harbour. "So you two didn't mean to have her? Or to move back here? Then—"

"Why did we? Might be easier to show you." Dom led the way out of the bedroom, pausing at the top of a staircase lined with framed photos. "We gave staying together one last go, but we both knew it was over. A month or so after first deciding to split, Gemma called me. Told me . . ." He touched the edge of a photo of a sweetly scrunched face wrapped in baby blankets.

"Maisie was on the way?"

Dom nodded. "And just like that, everything changed. Didn't grasp that until I held her. I think I said that loving a child is like having your heart beat outside your body." He tapped the photo-frame edge. "No ribcage to protect it. That's how I felt when I held her. Gemma too. We were both shit scared in our own ways. She was tiny, you know? We were even more scared when . . ." He swung to face Austin, and there—*there*—was a reminder of what he'd seen running towards him on the harbour, fear so sharp it knifed him. "When they told us about Maisie's issues."

"Issues?"

"It started with her low birthweight," Dom said before backtracking. "No. Actually, some of her measurements were off before she was born."

"Measurements?"

"Yes, when she was scanned. They do it a couple of times. Maisie ended up needing a couple extra. Something about the circumference . . ." He touched his forehead, and Austin might not have noticed the slight tremble of his finger if he hadn't made watching Dom a habit. Now he couldn't unsee this hint of a strong man shaking. Also couldn't miss that Dom only met his eye again briefly before resuming.

"Once she was born, she looked perfect to me, you know? Just tiny. But aren't a lot of babies?" He didn't wait for an answer. "So, yeah, she's still a bit wee compared to other kids her age, but it was hardly noticeable when she was an infant." He took a few steps down the staircase, pausing at another image of Maisie pointing at balloons celebrating a first birthday, her hair a curly halo like the woman who held her. Dom's finger didn't shake now, but his touch to both sets of curls looked gentle. "You know Gemma's been away since the accident?"

Austin nodded.

"I had to get down on my knees and beg her to go. Needed to plead before she'd leave Maisie to go to this place Vanya found for her. Somewhere to talk and listen with people who weren't me about some news we recently got. You know when I took Maisie to visit, before the swimming party?"

Austin nodded.

"That was the first time she ever told me that this day"— he touched the photo of a first birthday again—"was a low point for her. Gemma started to sink with me right beside her. I had no idea. It was a party, right? Nothing to be unhappy about, yeah?"

Again, it didn't sound as if he expected an answer.

"She was a year into being a mum, but this was the point when a final penny dropped for her, she said. All the kids there were from her new mums' group. All born the same month, and every single one of them was miles ahead of Maisie. They were pulling themselves up. Some of them were already walking. Maisie just . . ." He touched another photo,

Maisie lying on a rug pointing at the same balloons, face split by a smile just like her father's.

Or, like her father's would be if he didn't move on, taking a few more steps down, frowning. "I didn't notice as much as Gemma. We were living separately then." The next photo he stopped at documented another milestone, Maisie in Dom's arms this time, a fairy-tale castle rising behind them. "I was a bit of a Disney dad for a while. You know? Turn up on the weekends and do all the fun things with her, as if that's being a good father? Of course I didn't see what Gemma did every single day. Now she says that's when she started internalising."

"Internalising?"

"Noticing every missed milestone. Blaming herself for them. Little things at first, like Maisie not rolling over. Or like . . ." He made a pincer movement, thumb and pointer finger meeting, Austin reminded of Charles again, and not only for his teasing at Porthperrin's rock pools but for all the classroom activities he'd created to help—

"She still struggles with her grip? Like to hold a pencil properly?"

"Yes." Dom reached the bottom of the stairs next to a family photo of him and Maisie beaming, the woman beside them also making a sterling effort.

But her smile doesn't touch her eyes. Doesn't even come close.

This was a stranger, not someone he knew well, but Austin could have looked in a mirror, seeing the same pinched expression Charles had captured during that rock-pool visit.

Maybe that's what Dom focused on now too. "We'd moved back here by then, but I didn't grasp that she'd started to stack up each milestone Maisie missed like bricks." He focused on Austin next. "You know what happens when you stack those without a firm foundation?"

"They fall?"

Dom's nod was short. Swift. As blunt as what he next said. "Stack them high enough and it doesn't take much to make them topple. You'd never have known she was struggling. Gemma, I mean." He scrubbed his face, seeming to speak to himself. "Or maybe that's me kidding myself, but she was so on it regarding Maisie, you know? Always finding classes to stimulate her when she was a baby. Always reading. Always trying to improve—" For a moment he struck the same pose as his daughter had at the end of the sea wall, arms outstretched.

"Maisie's balance?"

"You noticed it's off?"

"But all kids fall ov—"

"Maisie's not going to stop."

Dom did though. He stopped dead then for a long, extended moment before dragging in a slow breath.

"Gemma's the one who never stopped. Never stopped searching for answers, but it's tough to get a definitive diagnosis with some kids until they're older. Until then, they're just behind the curve. That's what the paediatricians told us. Watch and wait was the verdict, but watching and waiting wasn't in Gemma's nature. She's like a lioness about Maisie, you know? Fierce. Protective."

He might as well have described himself, standing like he had so often, braced and steady with his arms crossed, but for once he sounded uncertain. "Then she found out about some genetic testing. Got it done just before the end of the school year. Going private cost a fortune, but we could afford it, so where was the harm, right? Besides, Maisie's teachers kept sending home notes wanting a discussion about holding her back again. That felt like another nail in a coffin for her progress."

"They just wanted to talk about what might be best—"

"Didn't matter. Before the testing, we didn't have any answers for them." He closed his eyes. "Part of me wishes we still didn't."

Dom moved away from the foot of the staircase as if trying to leave that behind, opening the front door, the crash of the sea suddenly louder. "Yes, some disorders are only passed on by one parent, but Gemma didn't need to know that, did she? Finding out that it was genetic—could only have been passed on by her, and that Maisie won't ever . . . That she'll actually get more . . ."

He struggled again, his voice so much hoarser.

"I found it tough then, being alone, no one to share being scared with. I couldn't make myself tell Dad right away, and that felt awful. But for Gemma, it really was one brick too many. She looked like she was dealing with it, but she wasn't. The bricks fell and they crushed her. I mean, she kept it together whenever she had Maisie. She's such a great mum. I could have been a better father."

His jaw clenched.

Austin wanted to touch where it ticked. Wanted to grab him by the shoulders and shake. Wanted to tell him that being better didn't seem possible from his perspective, but Dom wasn't done yet.

"Or at least I shouldn't have believed her when she said she was okay. Could have dug deeper after I started to get phone calls from the school to come get Maisie when Gemma should have. Turned out that when Maisie was at school, Gemma had too much time to think. Got lost in what-ifs. Lost track of time too when she was researching treatment options, and believe me, there's so much bullshit online to get lost in. That's why I was late so often. I didn't know she was blaming herself so much. That she felt like she had to fix it."

That rang bells for Austin.

He nodded, but he pictured his mother poring over a spreadsheet at their annual meeting. Pictured himself totting up each and every bonus, and nodded again, harder.

Dom frowned as if Austin might be agreeing that blame lay with a woman who actually reminded him of them both. For the first time, Dom sounded angry. "Gemma didn't do *anything* wrong."

Austin blinked. "I'm not saying she did." He didn't know how best to phrase this. "But blaming ourselves is what we do, right? It's human nature." This next part was harder to acknowledge but needed saying. "Only guilt isn't rational, is it? It takes over. Shapes all kinds of decisions." The sea crashing outside wasn't enough to drown out what he said next. "Trying to put things right can become an obsession."

"Yeah." Dom scrubbed a hand through his hair, anger gone as quickly as it had risen, something like relief its replacement. "Yeah, that's it exactly. I had to do something for her. Intervene, because . . .." He shut the front door, not ready to leave yet, scanning the wall at the foot of the stairs. He settled on a final photo, this one taken in a restaurant, Maisie grinning over a huge bowl of spaghetti, and he said a word Austin now realised he'd never mentioned.

"Her disability is pretty unique. When we got the results of the genetic testing, we were given a sheet about it. And about how any disability can be a big adjustment for new parents." He touched the bowl in the photo. "Compared it to planning a holiday to Italy because you want to see Rome and the Coliseum but getting off the plane to find you've landed in Holland."

"Holland?"

"Yeah." Dom touched Maisie's smile next, sauce on her chin familiar. "Nothing wrong with the Netherlands, it's just not what either of us expected. Sure, it doesn't have Rome or the Coliseum or a million other things we'd expected, but it's lovely in its own way, like her. And maybe that's a good thing." For the first time, his eyes held a hint of humour. "Maybe the Dutch drive a bit slower than Italians, but they still get to their destinations. Might even enjoy having more time to make the journey. It's a mental adjustment for parents, though. Learning to let go of expectation. Learning not to compare. Celebrating small wins instead of perceived losses. Getting used to a different timescale."

Like for reading, Austin guessed, remembering Dom's fist-pump reaction to Maisie reading a single word back at the pool, so slow in comparison to Austin's sister.

For a moment, he stood again in the library close to their home, willing Tamsin to hurry.

I should have slowed down too. Enjoyed the journey. Learned to have much more patience with her.

And for another moment, Austin didn't stand in Dom's hallway.

He sat next to a little girl in Glynn Harber's dining hall instead, helping her to twirl spaghetti.

Had he ever hurried Maisie like he had his sister?

No.

No, he hadn't.

Not even once.

Maybe losing Tamsin did teach me something.

His eyes welled and Dom noticed.

"Don't be sad," he said, gritty. "You know, you keep saying kids or a family's the last thing you're cut out for, but"—he rubbed the pad of his thumb under Austin's eye—"I can't help thinking this says different."

Dom kissed him before repeating what he'd said as if Austin needed to hear it again.

"Don't be sad. Yes, it's a different journey, but it's Maisie's, and I'm learning to love it."

―――――――――

DOM SHARED MORE on the way to the station, seeming to find it easier to talk while driving. He listed the impact of Maisie's condition, describing what she needed, his gaze fixed on the road the whole while.

So he doesn't have to look at me while he does it.

Something inside him coiled tight then, remembering Sol doing the same thing in what seemed like another lifetime. He'd stared ahead too on the way down to Cornwall while explaining that he wasn't only Cameron's uncle. He was his only option. His nephew's final chance for a family.

Family.

Austin shifted in his seat, that word still getting to him.

Why?

Because of what happened to mine?

No.

Because of what I did to it.

His hand rose to clutch his seatbelt as if Dom drove fast instead of crawling behind camper vans and slow-moving tourists.

Dom glanced his way, but at least a ghost of a smile

emerged. "Hey, what's with the death grip? I wasn't driving anywhere near the speed limit let alone over it."

"I know." Austin tried to peel unwilling fingers. Couldn't make them let go. Covered that failure by snapping out of nowhere. "I didn't say you were speeding."

Dom ignored that version of Austin yanking back tender feelers. He reached out instead, eyes still on the road, his squeeze to Austin's knee brief, and when had he learned to do that? Learned to ignore what kept others firmly at bay?

"The white knuckles were a giveaway, Aus. I get it, okay." He glanced Austin's way. "Not that this rust bucket could do more than fifty, but what I'm really saying is that you made it clear enough times already that being late for Maisie was no excuse for putting my foot down." He blinked. Glanced Austin's way again before admitting, "Can you understand why I was late now?"

Austin nodded.

"That's when Gemma was really sinking. It crept up on all of us. I couldn't ignore it after Maisie fell in."

They left the coast road behind, the station close now, and Dom reminded him of what he'd first told Austin on a date at the Anchor that seemed years ago, not only weeks.

"It was an accident. A miscommunication. But Gemma reacted like it was her fault too. Like she'd dragged Maisie to the end of the sea wall herself and shoved her in. Every single one of those stacked bricks that fell when she heard the test results crushed her all over again. Didn't matter that she spent the last six years fighting for her every single minute. And it didn't matter that she never stopped searching for ways to help her. It was a final straw." He slowed over speed bumps as they approached the station, care evident like it was in his description of what sounded like a breakdown Austin could all too clearly picture.

Dom parked at the station. He turned off the engine and twisted to face him. "But it was also good, because now we can rebuild."

And wasn't that what he did best, surveying ruins but seeing potential?

"That's what you gave me, Aus. Can't say it enough times —a second chance to rebuild my family. Renovate it into something better. Stronger." He drew in another of those slow breaths before letting it out in a hurry and blurting. "I know we said this—you and me—was only for now." He labelled something that felt far from insubstantial. "But you've got to know how I feel about making additions." He smiled then kissed him, his lips soft, stubble a brief, tingling rasp. "If you stayed, I think you'd make a good one."

He got out of the van to get Austin's case from the rear.

Austin followed. "A good what?"

"Addition," Dom repeated, wheeling Austin's case for him to the ticket machine where Austin fumbled his card, which fell.

Dom bent on one knee to scoop it up, a surprise reminder of the first time he'd knelt for Austin.

That time had been down to desperate relief. This time it came with three words that should send Austin running.

"To our family."

Dom stood, and it didn't matter that there weren't even hospital curtains between them and the rest of the world, he kissed Austin regardless, ending with their foreheads touching. "I didn't expect to end up in Holland," he said, huskily. "Didn't expect to learn to love it. You could come with us if you wanted. Maisie's smart enough to already love you. To trust you. So maybe think about that in London, yeah? A slower journey might also suit you better."

Everything inside Austin wanted to nod.

Wanted to jump into arms he knew could take his weight and hold him.

Instead, he said what he had to. What had always been coming. His one cast-iron commitment.

"But slow won't come with a bonus package."

"You know that money—"

Austin stopped Dom then. Had to before he offered to make his life far too easy. "No, this time I can't take your money." He backed through doors that slid closed on the end of his sentence. "Not when it's my debt, not yours."

23

W hat felt like the longest journey of Austin's life started then as he boarded the Penzance train bound for London.

It should have been more than enough time to prepare for an interview he needed to go well.

He scanned investment bank facts and figures on his phone, but precious few of them computed—couldn't while he kept seeing Dom's face before the station doors had closed between them.

How would he describe what had flickered across it?

Surprise?

That didn't quite fit.

Disbelief.

He saw that over and over. Replayed it as the countryside shifted from wild to cultivated, Cornwall merging with Devon, only the sight of back gardens like his mother's as the train rattled into Exeter bringing him back to the present. The urge to get off there instead of continuing was almost overwhelming. He stamped on it quickly. Going home earlier than expected wouldn't help. Calling Dom wouldn't either.

What would I even say to him?

Besides, everything he'd heard suggested that Maisie needed consistency, not someone who'd leave her.

The train pulled out, picking up speed, light flickering on the window like those justifications, somehow insubstantial. Not nearly enough reason to walk away from a man who . . .

Makes me happy.

Different images flickered then.

Flecks of glitter in Dom's stubble in a Porthperrin back garden.

On the wings he'd made for Maisie too.

The pool water at the Haven had sparkled as well, like Dom's smile at his daughter inching deeper.

He saw that all over again. Heard laughter too. *Cameron's*, he remembered, echoing and so happy it had almost sounded like . . .

Forgiveness.

So maybe . . .

He focused on something more concrete, opening a familiar spreadsheet tracking a target this interview could help him catch up with. Maybe exceed, if he negotiated a package with no loopholes, this time.

That was another Cameron reminder, keeper of a watch that hadn't been worth anywhere close to what he needed. But something else Cameron had told Austin flickered, receding like the trees bordering this stretch of train line only to rush closer again as he remembered.

The only way I could ever disappoint her was by missing a chance to be happy.

Austin's fist clenched around his phone then, tightening when it pinged.

Dom: *Sorry. I was too full on.*

No. He'd been perfect.

Dom: *Been thinking it for a while.*

Dom: *Every time I see you with Maisie.*

Dom: *Now I can't imagine you not being around to see her make progress.*

Austin couldn't either.

Fuck no, he really couldn't.

Dom: *Forgot to tell you good luck. Not that you'll need it.*

Dom: *You're brilliant. x*

Austin sat surrounded by strangers, not seeing anything but that single x at the end of Dom's last message, startling when another message pinged in, from Charles this time.

Charles: *Is it wrong to wish you bad luck?*

Charles: *Like, I really hope Heligan doesn't fancy your pants off and offer you a job?*

Charles: *But regardless, don't let him faze you.*

Austin got up. Made his way to the quieter space between carriages and called him.

Charles answered right away, whispering, "You really missed my voice so much you had to call instead of texting?"

"Miss you? Not likely." He had though. So much.

It struck him then that this train wasn't only carrying him away from Dom. A whole host of friendly faces filled his vision until he blinked hard again a few times.

"Of course I don't miss you, Charles. And why are you whispering?"

"Because they're interviewing Hugo in the next room, then it's my turn. They'll ask all those awful questions like what kind of animal would I be if I could choose. What would you be?" He answered for Austin. "A hermit crab, obviously."

"I know, I know. Too snippy."

"No." Charles sounded puzzled. "That's not the real you, is it? I just mean your old shell didn't fit so you've been looking for another, haven't you?" He made complex things so simple. "That's what hermit crabs do too, isnt it? Search for the right size shell to grow into? Now help me choose one, won't you? What kind of creature is fun but slutty?" Charles also answered his own question, laughing. "A Labrador, of course. Loyal unto death, but greedy. For love," he added. "Like me. Now why did you call? Be quick."

Austin swayed with the train's movement, bracing against a carriage wall. "Tell me why I shouldn't let your friend faze me?"

"Heligan? Because he's got a bit of a serial killer vibe but he's actually a sweetheart. One of the few boys at school who didn't flush my head down the toilet. Just don't let him fuck you."

"That bad?" Austin switched screens, googling, his eyebrows raising as the search loaded to show someone far from murderous, although those cheekbones did look sharp enough to draw blood.

"No," Charles said, almost purring. "That good. I don't call him Fucking Fabulous just because he bought me after-shave as a post-sex thank you. His cock's made of magic." Charles sighed fondly, forgetting to whisper. "One of my rare repeats, obviously, before I became a born-again-for-Hugo virgin."

"Obviously."

"So just stay out of Heligan's pants because believe it or

not I would actually like you to stay in Cornwall. Don't let him hypnotise you with his lovely penis—"

Another voice spoke then, muffled, like the answer Charles gave. He came back on the line a moment later. "Well, that was unfortunate timing." He rallied. "Or maybe it's better they know what they're getting. Not that I'm holding out much hope. The parishioners have already given Hugo a hard time about his stance on refugees during his question-and-answer session."

"Doesn't sound very Christian of them."

"Quite." Charles went quiet for a moment, the view out of the window more built up now, Paddington fast approaching. "Listen, talking about sex, what about Dom?"

Austin took a turn at being quiet then.

Charles sighed. "I was hoping he was the one who'd hypnotise you with his willy." His next sigh gusted. "Didn't you two click at all?"

"It isn't a matter of not clicking." Austin wasn't sure how to explain that sex with Dom had been a mistake for different reasons. One slipped out as Charles listened. "It's going to make leaving harder, that's all."

"So don't." Charles returned to animated. "Hugo isn't going to get this gig if they hate me, which means we'll get to have at least another year together! I'll call Heligan right now. Tell him that you got a better offer."

No.

He'd already had one from Dom but hadn't taken it.

Austin closed his eyes then, seeing a hundred different versions of someone this train carried him further away from.

Dom, checking his reflection that first time, nervous.

Dom, rolling his eyes at his father, standing in a kitchen he'd hand built for his mother.

Dom, guiding Austin's key into the right hole when his hand had shaken too much to do it alone.

Alone.

That's what he said was hardest.

Now I've left him alone all over again.

Charles brought him back to the present. "I'll call him right now for you."

That took a moment to process, his head not only full of mental images but with regret. "Call who? Dom?"

"No," Charles said softly. "But isn't it interesting that he's the first person you think of? I meant Heligan. I'll call him and cancel."

Austin straightened up, pulling himself together, which should be easier, surely? Now it felt as if every bone in his body needed setting. "No. Don't. Thanks, but I'll see it through now I'm here."

"Then you'll go to your mother's?"

Austin nodded as if Charles could see him, and maybe they'd shared close quarters for long enough that somehow he could.

"Come back right away afterwards, yes? Oh, it's my turn for the firing squad now. Wish me luck?" Charles lost any trace of laughter, saying exactly what Austin felt too. "Really don't want to let him down."

And that was the crux of it.

Going to this interview felt like letting down Dom.

But not grabbing the opportunity with both hands could let down someone he'd already done much worse to.

THE MAN CHARLES listed as *Mr Fucking Fabulous* in his phone contacts seemed far from that when Austin met him.

Oh, he was good-looking, all right. Austin hadn't expected anything less from the sex-on-legs description Charles had given or from those online photos. But the man whose office he was shown to was preoccupied, frowning, gesturing for him to take a seat while he was mid-phone call.

Austin sat, listening to an interest rate negotiation, aware a printout of his CV lay between them. Aware too that this office was exactly what he'd aimed for, its corner windows offering not only a view over the City of London's narrow streets but of a sliver of St Paul's in the distance. The cathedral dome shone in the afternoon sunshine while the streets below were shadowed, red double-decker buses the only spot of colour, so different from the view outside his Glynn Harber study window.

This man was in exactly the kind of seat he'd wanted. That he'd planned for, each rung getting him closer to what he needed.

Needed?

The word *owed* fit better. It also prodded something deep inside him he shoved down, still listening.

Heligan's side of the conversation was familiar. Aggressive in a way working with Luke meant he'd half forgotten. Hearing the cut and thrust first-hand was a stark reminder that working with Luke had been nowhere near as pressured.

Didn't mean we weren't productive.

He admitted something he'd made himself stave off.

I did some of my best work there.

Some?

Everything he'd done in Cornwall had felt more worthwhile than number crunching for bigger organisations. Yes, the grants he'd found wouldn't count for much here where transactions must total multimillions, but—

He heard Dom then.

"Turns out money can't buy everything I thought I wanted."

It really couldn't.

He heard him again, as clear as a bell over the drone of a conversation about profit and loss, Dom's voice coming through louder. Clearer. Touching a nerve that tingled.

"These days, what I value most costs little."

He'd meant Maisie, of course. And all of those ways to help her that he'd fashioned from offcuts of wood with his father, building an obstacle course to help her develop.

Austin's thoughts skipped to another huge return from a pint-sized investment while half listening to Heligan mention totals that could cover Glynn Harber's costs, and then some.

I loved hunting down cash for more free places.

Maybe Heligan saw some of that realisation cross a face Austin quickly schooled to be less expressive.

And when the fuck did I start showing how I feel to all and sundry?

Being open someplace like here would be as good as spilling blood in shark-filled waters.

That must have shown too, Heligan tilting his head in what might have passed for concern if Dom had done it. Now it came with a raised eyebrow. With a stare too, Heligan's gaze cool. Piercing. Steel instead of faded denim.

His voice was sharp too, a steelier version of Charles, who'd shared his schooldays. "Be with you in a minute, Russell."

Being called by his surname shouldn't throw him. It was usual in this environment—expected—so why did it set off a whispered warning as if he'd held a shell to his ear, not hearing the sound of the sea, but a clear order.

Go.

Leave now.

He had to grip the armrests of his seat to keep from doing just that, holding tight because, yes, this man might be someone with access to corporate sponsorship or big bonus potential, but...

I can't work somewhere soulless where first names don't matter.

When had he changed that opinion?

And fuck telling Sol that shortening mine was unprofessional.

Another whisper curled around him. Through him. Found the coil that had pulled tight on the way here, tugging until it started to unravel.

I never told Dom not to call me Aus, did I?

He almost shook his head, reining in that movement because the man Charles had hooked him up with said, "Russell?" again, before offering his own surname like Austin had heard at a hundred networking events. "Heligan. Shall we get this over with?"

Austin stood to shake with him, but Heligan's phone rang.

"Damn," he said, checking its screen, his voice clipped. "Got to take this. Sorry." He scrubbed at his face, composure gone for a brief moment. "Yes, yes, yes," he said to whoever had called. "Any chance of you getting to the point anytime soon, Pops? Only I've got someone with me—"

He broke off. Laughed. And there a glimpse of someone Austin could believe had appealed to Charles once because that burst of laugher rang out. "No, Pops," Heligan said, his gaze meeting with Austin's once more, this time a touch less steely, if not quite warming in a way Austin wished to God he'd taken one last long look at before leaving. "No, it's not a pretty girl. And thank fuck you finally retired and never leave the island, you sexist bugger, or I'd spend all day in tribunals." He rolled his eyes, surprising Austin into a smile of his own.

Maybe that was a mistake.

Heligan sat forward. "No, not a pretty girl," he said almost under his breath. "It's someone I'm seeing for a friend as a favour." He paused, listening. "A favour for who? Heppel. No, not George. The third one. Christ, why do you always need to know every single detail?" He leaned in to snatch Austin's CV from the table, casting a cursory glance that couldn't have gone much further than his education because he said, "We didn't go to the same school." He dropped the CV back onto the table. "You won't know the family."

That was enough.

Austin was done.

He'd seen and heard enough to know that coming here had been a mistake.

He got up, Heligan also rising. "Where are you going?"

"Back where I belong." That felt both right and wrong as soon as he said, "Home."

Maybe that showed on his face too, but it prompted something surprising.

Heligan spoke again into his phone. "Pops? I'll call you back." He lowered it, head tilting again. "Go on," he urged, nothing sharp about him now.

"With what?" Austin asked, flustered.

"With telling me where you belong, because now that you mention it, Heppel said he thought that you should stay where you were." He squinted. "And that's why he thought you might be useful to me. He also said we'd probably get along over a glass or three of Châteauneuf." He gestured at the exit. "Shall we?"

THEY WENT to a nearby wine bar, Heligan leading the way to a table before securing a bottle and two glasses. He poured extra-large measures, taking a quick sip followed by a longer one, his Adam's apple bobbing. "That's more like it," he said after a third deep sip, relief a reminder of office stresses Austin hadn't felt once at Glynn Harber. Then Heligan sat back, his gaze frank, and although he needed to speak up against the din of where this city really did its business, his tone changed, cut glass almost softening. "I've got a lot of time for Heppel."

Agreeing to that was easy. So easy. Austin nodded. "Me too."

"That's why I listened to him." Those sharp eyes crinkled, a surprise reminder of Dom, there and gone in a split second. "I would have contacted you eventually, but the photo was a nice incentive. He said you'd suit me, and he was right."

"Suit you?" Austin set down the glass he'd been about to take a sip from. "I'm not—"

"Looking to hook up like Heppel and I used to?" This smile also surprised Austin, nothing shark-like about it. "No, I'm looking for someone with a different set of skills." He raised his glass to lips that quirked after he'd sipped. "Mind you, if both are on offer—"

"They're not." Whatever had unspooled inside him on the way here reached its limit, a sharp tug at his insides almost painful. He shifted in his seat, an inch closer to the door than to this man who might hold the keys to his future. Keys he'd so badly wanted.

Needed.

Now I don't want them.

He shouldn't be able to hear his heart pound while businessmen brayed at the table behind him. Shouldn't be able to hear his watch ticking either, not while Cameron had it.

Another realisation landed, leaving him winded.

I don't want my watch back either.

Not even if selling it is the only contribution I can make towards my target.

Hitting it will never make me happy.

He pictured a near-empty perfume bottle, safe in a drawer in Luke's study, hidden under a pack of Kit Kats, then grasped his wine glass tighter.

I need to go home.

He said so.

"Neither are on offer. Not a hook up nor me coming back to work in London." He pushed his glass away. "Didn't know until I got here. I've wasted your time. Sorry."

"Interesting." Heligan watched him over the rim of his own glass. "And potentially a real shame, but if I'm honest, I'm not sure anyone could match up to Heppel. I've looked. Given up any hope of finding someone who makes me laugh as much while fucking. Bit of a hopeless prospect, so I've stopped trying." He leaned forward, elbows on the table, steepling fingers that weren't as thick or work roughened as Dom's. That likely woudn't be half as gentle either. "But Heppel did tell me about your skillset. You're good at audits, yes?"

Austin nodded.

"Good. That's what he promised. Heppel said nothing got

past you and that's what I'm on the hunt for to rein in a different kind of hopeless prospect. My grandfather. He has an island estate, Kara-Enys, off the coast of where Heppel says you belong."

"Belong? Where?"

"Cornwall."

He described a work opportunity that might have been intriguing if not for ticking that got louder instead of fading. That internal tugging didn't ease up either, pulling Austin to his feet, rising like the arch of Heligan's eyebrow.

"So, Russell, that's it in a nutshell. The old man needs a financial minder to find out what he's blown a fortune on lately. Someone to audit what's bleeding the estate dry all of a sudden. What do you think?"

"I think I need to run for my train." Austin extended his hand, shaking before grabbing his case and throwing a quick, "But it was good to meet you," over his shoulder.

If Heligan answered, Austin didn't hear him.

The door swung closed behind him and he took off running.

24

A ustin slid his case into the boot of a cab in Exeter, his taxi driver moaning all the way to the address he gave him. He started with the weather before moving onto football.

"You see the price of Grecian tickets this season?"

"No," Austin murmured, intent on his phone, thumb hovering over Dom's contact like it had a hundred times since making it onto a packed train by the skin of his teeth. He hadn't been sure what to text as he'd caught his breath, swaying with other standing commuters until a seat came free, once past Reading. Then he'd sat, only hearing Dom say, "Maisie trusts you," over and over instead of tinny dubstep from his seatmate's headphones, his quiet, "She loves you," somehow louder than a blaring Disney movie from further down the carriage. Precious little of that background noise had sunk in, like the cab driver's football conversation.

"They've put the price up again. Fecking extortionate."

Austin's hum must have been too non-committal. His

driver only griped even louder. "Like the price of diesel. Fecking—"

"Extortionate too?" Austin looked out of the window, then away, the cab almost at his old school, always tough to revisit, especially passing by as slowly as the speed limit forced traffic to crawl now.

His phone lit with a distraction. A message from the man who'd filled his thoughts all the way here.

He opened it to find a photo rather than text, a smile he couldn't help returning, and whatever had tugged inside him yanked so much harder. Seeing this snap of Maisie next to a rock pool with her best friend, both holding crabs and grinning, did something to him. So did the words that appeared beneath it.

Dom: *She's back at sealife school with Tor, can you believe it?*

Another message arrived.

Dom: *Thank you xxx*

He would have replied but something else yanked him from the moment. "Sorry," he said to the driver. "What did you just say?"

"Me?" The cab driver glanced sideways. "I said, fecking speed bumps."

"What about them?"

The driver blinked. "Well they're ridiculous around here, aren't they? Way too many of them. And too high." He gestured ahead. "Like these. Wrecked my exhaust a couple of times already, and I wasn't doing much more than thirty. Traffic calming they call it." He steered through a winding chicane that hadn't existed when Austin had been a student at the school they drove past. "Traffic calming," he chuffed. "Traffic hell, more like it, and all because some local busybody won't stop pestering the local council."

Another message *pinged*, but Austin's focus had switched, his voice dropping like his phone did into his lap. Like his heart did too, remembering. "You want to know what real hell is?"

Now the driver fell silent.

"Hell is knowing that your seven-year-old sister might have made it if the car that hit her had been going a few miles an hour slower." His cheeks heated, weird when the rest of him turned icy. "Did you know that only half of the kids that get hit at thirty miles an hour live?" He pointed at the twenty mile per hour sign they passed, knowing exactly how much each one had cost to purchase. To erect. To maintain.

I know down to the last penny because I watched Mum research the costs.

Saw her draw up the first budget.

Watched her set a target for one speed bump and street sign where Tamsin was hit.

Saw how long it took her.

What it cost her to ask strangers for money that the council promised to match.

I had to take that load from her.

"Traffic calming drops that percentage to ten per cent."

That statistic was still painful, his sister so much more likely to have made it if the car that hit her had been slower. He added a quick, "I'll get out here," paying fast and grabbing his case, walking the rest of the way until he saw what his mum had mentioned, the cherry tree in the garden shading the whole front of the house, overgrown, a branch still dislodging a gutter.

Because I keep putting off coming back here.

He knocked on the door, his mum taking a moment to answer, surprise registering first before delight.

"You're early!" Her rare smile was a blast from the past, his own instinctive one fading just as quickly when she added, "Good, because I took a look at the annual results for the company you work for."

Supernus.

A frown flickered, his mum's forehead lining. "Looks like they forgot to list Tamsin's charity in their matched-giving list. Can you call someone in your office? Check we haven't slipped through the net and are still on track to hit this year's target?"

And this is what I avoided.

She went inside.

Austin followed much more slowly.

HE SAT in a kitchen he'd once described to Dom as in need of updating, steeling himself for a conversation he'd dreaded. His fingers found a mark Tamsin had left on the table after finishing a piece of artwork, the pine dented by initials he traced before covering them with his tablet.

"Mum, I need to—"

"Tea?" She flicked on the kettle.

"No, I'm—"

She'd already opened the fridge for milk, a sketch held by magnets catching his eye as she closed it, a butterfly drawn in black ink that hadn't been there on his last visit.

"That's new."

"This?" She moved a magnet aside, bringing the sketch to him. "I printed it out after the last council meeting. Look at what we started."

Anyone else might have heard pride then.

Austin heard something different.

"What *you* started," he said, gritty, taking what was far from a drawing of a butterfly from her. It was a plan, he now saw. An aerial view of the streets around them.

That central part wasn't an insect's abdomen and thorax, as he'd first thought. It was the school building his cab driver had crawled past next to a play park Tamsin had loved. Streets extended from each side, winglike.

His mum touched the far edge of one. "Every single speed bump. See?" She pointed. "Here's the very first one." Her finger touched the spot Austin could see as clearly now as when he'd . . .

He shook his head as she listed street name after street name.

Closed his eyes.

Must have kept them shut long enough that his mother noticed, opening them to his mum's hand on his shoulder, her voice surprised and worried.

"Sweetheart? What's wrong?"

He shook his head again, then stood, taking the hug she offered—that he still needed, closer now to thirty than to the thirteen-years-old he'd been when slowing traffic through local rat runs had made his mum's grief productive.

When had that turned into a yoke across both their shoulders?

As soon as I earned my first bonus.

Felt like I could finally pay back what I owed her.

Thinking that was hard. Saying it was too. As hard as it had been to tell her what he'd done to their family. He whispered it into her hair.

"Supernus won't put Tamsin's charity on the matched-giving list, Mum."

"No?"

"No," he admitted, that lump in his throat back, bigger than ever. "Because I don't work there anymore. I left." And here was the part that he'd come here to say. "And I won't work for another company like it because I don't think Tamsin would want me to. She'd want me to be happy. You too."

It was that simple, a realisation that came with a slideshow of people he saw as he pulled out his phone. His sister came first. He scrolled to the photo his mum had sent of her in wings he'd done his best to recreate for Maisie. Austin had held Tamsin's hand in that old photo, grudging at the time, most likely. He couldn't remember. But even that had been a lesson.

Because I learned to love it every time Maisie needed my hand to balance.

It had been a second chance he hadn't known he'd needed.

"You see," he said, scrolling away from that reminder. "There's a little girl who I want to be around for. One who needs a bit of support now. Who might need more in the future." He moved on to the photo taken in Ken's hallway, Maisie's hands on her hips, so like her daddy. "I can't do that and keep climbing the same kind of ladder that helped me hit our targets." He quickly backtracked. "I mean, I'm sure I can still raise funds like you, but . . ." Austin met eyes the same shade as his sister's, which turned glossy. "But I'm not sure you continuing to do that is good for you either." He gestured at the kitchen. "You deserve nice things, Mum. Life's short."

He fixed his gaze on his phone rather than be the cause of more pain, the screen blurring until he blinked it clear just as his mother reached for it. He must have scrolled back because now Dom filled the screen, Maisie sleeping safe in his arms despite thunder, and Austin had never wanted anything more than to crawl in bed beside him.

Or, almost anything.

If his voice had turned gritty before, now he spoke through glass shards. Through guilt that still bled, turning each word crimson.

"I'd bring Tamsin back if I could." This truth was always the worst. "I can't. You can't either." He touched the printout again. "This is such a tribute. It's amazing. A legacy to be proud of." So many potential lives saved. So many other families shielded from pain tethering him to work he'd hated.

Now he had to cut it.

"Mum, I've always felt that Tamsin dying like that was my fault."

"Yours? No." Those glossy eyes welled. "Of course it was my—"

"Fault that the car hit her? How could it be? I was the one walking ahead instead of beside her, like you always told me to. Like you would have done, if you'd been walking with her. If I'd held her hand instead of being pissed off at how long she took choosing her books at the library, I'd—"

"Have been hit instead of her? You were, Austin. It hit you as well, remember? Yes, that car hit Tamsin first, but it fractured your skull too. I nearly lost you both." Devastation hoarsened her voice. "Your fault? No. Never."

For a last time, he felt Tamsin's fingers curl around his, ghostlike, while his mother shook her head. They let go as Austin said, "I'm just saying what both of us must subconsciously do every time we have this meeting—blame ourselves for something random. For bad luck due to

someone checking their phone while driving at thirty instead
of twenty. Bad luck that you managed to turn into something
different." He saw much more than a butterfly in that
printout summing up years of tireless effort. Had it cost her as
much as it cost him, each fundraising target he smashed only
raising the bar even higher?

He met her gaze then. Saw it swim. Pulled her into
another hug and spoke into her hair once more.

"It's Tamsin's birthday tomorrow."

She nodded, her arms coming around him.

"She'd want us both to be happy," he murmured. "I could
be happy where I work now." So happy in ways he didn't have
words for. "But I'm going to find it tough to let myself if you're
still here feeling guilty about something neither of us knew
was coming."

He paused, feeling her shoulders hitch, also feeling her
try to stifle that movement as he continued. "So this year, can
we make her birthday different?"

She nodded, her shoulders shaking again as Austin
suggested a way to make that happen.

LATER, they rooted through what Charles had described as a
cupboard of doom, unpacking what had taken up space for
too long. Or maybe it had stayed filled for exactly as long as
they'd both needed because his mother shared while looking
for what Austin had requested.

She set aside one of Tamsin's old dolls. A teddy too,
before saying, "Ah. Here it is." She opened a box crammed
with old art works that she dug through. Some came apart in
her hand, glitter scattering on the upstairs landing carpet. "I

don't know why I kept all of this when I finally redecorated her bedroom," she admitted, a few seashells dislodging from a craft project despite the gentleness of her touch.

Austin had a pretty good idea, in hindsight. "That was the autumn I went to uni. The same month *he* got out of prison." He didn't need to name the driver who'd killed his sister.

"Yes. That's when I really ramped up the fundraising." She stood. Took the box to the kitchen where she unpacked it, the pot of glue she found long dry, the glitter still shiny. "Starting the charity kept me busy, but did it . . ."

"Did it what?"

She met his gaze, her own bare.

Raw.

Worried.

"Did it put you in a different kind of prison? You know I never expected you to raise so much money, don't you? More every year? I thought you must want to."

"I did." He'd needed to in order to pay a debt he now grasped neither of them owed. "But recently I met someone who—" He ran a hand through his hair, confused for a second that it snagged his fingers, it had been so long since he'd worn it slicked back to fit a mould he wasn't cut out for.

"You met someone?"

"Yes, someone who talked to me about guilt." Because that had been Austin and his mother's taskmaster. He knew that now. Could see it as clear as day in each ladder rung he'd clambered. And in how he'd walled himself off from Sol and Cameron. "The person I met says it can stack up like bricks." The walls they'd built together needed to be demolished. Or most of them did, at least. He touched that butterfly aerial view. "I mean, some bricks *can* be constructive. Can build something worth celebrating if they start with firm founda tions. The only way to know for sure is to check that you're working from the same blueprint. To talk instead of assuming."

He found a sheet of paper and a paint palette then, the colours dull and bone dry until he added water, turning vivid as if time had stood still since his sister had last used them.

In some ways it had.

And that's a shaky wall right there.

"We could talk about the charity while I make this, if you wanted? How it started and where to go next? Take it in turns so we're clear that continuing is what Tamsin would have wanted?"

His mother nodded. Found him the paintbrush he needed. Nodded again when he said, "Do you want to start?"

She hesitated, seeming lost.

That lump in his throat finally dissipated. "Ask me anything, Mum. Doesn't have to be about the charity or Tamsin. Just get the ball rolling, yeah?"

"Anything?" She drew in a slow breath he recognised as his own coping mechanism, finally asking, "What . . . what are you making?"

"An invitation." He flashed a quick look across the table, wary. "Not to Tamsin's birthday. I know we don't exactly celebrate that." He wasn't sure now if their annual meeting falling on the same day each year had helped either of them. "It's an invitation to tea. That little girl in the photo invited me to tea a while back. I'll invite her to come here, to return the favour, if that's okay with you. If not, that's fine too. I can invite her to the school where I work instead."

"You've been working at a school?"

"That's where I met . . ." *My boyfriend* felt presumptive. Also didn't feel big enough to describe what welled inside him. "Her father. He's called Dominic. Dom. She's called Maisie. She loves glitter. Anything bright and sparkly. Really loves a party." Austin focused on that aerial view again, then outlined some butterflies of his own with clumsy brushstrokes he guessed Sol would smile at. "They come as a package, Mum. She's pretty special."

What had welled inside spilled over, no way to hold back what felt this true.

"They're both special to me. Special enough that I want to stay in Cornwall to see where we're headed. So I'll take a photo of this when I'm finished. Text it to him and hope he's got time spare." And he'd also hope that Dom read the real message behind it.

I want you both.

"So, that's what I'm making. Not sure if he can come. He's got friends visiting, but the hardest part is asking, right? And what's the worst that can happen?" He winced. They both knew the answer to that question. "So, it's my turn to ask a question now, okay?"

His mum nodded for a third time, found a paintbrush of her own, adding colour to the wings he outlined, the soft blue she selected perfect.

Austin asked, "So how do you see the charity working in future, if I stay in Cornwall long-term?" Then he painted, ready to listen.

25

Austin woke late the next morning to the sound of something scratching at his bedroom window.

Those cherry tree branches.

He rolled over to see them silhouetted against the curtains, blocking most of the bright sun behind them.

Too bright for it to be early in the morning.

He fumbled for his phone then and checked it—almost ten o'clock already, a text from Dom waiting, sent hours earlier.

Dom: *Showed Maisie your invite when she woke up. She's excited. Also stroppy. Can't believe you're making her wait until teatime. Kid's got no patience.*

A photo followed, Maisie sitting cross-legged in her grandfather's hallway, the light streaming through the front door's glass panes burnishing a halo of curls. She'd look angelic if she wasn't pouting.

He smiled. Couldn't help it. Smiled even more at the message that followed.

Dom: *Then Dad told her she better behave in case Santa was watching.*

The next photo showed Maisie flat on her back, arms and legs a blur, meltdown in progress.

Dom: *Just so you know what you're getting into.*

He didn't need that warning. He'd seen the best and the worst already and wanted it all regardless.

And now I might get to have it.

Austin stretched then, bones cracking, still bleary but with something new tugging at his heart this morning. This rope wasn't constricting. Didn't cinch tight and yank him. It tugged gently and Austin went with it, heading still half-asleep to the bathroom, almost tripping on the way there.

The boxes he and his mum had pulled out last night spilled across the landing, some propping open a door that usually stood closed during his visits.

Today he surveyed Tamsin's bedroom and it didn't matter that the essence of her had been stripped from it years before —that it had been redecorated, the furniture reconfigured. He still saw her. Maybe he always would, and that was okay. He could breathe around that now he'd touched a few of the things she'd treasured. He and his mother had placed them on a shelf last night, out in the open instead of hidden.

There were more boxes to sort through that he nudged aside on his way into the bathroom—more bricks that would take longer than one night to dismantle—but at least they'd started.

He turned on the shower and hunted for a toothbrush. Met his own eyes in the mirror before steam could cloud it. They were less shadowed this morning. Everything was when he finished showering and dried off, walking back into a brighter bedroom.

So much brighter.

He blinked in sunshine that had been blocked by branches when he'd woken. Now it streamed, only hindered by curtains he yanked open to see the reason for the difference.

Austin saw the van first, Dymond and Son on its side peeling, and he laughed. Laughed again as he opened the window.

Dom stepped away from the base of the tree, a wood saw in his hand, shoulders speckled with sawdust and splinters from the branches he'd cut back already, grinning.

"Morning, sleeping beauty. You got my texts?"

Austin nodded, speechless.

"Turns out Maisie wasn't the only one with no patience."

Austin meant to ask, *What time did you set off?* Something different popped out.

Dom dropped his saw.

He went back to the base of the tree and grasped his ladder, which he repositioned.

Then he climbed, sure and steady, filling Austin's window, blocking the light for the best of reasons. "What did you just say?"

"I-I said, I love you?"

Maisie wasn't the only Dymond whose smile could rival the sun. Dom's did then too, not dimming a fraction as Austin quickly backtracked. "I mean, I could probably fall for you, if you wanted."

"Probably?" Dom climbed inside the bedroom, an audience across the street watching, Austin noticed, once he cleared the sill. "*If* I wanted?"

"Christ, the neighbours saw that. The police will be here any minute."

"Over the road? Nope. Your mum talked to them. Introduced Maisie before she took her to the shop. For party food, she said." He came closer, touching Austin—his face first, cupping his jaw, his own head tilting. "Maisie went to her right away. You've got the same eyes. Soft as butter."

"I've been called a lot of things." His breath caught at Dom's hand lowering to where he'd left a mark the last time they'd been this close with only a towel between them. "S-soft isn't one of them."

"Soft as butter," Dom repeated, thumb brushing his love bite. "Kind as well, like your mum. Maisie was sad when we got here. Forgot to bring her dolly." His hand slipped to the nape of his neck, exerting gentle pressure. "You know what your mum did while you were snoring, Sleeping Beauty? She magicked one out of nowhere." His lips brushed the shell of Austin's ear, the tingle another kind of magic, his cock stirring. His heart too, which swelled because Dom quietly rumbled, "That's how I know she'll take good care of Maisie. You must have learned how from her."

"I'm . . ." Austin angled his head, seeking more sensation. "I'm actually quite cut-throat."

Dom laughed, a breathy warm gust, and Austin melted.

"Sure you are." Dom breathed, his lips soft where they next landed, exploring, dotting a trail back to his mouth. "So cut-throat I fell for you too."

For a second time since meeting, they stood next to an open curtain and embraced.

This time, doctors and nurses didn't pass by as their mouths connected, and if the neighbours across the street still looked, they soon lost sight, Dom going where Austin pushed him, the bed creaking as he sat on its edge.

If it creaked again as he climbed onto Dom's lap,

Austin didn't notice. All he heard was Dom murmur, "So you decided against London?" and felt his hands skimming his sides too, big and broad and all his as he nodded.

Austin nodded again, harder this time. Kissed him and couldn't stop, apart from saying, "I got a better offer."

He wound his arms around Dom's neck, holding him tight even though rough splinters of sawn wood dug into his bare chest, wanting Dom even closer, ignoring where they poked him.

Dom didn't ignore it. He pulled his T-shirt over his head and tossed it to the side, brushing rough flecks off Austin's skin, kissing where they'd dug in. Then he shifted him off his lap, pushing until Austin lay flat and let Dom unknot the towel around his waist to kiss each bare inch from his throat to his pelvis.

If Austin had thought something inside him had pulled tight before, he'd been wrong. Now whatever it was didn't yank or tug or tighten. It snapped, freeing him for good.

Maybe Dom felt that happen, sensing that Austin was all in. That what he'd blurted before Dom climbed in through his window had been honest. Heartfelt. That the *I could probably fall for you* he'd added was bullshit. He'd already thrown himself headfirst in love with the man kissing his way back up his body.

Now Dom lay across him, kissing Austin deeper, his mouth open and hotter. Wetter. His breathing was heavy, his weight grounding as he promised, "Love you too, Aus."

Austin had never got a hand between them faster, grasping Dom's belt before asking, "How long ago did they leave?"

"Your mum and Maisie? Five minutes? Maybe ten?" Dom

kissed his throat, mouth finding that spot that made Austin curl around him, arms and legs tightening.

Around him? I'd crawl inside him like one of those fucking crabs Charles showed me and never leave, if that was an option.

Dom lifted his head, black ink of his pupils spilling over the same blue of the butterflies Austin had painted. "She said they'd stop at a play park on the way back. Let Maisie run off some steam."

That gave them enough time for Austin to push back and unfasten Dom's trousers, getting his mouth on him, but only briefly. Then he moved where Dom steered him, making the most of a shared favourite number.

Dom's mouth was warm on the head of his cock as Austin knelt over him, his knees shaking at the sensation until Dom pulled off, his voice hoarse. "Feel free to join in anytime you're ready."

Austin laughed then, not caring if the sound carried through the still wide-open window, joy rising like Dom's cock did, pleading for attention. He gave it plenty, lips stretching, tongue flicking then pressing, doing his best to take him as deep as he could without collapsing at Dom doing the same, his hands gripping the cheeks of Austin's arse and squeezing before finding his hole with the wet tip of a finger.

Austin let out a groan then, choking around his mouthful, and Dom rolled him, gasping, getting his mouth back on Austin's cock once he was flat on his back. Dom knelt at the side of his bed as if in worship, his head bobbing, their eyes meeting as Austin lifted up onto his elbows, gaze holding until he pulled off and made a promise.

"Going to give you everything you ever wanted."

That's you.

Austin's head fell back, Dom sucking him again, his lips

bumping against fingers that wrung out pleasure, his head bobbing faster, maybe aware Austin's climax was on the horizon. Aware too that they needed to hurry.

Austin saw his other shoulder moving.

"You getting yourself off?" He didn't wait for an answer, wriggling until he could reach him, cupping balls that pulled up as he got a hand on them, Dom close to the edge as well. He felt Dom's touch stutter. His head slow its bobbing. Felt him start to come, a wet pulse striping Austin's wrist as Dom groaned, lifting his head, leaving Austin's cock wet with spit and shining. Aching until Austin got himself off too with Dom watching.

His hand flew, his breath catching, unable to look away from a man he wanted to wake up to every morning. Be the last thing he saw each night before sleeping.

"Yeah," Dom said as if he agreed, and Austin's orgasm washed in, waves of pleasure so strong he couldn't breathe for a moment, so deep he saw stars at the edges of his vision, time stopping when maybe he should pay attention, but that was okay.

He could float for a while longer—let himself drift with Dom beside him—happy as they came down, kissing.

———

THE PLAY PARK wasn't far from the house.

Austin's steps slowed halfway there, then stopped, Dom taking a moment to notice.

He backtracked. "You forgot something?"

"No. I was remembering." Austin pushed back still-damp hair and pointed to the building beside them. "This is the library I took my sister to every Saturday."

Dom surveyed the building, maybe guessing it meant more than bricks and mortar to Austin. He nodded, saying nothing, waiting.

I love how he does that. Doesn't ever hurry me to share.

It made him want to.

"It's where we were the day she was hit."

Dom's gaze landed on speed bumps that now forced drivers to slow down. "By a car?"

Austin nodded. He resumed walking, stopping again fifty yards or so later. "Right here." He reached out to wrap a hand around the first twenty-mile-per-hour sign his mum had campaigned for.

Again, Dom paid attention, waiting.

Austin drew in a slow breath. He pointed to a low wall that had been rebuilt enough years ago that it didn't stand out now. "The car hit her first. She wouldn't have known a thing." He closed his eyes, hoping. "Hit me next. Not sure if the wall broke my skull or the car did."

"You were hurt?" Dom moved then, sweeping hair from Austin's forehead as if a reminder would still show on his outside. Nothing did, not from Porthperrin's rocks or from an accident he now let go of blame for. Or at least tried to.

"I was hurt. It healed quickly, but I stayed hurt in here for a long time." He tapped his temple. "Because I couldn't stop thinking that it should have been me." He couldn't look at Dom then. Couldn't handle the sight of that much caring. His gaze flicked across the street instead at his old school. "Kids can be cruel, right?" Not all schools were Glynn Harber. "I was already a bit of a target for bullies." He lifted his chin. "Small and skinny? Liked statistics instead of sport? Not interested in girls?" He shrugged. "They didn't get to me until . . ."

Traffic passed.

One car.

Two.

Both driving slowly.

Safely.

"What did they do, Aus?"

"Made sure I got reminded every single day that I'd let my sister die. That I didn't take good enough care of her. That I was the one our dad must have hated the sight of because he left right after the funeral." He flashed a look Dom's way. "He didn't leave because of me." Austin knew that now even if he'd internalised a different version after years of taunting. "People handle grief differently, that's all. He and Mum weren't like you and your dad. They pulled apart, not together."

"Still tough for . . . How old were you again?"

"Thirteen." Still very much a child, in hindsight, now that he remembered Cameron not coping with bereavement.

I was so tough on myself.

He let go of that now like he did the pole to continue walking with Dom beside him. "Bit ironic that I ended up spending most of my time in the school library after that. It was my safe space even though I could never make myself go back in there." He gestured back at the public library they'd passed. "But the school library was different. That's why once the art building renovation is finished, my next project is going to be extending Glynn Harber's library. I'll find the funding to make it bigger and restock it." Make sure it offered the same kind of soft and squishy reading areas that his sister had loved.

He saw Tamsin then, sprawled on cushions, taking her time choosing books, and in his mind's eye, he let her, sitting beside her as if no clocks ticked. He turned pages as slow as she liked, not in any hurry, like he'd get to do from now on with Dom's daughter.

I love her too.

"Extending it?" Dom asked, talking easily as if he didn't notice Austin rub at his eyes. "You planning on a rebuilding project?" He slid an arm around his shoulders. "Tell me all about it before we get to the play park?"

Austin did, walking towards the sound of Maisie's laughter, sharing happier plans for all their futures.

EPILOGUE

Porthperrin
Nine Months Later

The day the art building reopened, Austin rolled over in Dom's cramped boyhood bedroom, not sure why he'd woken. He grabbed his phone, blinking at a blank screen. *I didn't miss a call.* He blinked at the bedroom window next. *And it's definitely not the seagulls.* He'd spent enough nights here now for them not to wake him.

The source finally registered.

"Shit."

He lurched bolt upright.

"That's the front door sensor."

Austin scrambled, rolling out of bed so fast he stumbled, almost colliding with a wardrobe too big for the small space. The curtains fought back next instead of opening, the window latch also uncooperative, until one finally swung open.

The street below was empty, only bunting fluttering, no sign of—

"Maisie!" he bellowed, seagulls taking off from surrounding roofs, shrieking.

"She's with Gemma, remember?" Dom answered from the doorway, a tea tray in hand. "Dad's gone to collect her and forgot to turn the alarm off, but ten out of ten for that foghorn impersonation."

"Ah." Austin breathed again then, heart still hammering. "I thought—"

"That she'd snuck out for a Saturday morning stroll along the sea wall?" Dom teased, but he set the tea tray down to squeeze Austin's bare shoulder, aware too that time might be a healer, but some scars never faded. His voice gentled. "Sealife school starts early today, remember?"

"Because of the tide," Austin remembered. The rest of last night's conversation also washed back in. "It'll be higher than usual. She'll be okay?"

"Dad will bring her back if she wobbles. One small step at a time, right? Either way, she'll be back in plenty of time to come to the station later. I don't know who she's most excited to see out of your mum and Vanya." Dom untied his robe, and nine months hadn't been long enough for complacency to set in at the sight of his jersey boxers clinging. "You okay going without me? I've got to shoot off. Jason's found a leak at the art building."

"A leak? Around one of the restored windows?" That was surprising, the filigree of ironwork still spiderweb fine, but no longer brittle.

"Nope, a pipe leading to the new sprinkler system. Better

to find it now while the building's empty than when it's full of artworks later. It's one of the joys of renovation—fix one thing, find three more issues." He took a quick sip of his tea before checking the time and gulping another. "It's nothing that a bit of copper pipe and solder can't put right, but I need to leave in twenty minutes if I'm gonna fix it before Luke's final inspection."

He passed a mug to Austin, maybe noticing the remains of a tremor as he reached for it. "Hey," he said, quieter, not letting the mug go yet. "Sorry you had a shitty wake-up, but you know you don't have to worry about Maisie getting out without anyone noticing, don't you? This place and Gemma's are like Fort Knox now. Cliffside too, even if staying in Porthperrin is all Maisie's comfortable with right now."

His gaze switched to the window at a house visible along the coastline. "She'll want to stay there again with me one day. Soon, hopefully. It'll be empty now Jason doesn't need a base here." He added, "Small steps," as if reminding himself of what he'd just told Austin. "Until then, I can put up with a tiny bedroom if being here makes Maisie feel cared for."

Austin knew that. Had stayed over often enough to see the same care in action he'd also witnessed at Glynn Harber, Maisie making steady progress now the teaching team knew her issues.

Perhaps the same care showed on his face.

Dom wrapped Austin's hands around the mug. Covered them with his own. "Just wish we got more time alone without my dad or your housemates one room over, so drink up," he ordered. For once, Austin didn't argue, early wake-up heart rate finally slowing only to pick up again when Dom kissed him between sips, his lips cool against Austin's tea-warmed ones. "Done?" he finally rumbled.

Austin took a last gulp, nodding.

"Because I'm not." Dom took his mug and set it aside. "Not while something else has got you worried. Apart from Maisie, I mean." He kissed him again, if only briefly. "Because something had you tossing and turning all night, so hurry up and spill it because how often do we get this place to ourselves?"

"Almost never." Like at the stables, privacy here was rare and precious. "It's nothing." Austin met a gaze that didn't waver and the floodgates opened. "Okay. Okay, I'm nervous, which is stupid, but Mum sounded lost the last time we spoke, and I'm not sure how to help her. Not like I used to."

"Because old habits die hard?"

Austin nodded.

"You know you don't have to solve every problem for her, don't you? She'd hate hearing you thought you had to. Wouldn't surprise me if she's nervous too." He opened his arms, which Austin stepped into, breathing easier for the first time since waking. "So, yes," Dom murmured, "Tamsin's charity was a huge part of her life for a long time. No wonder it's left a gap, but the right thing will come along to fill it sooner or later." Dom let him go, tilting his head. "Maybe solving a problem for me might take your mind off it?"

"You've got another problem aside from the leak?" Everything inside Austin came to attention. "What is it? Maisie? You don't need to worry about her. I'll look after her, I promise."

"I know you will. Here's my real problem." Dom backed off before shrugging out of his robe and dropping his boxer briefs as well. "Is twenty minutes long enough to get us both off, get showered, and have a shave too?"

Austin smiled then, stifled it fast, and tried to sound his

old version of prickly. "Well, that's quite a steep target." Narrowing his eyes was pointless while Dom's twinkled. "But I do like a challenge." He tilted his head like Dom had just done. "Want to know my answer?"

Dom nodded, palming his cock before mirroring a grin Austin felt spread without permission, all his worries slipping.

"We should prioritise. Only do what's most important." Austin led the way to the shower room, mirror reflecting a traffic stopper he barely noticed, too intent on turning on the water. "Besides." His voice echoed as he stepped under the spray, tugging Dom in to join him. To kiss him. To find his ear and whisper, "I like your stubble. And not shaving will give you at least five more minutes to blow me."

Dom laughed, and everything felt better. Brighter. Warmer.

Steam rose and Austin did too, Dom's hand on his cock distracting him from a clock that must still be ticking. But here, in a bathroom remodelled by the same hands now drawing pleasure from him, Austin hoped that clock would stop, or at least slow so he didn't have to rush running soapy hands of his own over each of Dom's solid contours.

He reached too far, slipping. Almost falling.

Dom caught him.

"I've got you."

He did, both feet firmly planted, water running down legs that were as steady now as that first time on the harbour. Only his shoulders had shaken that day with the strength of feeling Austin couldn't have guessed would ever aim in his direction. Or that would build into something far too big for occasional nights sharing a cramped Cornish bedroom, not when Cliffside would soon stand empty, waiting for a family to fill it.

Small steps are what's best for Maisie.

Taking it slow.

But the minute she's ready, I'd live with him there full time in a heartbeat.

Wanting that so much prompted a shiver. Dom steered him under the water as if he needed warming, washing soap from Austin's torso, his mouth following, lowering as Dom sank to his knees. He held Austin's cock then and mouthed it, sucking for a slow, delicious moment only to wipe water from his eyes before taking him deeper, his dark hair plastered flat and glossy. Austin ran his fingers through it, pushing it back, gaze fixed on eyes that might have been what he'd first fallen in love with.

Fuck it, I've loved all of him since . . .

A thousand memories flickered.

So many stolen moments, like doing this in the studio at midnight, the building shrouded mid-renovation, glass reflecting a hundred versions of this man kneeling. Sex in the back of the Transit van too, so desperate for each other, Charles teasing him for sawdust in his hair was worth it. And rare lazy mornings at Cliffside, Jason not there and Maisie safe at home with Gemma. The sea stretched beyond the bedroom window there forever, like he wanted with Dom.

Austin's head tipped back as sensation mounted, not seeing the room they filled with steam now. Instead, he clutched Dom with his eyes closed, oblivious to whether he grabbed his hair or shoulders, close to coming in only minutes.

Fast is good but, yeah, I want the chance to go slow with him more often.

Downstairs, a door slammed, Ken's call of greeting another seagull-scaring bellow. "Hope no one's been naughty while I was gone. You never know when Santa Claus might be watching!"

Some privacy would be good too.

Dom nodded as if he agreed, eyes dancing with silent laughter before focusing on getting himself off fast too, his head still bobbing, lips a tight ring of pleasure that suddenly loosened. He came first, gasping, and if his release spattered Austin's legs, he didn't notice, too busy finishing what Dom had started.

He tightened his grip on his own cock, fist flying, heart racing for the best of reasons.

Dom smiled up through falling water, sucked a finger, and helped him to hurry.

DOM HAD BEEN RIGHT, Austin decided on the way to the station. Old habits did die hard, apprehension mounting the moment he started the Range Rover's engine. He'd also been right that Maisie would be a good distraction. She bounced with excitement that exploded on the station platform at seeing two of her favourite people.

Austin hung back as she gave Vanya a one-armed hug before leaving him holding her dolly, freeing both arms to do something that drew Austin closer.

"Oof!" his mother said as Maisie threw herself without hesitation, trusting another Russell would open their arms and catch her. "Well, that's what I call a warm welcome." She met Austin's eyes over a narrow pair of shoulders that were somehow like her father's broad ones, holding a family together. "I don't know why I was nervous."

Austin breathed easier after a hug of his own, reuniting on new terms easier with a Dymond in the mix, no way to stay in the past while Maisie dragged them forward with constant questions.

"Yes," his mother said on the way to Glynn Harber. "I am staying for the whole weekend."

"Where?" Maisie sounded hopeful. "In one of my bedrooms?"

"No. But I'd love to visit, if we have time. You could show me how your wings are holding up." She lowered her voice to almost a whisper. "I've brought some extra sparkles with me in case any of the old ones fell off."

Austin glimpsed Maisie wriggle in the rear-view mirror, squirming with joy, and a second real smile of that morning cracked wide open. "You'll like Cliffside though, Mum. It's less than a half mile on from Porthperrin. Only a ten minute walk along the coastal path, and the views are spectacular."

Vanya murmured his agreement, Russian accent soft and rolling. "Is very beautiful location. The house too. My husband calls it his very best renovation." And not just of a building. Would Dom have known how to rebuild his family without learning to talk his way through pain there and come out with something stronger?

Austin glanced sideways to see Vanya watching, and nodded. "Dom loves it."

Vanya murmured, "Would be best as a family home." He glanced over his shoulder at Maisie who still chatted, keeping his own voice low. "How is she doing? I know you made progress with water, but is she feeling easier around the sea yet?"

Maisie couldn't have heard his question, but the secret she whispered to his mother was as good as an answer. "Do you know what's at the end of Cliffside's garden?" She wiggled fingers like anemone feelers and applied the same volume control as her grandfather. "Rock pools!" She added a quieter, "I could look in lots of them if Daddy lived there again. Mummy told me."

Austin tucked that away as he drove into Glynn Harber, heart lifting at Gemma raising the subject like the car did over brand-new speed bumps. Lifted too at her feeling ready for more distance—another small step to build on.

That's what mum and I did too. Built something together, only it took over.

Maybe because we didn't talk like they all do now.

There were reasons for that, he thought as they drove past Cameron and Teo who carried easels to one of the school's minibuses, both of them seventeen and man-sized.

Thirteen was far too young to know I was drowning in guilt, or to know how to tell her.

They passed Sol next, the same dark eyes as his nephew warm with greeting.

And Mum had to deal with bereavement and with me too. No wonder fundraising was easier than dealing with her feelings.

Today, talking came much easier, especially with Maisie shouting, "Diamonds!" as he pulled into a crowded car park.

His mother asked, "Is that . . . ?"

Vanya turned in the passenger seat. "The art building? Yes. So much glass, and now none of it is broken. Look at before and after." He opened the Balfour website on his phone to show her.

Austin switched off the engine and turned in his seat to peer where Maisie pointed, and yes, it did look as though diamonds sparkled above the tree line, gleaming like Maisie's eyes. Once out of the car, she almost slithered out of Austin's hold to rush towards it.

Austin caught her. "Hey, you be careful, yeah?" He held her hand. "There's lots more cars here than usual today. Besides, you need to take a drawing with you, remember? For the first art show in the new building?" He went to check a watch he hadn't worn for so long he surely should have lost the habit, letting go of her hand to check his phone instead. "There's still half an hour until it opens, so let's go and choose one of your drawings from your classroom—" He looked up from his phone to find he talked to thin air, no sign of the little girl he'd promised Dom he'd look after.

"Maisie?"

He looked around, only seeing Vanya talking with his mother, panic spiking until Vanya moved, Maisie there behind him, her arms around a new arrival.

Tor.

He let out a relieved sigh, following them around the building where he promptly lost sight of both children.

A bottleneck had formed, crowds admiring artworks by older students that lined the pathways. Austin edged around them, the hand Maisie had held curling, emptiness feeling all wrong. It also felt wrong that he'd lost sight of her twice within minutes of arriving.

Fuck, shit, bollocks.

A squeeze to his other hand caught his attention.

"Isn't this lovely?" his mum asked, voice raised over the buzz of the crowd. "So many people!"

Austin would agree if not for a reoccurrence of his heart pounding like it hadn't since the first time he'd lost sight of her, Maisie swallowed up this time by waves of people instead of water. Maybe his mum felt it skitter. She squeezed his hand again, sympathy so clear it stopped him despite his urge to hurry. It also made him get honest.

"I know she's safe here. I just . . . I just don't like it when I can't see her." He focused on the art beside them instead of maintaining eye contact. An older woman laughed out from the canvas, her dark eyes merry and familiar, confirmation of that scratched in the portrait's bottom corner, signed *Cameron Trebeck*.

His mum didn't let go of his hand. She held it tighter, standing shoulder to shoulder with him. "This is the hardest part, love. Giving them the freedom to spread their wings a little. You know the statistics—accidents are so rare." They both knew that didn't stop the rare ones from hurting. "But enjoying life is important." She touched a label naming the portrait. "Being happy."

Austin nodded. Nodded again as she raised the subject that had been on his mind that morning. "I've been thinking about what you said about doing something different with my free time." She touched the label again. "About choosing what makes me happy as well." She met his eyes. "That means doing something useful. I've learned too much to waste it. Only next time . . ."

"You'll pick something not so all-consuming?" He drew in a deep breath, lungs unlocking, remembering something Jason had mentioned over dinner. "Come with me." He drew her through the crowds to the outdoor classroom where Maisie and Tor knocked on the glass doors until Charles let them in. "Vanya," Austin called before he could follow them in. "Are you still running those storytelling sessions?"

"Yes." Vanya held the door open for Austin's mother, talking quietly when the children picked out artworks. He gestured to a comfy reading corner. "At my school, this is my children's favourite place in my class. They love stories." He stopped by a bookcase. "Just wish I had more books for the ones who don't speak English so their parents could read to them."

Charles asked, "Is that many of them?"

"Children who don't speak English? It's most of them." His accent thickened. "Nearly all are new to Britain. Lots seeking asylum like I did. Friends helped me learn English, but it's harder for children if their families don't have friends yet. The kids lose progress each school break." He touched the spine of a book. "That's when I run storytelling sessions in local libraries, the one place that's free for families with no money. A safe place for children. They all love going."

Like Tamsin.

Austin met his mother's eyes, wondering if his own reflected the same depth of feeling as hers.

"Parents come with their kids and learn too." Vanya's voice roughened. "Only wish I could run more sessions." He shrugged. "But can't be in two places at once. Or three. Or four. Would need to pay storytellers. Train them not just to read, but to listen. How to make books too."

"You make them?"

"With the children, yes. That's how I start each session, translating what they draw into English. Stories where they are heroes, not washed up somewhere they're not welcome. Give them words to feel powerful and wanted."

Austin's phone buzzed in his pocket as his mother said, "That sounds like it takes a lot of resources." She tapped a finger over her lips in a move he'd seen hundreds of times over the years, her head bent over budgets. "Have you had any luck accessing community grants? I could talk you through some shortcuts if you wanted?"

Happy wasn't only the title of a portrait, Austin decided. A bubble of that feeling rose behind his ribs as he backed away to leave them to it, another bubble joining it once he'd read a text message. "Sorry," he interrupted, "but can you keep an eye on Maisie? Dom needs me up at the art building." He checked his phone again. "Something last minute's come up."

He left them to weave through crowds but still felt lighter.

Mum really could help Vanya.

No.

They could help each other.

That thought carried him almost to the top of the hill, only the sight of the minibus outside the building making him stop. Or the sight of Cameron, to be specific, and although it had been nine months since Luke had matched them at Whisper Tor's base, he heard him all over again now as if he stood between them.

"When you're ready to let go of whatever's held you back for good, you'll recognise the perfect moment."

Austin approached Cameron, who looked wary. "Can I talk to you about our matched giving?"

"Now?" Cameron set down an easel. "You decided you want your watch back? It's down in the old art room in my bag." He crossed his arms. "Does that mean you're leaving now the renovation's finished? Can't think of why else you'd need to know the time all over the world. Got a new job slashing some international budgets?"

Once, Austin would have reeled back from those punches. Now, he knew better. "Not a chance."

He remembered what else Luke had promised. *"These partnerships tend to last, whatever happens."*

Seeing Cameron's arms uncross encouraged him to keep going. "I'm not going anywhere because I want to be around to see what you do next. Where you go next, Cameron. Someone's got to chart your progress."

"Oh." Cameron blinked, almost smiled, and settled for tapping his bare wrist and grumbling. "So you want it back because . . . ?"

"I'm happy." Another of those bubbles swelled inside him. "Really happy, like you said your gran wanted for you." Cameron nodded, so he continued. "And I didn't say I wanted it back. I asked if we could talk about it. About you keeping it so you know what the time is at home wherever you are in the world." Because he did have the kind of talent that could take him global.

Like usual, Cameron didn't make anything easy. "What do I need a watch for? I can always google time zones."

Funny how saying this was easier than Austin could have ever imagined. "Maybe I want to think about you checking it before calling home one day, knowing that more people than your uncle or Jace would answer. I'd pick up if you called me. I'd want to hear from you and find out how you're doing. Never stopped thinking about you before." He shrugged. "Not sure I can quit now."

He watched that have impact. Cameron rubbed his chest and his voice cracked. "Y-you don't want the watch back at all? Isn't it worth a lot of money?"

Austin shook his head. "Not to me." What he valued was right here. He glanced at a building fit for another century of Glynn Harber's students, wondering how many he'd get to see flourish like Cameron. Like Maisie too, who would, in her own unique way, now that both her school and home family communicated.

His phone buzzed again, Dom sending a single question mark followed by the words *tick-tock* that made him snort and hurry. He cast a quick instruction over his shoulder. "Your envelope's in the study if you want it. Second drawer down, under the Kit Kats." But Cameron was gone, disappearing just as fast as Maisie had managed.

The door into the building opened without creaking these days, no scent of damp offering a mouldy welcome. Dom didn't greet him either, Austin's footsteps echoing alone, the restored studio empty until he looked up.

Today a crumbling ceiling didn't block the light from flooding the space. The sun shone through an atrium where Dom stood high up on a maintenance walkway.

"I thought the leak was in a water pipe?"

"It was."

"So what are you doing up there?"

"Come and see." Dom leaned out, pointing at a ladder. "Quick, because I need to put that away before the kids get here."

Austin hesitated at the bottom, one foot on the first rung. "I thought my ladder climbing days were over."

"Come on up," Dom said. "What I've got to show you is worth it, I promise."

Austin did climb then, taking the hand Dom offered, steadying once he'd caught hold and didn't let go. "See?" Dom said. "Worth the climb, right?"

He was. Austin scanned a face he loved more now than ever, reaching out to touch freckles of paint a last-minute touch-up must have gifted. "Yes. More than worth it."

Way up above the studio, Dom's laugh rang out, eyes rivalling the shade of sky behind him. "I meant the view."

"Oh." Austin turned. Caught his breath. Must have tightened his grip, Dom needing to unpeel his fingers before sliding his arm around Austin's shoulders. If he asked another question, Austin didn't hear it and couldn't have answered, breath stolen by the view of Glynn Harber's valley as a bird might see it.

There was the chapel and the boarders' building, safe spaces for so many more children these days. The peak of a cottage roof too, Luke and Nathan's bolthole. Only the stables were hidden behind the main school building, but he didn't notice, too busy counting windows until he got to the ones of a study where his journey to happiness had started. "It's amazing."

Dom kissed his temple. "Now, look this way." He turned with Austin.

"That's High Tor?"

"Yes."

From this angle, a ribbon of moorland stretched between them, wild and rugged. "Now come here." Dom drew him to the left where sea-green water glittered, and maybe enough time had passed to see its beauty, because when Dom said, "What do you see?" answering him was easy.

Porthperrin clung to the shoreline, a grey and white smudge from here that he could clearly picture.

"Home." Austin backtracked. "Your home, I mean."

Dom's arm tightened around his shoulder. "Yours too, Aus." He steered him a fraction further, his arm dropping. "Or I think Cliffside could be, if you—"

Austin blurted, "Maisie wants to go back. She said so this morning. And Gemma sounds okay with the idea." He turned to add more, but for the third time that day, the person he looked for wasn't where he expected.

Now Dom didn't stand beside him.

He'd knelt.

"Look, I've got something here for you." Dom rummaged in a pocket of his jeans, pulling out a pack of tissues, eyes silently laughing like they had in the shower that morning, and tried again, this time digging out something metallic that shimmered.

"That's . . ." *A ring.*

His heart stopped, lurching when Dom said, "Nope. That's not what I was looking for either." He tried his other pocket.

"It's not for me?"

"What, this?" Dom held it up. "An off-cut of copper piping from my repair job? No, here it is." He pulled a folded sheet of paper from his back pocket. "Charles gave it to me this morning. Said I should look carefully at every detail."

He unfolded the paper, spreading it on the walkway, then grabbed Austin's hand, pulling him down beside him to see what was scribbled on it.

No.

Not scribbled.

Drawn by someone still learning to grip a pencil.

Austin touched two sweeping grey curves. "That's the harbour?"

"Yeah," Dom said. "Took me a minute to see it. Look." He pointed at a square. "That's Gemma's place." His finger traced a path Austin knew well.

"The alley."

Dom's smile touched so much more than his eyes. "Yeah. And look."

"Ken's place." Austin took over, finger following a path Maisie had taken so often between people who loved her, her handwriting the only shaky aspect when Dom pointed out stick figures. Austin read a heading. "My family."

"Mummy," Dom said, touching crayoned curls. "Grampy."

"What's he holding?"

"Dunno. A naughty list, maybe?"

Austin almost laughed. Would have if he hadn't noticed what Dom pointed out next.

"Daddy." Dom touched the outline of a man towering next to what might be a van, if Austin squinted. "And Daddy Austin." He met Austin's gaze. Held it like he'd held his heart for months now. "That's how she sees you, Aus. As someone who loves her as she is, like I do. Who cares and doesn't hide it, like me. Children don't believe what we say. They believe what we do, so she's believed you're Daddy material for a while now. Even changed her bedtime prayers to include both her daddies. Gemma told me."

Austin struggled to focus on a stick figure topped with a yellow scribble. Blinking didn't make his vision less blurry. He blinked again to see Dom hold out a different band of metal.

"Copper piping," Dom chuffed. "How about saying yes to some platinum?" He took Austin's hand, not hesitating as he slid a real ring on his finger. "Or you can choose something different. You know I'll give you anything you ever wanted, don't you?"

Austin kissed him.

Broke off just as quickly, nodding.

Kissed him again, having to swallow around happiness that almost stopped him from speaking. "You already have," he got out gruffly. "Like here." He gestured around them at a restored building that was so much more than a debt repayment. It was also about to reopen if the sound of people approaching was a signal.

They stood up together. "And there." Austin pointed out Maisie who sat on Jason's shoulders between his mum and Vanya. Sol too, who walked with Jace, Cameron between them, sun catching on the watch he must have decided was worth keeping. "You've already given me plenty."

"Plenty?"

Dom laughed, kissing him again.

"I'm just getting started."

The End

ALSO BY CON RILEY

Titles Set in the US

Seattle Stories

After Ben

Saving Sean

Aiden's Luck

Must Like Spinach

Salvage Series

Salvage

Recovery

Titles Set in Britain

True Brit

Be My Best Man

His Series

His Horizon

His Compass

His Haven

Learning to Love

Charles

Sol

Luke

Austin

Heppel Ever After

ABOUT THE AUTHOR

CON RILEY lives on the wild and wonderful Welsh coast, with her head in the clouds and her feet in the ocean. Injury curtailed her enjoyment of outdoor pursuits, so writing fiction now fills her free time. Love, loss, and redemption shape her romance stories, and her characters are flawed in ways that make them live and breathe.

When not people-watching or reading, she spends time staring at the sea from her kitchen window. If you see her, don't disturb her — she's probably thinking up new plots.

www.conriley.com
Twitter/Instagram: @con_riley
Facebook: Con Riley's Readers

Printed in Great Britain
by Amazon

22917022R00178